AN EX-NUNS OF DAYLESFORD MYSTERY

Better Latte Than Never

Sandra Broman

Write & Wrong

First published in 2018
by Write & Wrong
www.sandrabroman.com
Cover artwork by Sandra Broman
Text designed and typeset by Cathy Larsen Design
Edited by Jo Scanlan (Textpod)

 A catalogue record for this
book is available from the
National Library of Australia

Creator: Broman, Sandra
Title: Better latte than never / by Sandra Broman
Series title: Ex-nuns of Daylesford
ISBN: Paperback 978-0-6482512-4-8
               Ebook 978-0-648-2512-5-5

'Daddy wouldn't buy me a bow-wow' 1892, Joseph Tabrar 1857-1931

About the author

Sandra works from a studio/gallery
in Daylesford, Australia where
she makes all kinds of things.

For more information, visit
www.sandrabroman.com

Other titles by Sandra Broman
Built Like A Woman
Esther! A True Story
Diversions Most Obscure - The Art of Sandra Broman

Acknowledgements

Thanks to the people of Daylesford for forming such a varied population to draw inspiration from. Especially, thanks to the extraordinary pair who made me so excited I simply had to turn them into amateur detectives. Bill and Audrey could not exist at all if I hadn't met their real counterparts first. Having said that, I've given them their very own personalities.

Also big thanks to Roff Smith for the reading and encouragement, to Coby for the title and being generally helpful and to Jo Scanlan who edited the text and liked it.

Some locations are real, others imagined. Some existed when I wrote the story but have since changed. All characters are fictional, even if there is a biscuit maker with fabulous hair, a handsome bookshop by the lake, a chocolatier with fairylights and so on. There is absolutely no resemblance with the actual librarian in Daylesford, and I thank the library staff for being so helpful and knowledgeable.

Come and have coffee in Daylesford one day. You never know what might happen.

In memory of Britta and Lisa

CHAPTER 1

The door closed behind them with a snap as the lock settled back into the catch. Audrey's hand lingered briefly on the handle, the familiar feel of smooth brass etched into her palm. Through an upstairs window she saw someone looking down, but when she waved the figure disappeared from view. She turned to Jill, her friend of many years.

'Ready?'

'As I'll ever be.'

They turned and walked together down the gravel path towards their hire car, packed and ready to go. The distance between them and the car was not great, yet it seemed as if the ground behind them opened into an impassable gulf. Ahead of them was the whole world, an uncharted territory glowing and coming to life in the dawn light.

***

A little silver hire car wound its way towards the quiet little village of Daylesford, tyres sending sprays of water onto the verges as it passed by with some haste.

Daylesford is an exceptionally pretty place, clinging to a wooded hill in the highlands above Melbourne, resplendent in gold rush history. Abundant gardens burst with the power that comes from deep volcanic soil, locals nod at strangers in the street, and the houses are mainly old timber cottages in various stages of repair.

Now it was winter and trees stretched their naked branches against a solid grey backdrop. It had been raining on and off all day and the roads glistened with water, gathering in occasional puddles that reflected the milkiness of the sky above. Sitting inside the car were two women in their fifties, surrounded by all their worldly goods. And a much depleted bag of biscuits.

'There's one! And before you ask, yes, I'm sure,' said Audrey Pretty, who until a few hours earlier had been known as Sister Audrey. Tall and angular, her brown hair speckled with grey, she had a long and distinctive Roman nose and what her friends might have described as a regal bearing. Leaning as far forward as her seatbelt would allow, she thrust her face towards the windscreen and peered down the road with hawkish intensity.

'No, that was a bush, definitely a bush. Kangaroos move. Turn on the wipers, it's drizzling again,' said her passenger, the former Sister Jill, now just plain Jill Wicklow.

'They don't move if they're grazing. Or just sitting, thinking about things like grazing,' Audrey added triumphantly. 'You're not helping. Start looking so I can concentrate on driving. I want to get there before dark, dent free if at all possible. Now, find your glasses and stop eating.'

Jill, a short gently rotund woman with a pleasant face and curly hair put her hand in the bag and calmly took out another biscuit.

'Sure you don't want one? They're yummy,' she said, waving the biscuit in the air, sending crumbs all over the map which she was supposed to be following.

Audrey put on her sternest voice.

'Are you expecting to find the glasses in the biscuit bag?' She had worked on this particular voice for years and it could strike fear into most people.

'Pfft.' Jill, relenting, sighed and opened the glove box where her glasses had been all along. She popped in the last mouthful and brushed a stray crumb from her chin.

'According to the map, we're not far off now,' she said. 'Just another thirty minutes maybe. Wait, what's that?' Jill pointed to a large shape moving slowly in the distance among the trees by the side of the road. 'Kangaroo!' She pushed against the dashboard as if to brace herself for impact. 'Brake, brake. Oh, it's a man.

3

Let's ask if he wants a lift.'

The car came to a halt beside a man wearing a hat and handsome camelhair coat.

'If memory serves, there's an excellent optometrist in Daylesford,' said Audrey. 'You might need new glasses.'

Jill wound down her window. 'I thought you were a bloody great kangaroo,' she shouted cheerfully. 'We're heading to Daylesford, if you want a ride.'

'Thank you, my car broke down.'

'Hop in,' said Jill. 'You'll have to push that great big thing over a bit.'

The man took off his sodden coat and brushed a few empty food wrappers from the seat before wedging himself down next to a large black instrument case.

'I'm Hugo, Hugo Dubois.' He extended a hand between the front seats in greeting and smiled at his benefactors. 'It is wet out there, not the day for the long walk.' Although Hugo had been in Australia for many years his French accent was still strong.

'I am Audrey Pretty and this is Jill Wicklow. You look frozen through and through, let me turn the heating up.' Audrey twiddled the controls and a blast of icy air hit the back seat. The wipers increased their speed. 'Hang on, that's not right.' She fumbled some more. 'This is the best that I can do. If you lean forward you should get some heat between the seats.'

Hugo rubbed his hands in the warm blast.

'Ah, that's wonderful. Pretty is a well-known name around here. Are you related to Inez Pretty, by any chance?'

'My aunt,' said Audrey. 'Do you know her?'

'Of course I know the formidable Inez. Will you be staying long?'

'Yes, we think so. We're going to live with her.'

'Then we shall meet again. I have a book shop and cafe down by the lake, Le Bouquiniste. You must come and visit. Bring Inez one day, I haven't seen her around for ages.'

'How lovely, we will.' Jill held out the biscuit bag and rattled the remaining two temptingly. 'Lemon creams. Have one?'

'I will, thank you.' He picked one. Jill took the last one with relish and scrunched up the empty bag.

'You could have had another fifteen, but they are irretrievably ensconced in Jill I'm afraid,' said Audrey.

'It is delicious. I sell biscuits too, but not as good as these.'

'Oh, you are a flatterer. Let me make you some for your shop. It would be a pleasure,' Audrey beamed. 'I'm delighted that you like them.'

Jill looked at her and opened her mouth to say something but Audrey shot her a sharp glance, staring her down with a practised eye.

'Look out, kangaroo! No, another bush,' said Audrey to change the subject.

'Are you also related to Inez, Jill?'

'Me? No, no. I'm just a friend of Audrey's.'

Jill had none of the sharp features that ran in the Pretty genes. While Audrey had cheekbones you could cut yourself on, Jill's face had a softer oval shape with clear grey almond eyes framed by almost straight eyebrows. Audrey's eyes were pure Pretty, green with an ability to pierce. The two women did have one thing in common: gabardine. Their clothes bordered on identical in their drabness. White blouses under non-descript woollens and dark navy gabardine skirts. The light in the car was getting dimmer by the minute, but Hugo wished it was darker still when he noted the hideous dark brown buttoned-up cardigan worn by the woman on the left. It was an offence to expose your fellow humans to such a style disaster, in Hugo's humble, but very French, opinion. He wondered how long they would escape scathing criticism from the rather pointy Inez.

'Do you know Inez well?' he asked Jill.

'I've never met her, but I am very much looking forward to seeing her.'

Audrey's and Hugo's eyes met briefly in the rear vision mirror. He raised a quizzical eyebrow.

'Hmm,' he said. 'She can be charming, sometimes, and advanced age has mellowed her. Just remember that if she criticises anything you say or do, she is the kind of woman who kills snakes with her bare teeth and squeezes the venom out to use as eau de cologne. I'm sure she means no harm. Mostly.'

Audrey looked at him pensively in the mirror.

'Are there any other members of the Pretty family you'd like to insult while you're at it?'

'My apologies.' He shrugged. 'I just wanted to prepare Jill for some of Inez's more interesting qualities.'

The country road became an avenue lined with elm trees. Black Angus cattle grazed in a field to the side, and a hill rose up before them. A sign announced that they had now entered Daylesford, they should drive carefully, and visitors were welcome.

'Here we are at last,' said Jill with a quiver of excitement. 'We'll run you home first.'

As Daylesford was a small place, it didn't take more than five minutes to get to Hugo's bookshop on the edge of the lake. Between the quickening dusk and the fog they could not see much of the scenery, but they promised to come for a visit soon.

There were no traffic lights, just a roundabout at each end of the little shopping street. A few houses up from the top roundabout was an immense hedge, leaning precariously out over the pavement inset with an elaborate wrought iron gate.

'This is it. I'll be glad to stretch my dicky knee out for a bit. No regrets, Jill?' Audrey stepped out of the car and took a deep breath of the fresh wintry air.

'Of course not. The die is cast.'

In their view of the world, a decision should be made and then firmly stuck with, at least until a better option presented itself. Usually the first decision was the best one anyway. Wavering was only so much wasted time. They emptied the car of luggage and opened the gate, which creaked in response. A gracious two-storey stone building in Georgian style loomed in front of them, set off by splendid greenery. Soft feathery wisps of large shrubs, trimmed lavender and agapanthus jostled for space, and tiny seaside daisies squeezed themselves in wherever they found a spare inch of soil.

The front door was massive, with an etched fanlight above the doorframe which proudly announced to the world that its name was Stewart House.

'*This* is your aunt's house?' asked Jill. 'It's huge…'

'Used to be a public house, once.' Audrey pushed a handle which had PULL engraved on a metal label. A loud clanging was heard from inside. 'She's done that on purpose, so that only people who know how to work the bell can disturb. Good idea, really. She's pretty deaf so you'll have to speak up.' They had to wait a few minutes before the door opened to reveal a slight woman in a velvet dressing gown.

'Aunt Inez, how wonderful to see you again,' shouted Audrey as she embraced her.

'Welcome, Plum dear. You will break me, I probably

8

have brittle bones. You look more like your father than ever, ever such a gangly man. Was the journey tedious?'

'Lovely, thank you. You look well yourself.'

And she did, for her advanced age. Her eyes were green and bright and her long white hair was plaited and coiled high on her head without a single strand escaping. Inez's looks were as sharp as her mind and temper. The family resemblance was strong despite the age difference. The Pretty profile was unmistakeable.

'We met Hugo Dubois from the bookshop on the way. He said we should take you there for coffee.'

'Raving socialist,' huffed Inez. 'I will not set foot in his establishment. Stay clear of the revolutionaries. He was involved in the student riots you know. A ringleader.'

'Riots? Here? In Daylesford?' Jill was surprised.

'Paris – 1968. Don't believe anything the man says, he will want to introduce you to the wicked ways of the world.' She brayed, bumping Jill with her shoulder like a playful goat, making her drop her suitcase in surprise.

'Pleased to meet you. I'm Jill.'

'Bill? Funny sort of a name for a woman, what? Allowed in the convent, that sort of thing?' Inez peered at her curiously.

'No, I'm Jill,' she said loudly and looked at Audrey, who shrugged.

'Yes, yes. What on earth is that?' she pointed to

Jill's large music case.

'It's a tuba, E flat.'

'Being deaf is a splendid blessing,' Inez bellowed. 'I never could stand brass. In instruments or women. Your rooms are next to each other, I thought it best to place you where you can both hear my bell. James installed it for me.'

'Who?'

'James, one of the boys. I have two.'

'I think she means her helpers,' explained Audrey. 'I've never met them, myself.'

'I find the stairs rather steep, awkward hips, you see,' continued Inez.

'Absolutely awkward bloody everything,' muttered Jill and received a sharp elbow in the side from Audrey.

'I never go up there anymore. Go and wash off the travel dust, there's some food ready for all of us in the kitchen when you're done. You can bring the supper to my quarters. Plum will remember where it is. See you when you're ready.'

'Plum?' Jill asked when Inez had gone. 'Bill?'

'I have absolutely no idea. She probably doesn't even know my real name anymore. Don't worry about the Bill thing, she'll forget your name by morning and we can start again.'

'To be perfectly honest, I'm rather pleased to have a nickname. I don't think I ever had one before. It's a new name for a new part of my life. I might keep it.'

'Fine,' Audrey looked kindly at her friend. 'Bill it is. It will stick, you know. Nicknames do, for good and bad.'

Audrey led the way up a grand staircase in the middle of the hallway, faintly illuminated by whatever daylight still remained filtering through an enormous leadlight window. Bill struggled behind, slowly dragging the tuba case up behind her one step at a time. It was cumbersome in the extreme and hit her legs painfully.

'I'll have some bruises tomorrow. Do you mind if I leave the tuba here for now? I'll pick it up tomorrow.' Halfway up was a landing where the stairs changed direction. Bill went back down to collect her suitcase, and almost skipped with the ease of not carrying her beast of an instrument.

At the top of the stairs was a corridor with four doors. To the far left of this corridor were a handful of steps leading down onto a second smaller corridor with two further doors. Audrey had already managed to open and close them all while Bill went for her bag. Several rooms had no working lights, and appeared to be full of boxes and random dusty furniture.

'There's two rooms made up and ready. Which one do you want? They're very similar.' She went into one of the rooms and tugged on the pull cord. A lamp with a marbled glass shade illuminated what would once have been a grand guest room in the former hotel.

A huge ornately carved bed stood resplendent against one wall. Apart from a lovely marble fireplace and a freestanding armoire there was little else. The walls were papered in flowery medallion patterns, showing watermarks from past and possibly present issues with the roof. It all felt somewhat damp and cold.

'The wallpaper is different in the other room, some odd floral motif.'

'This one will do me fine,' said Bill.

The windows looked out over the road where a solitary streetlamp mistily illuminated the vague shapes of a stone church opposite.

'Catholic,' Audrey said. 'Wouldn't you know it? We are smack bang in the middle of the church precinct here. Another one on the corner, see? In the morning you'll be able to see yet another steeple up there on the left. I shall enjoy looking at all this churchliness from a safe distance.'

'Oh, it's cold. We have to light a fire.' Bill closed the curtains. She clicked open her suitcase to put away her belongings, which consisted of some clean and pressed blouses, a collection of underwear of the more sensible style, a few pairs of warm stockings, one gabardine skirt and one woollen one, a framed print of St Francis of Assisi, a knitted jumper and a pair of sneakers. A couple of nightdresses, a dressing gown, slippers and a zip-up bag of toiletries completed the packing.

'The bathroom is the door opposite us,' said Audrey.

12

'Great. I'll just wash my hands and face, then I'll be ready.'

Audrey carefully unpacked her own contents, which were almost identical. She unwrapped a picture from a layer of tissue paper. Hers was a print by Van Dyck, showing St Jude looking serious in dark and moody colours. She propped it up on the mantelpiece and patted him reassuringly.

Supper consisted of quiche, salad and blackberry tart. They put it on a tray and carried it through the draughty corridor leading to the old servants' quarters, now comfortably converted to Aunt Inez's apartment. The apartment, amply heated by a gas fire, consisted of a small sitting room lined with bookcases and a bedroom that was rich with oriental textiles and opened out to the garden. A reasonably modern bathroom off to one side completed her abode. A sleek grey cat was precariously balanced on the back of an armchair, asleep. It briefly opened one eye to peer at them.

'That's Lucy, say hello.'

'I remember Lucy. Hello,' said Audrey politely.

Bill just sneezed as she was ever so slightly allergic to cats. 'Your house is most interesting. These rooms are lovely.'

'Thank you dear. I find it so much cosier than the rest of the place, ghastly old thing. I haven't bothered to do anything to it for years, I only need this part.'

'Yes, the house is big, isn't it?'

'It used to be bigger still when it was a hotel, but there was a fire in the front bar and a wing got demolished. It had already been closed for several years when my grandfather bought it in 1902. No doubt you'll get the rooms you need to live in straightened out in no time. Paint it and whatnot. Air it out a little. You'll find some firewood in the little shed off the garage, and there are hot water bottles in the kitchen for tonight. Winter can be a bit grim.'

'I noticed,' Bill interrupted.

'Say what?' Inez held a hand behind her ear. 'I'm not wearing the hearing things.'

'I said I noticed,' repeated Bill loudly. 'Never mind.'

'Are you having hearing problems?' shouted Inez. 'I said that winter is grim! Furnish your rooms yourselves. There are plenty of things in the rooms around you, and in the garage. Speaking of garage, you can use my car when you've returned your rental. I haven't driven it for a long time, but it will start. It has started first time every time since I was given it on my 21st in 1947,' she said proudly.

'Is there anything you want us to do?' asked Audrey.

'Simon and James, utterly charming both of them, come now and then for the cleaning, gardening, errands and so forth so there's no need to worry about any of that. They usually cook things for me to heat up later on. Just do your own thing and I'll let you know when I want you. You'll want to go out and explore the village in the morning.'

Audrey gave Bill a quick tour of the downstairs rooms while they waited for the kettle to boil. Hot water bottles, they felt, were sorely needed tonight. The ground floor consisted of a sitting room, a library, a formal dining room, a second dining room and a breakfast room in a sort of lean-to construction opening onto a terrace.

The large old-fashioned kitchen featured plenty of battered copper pots and pans, speckled olive-green Formica benches from its last update in the fifties and an old wood-fired Rayburn stove. A pantry large enough to withstand the siege of Leningrad opened off one end. In the hallway was a door to what was once a cupboard, presumably, in which Inez's grandfather had proudly installed a toilet as a novelty in 1902. It was far too dark to see anything outside, but they found a basket left just inside the back door with enough wood to get a fire started.

'Hooray, firewood. Just the thing. Let's go up and warm the rooms,' said Audrey.

As they lit the fire in Bill's room smoke billowed in. Audrey opened both windows as much as they would allow. Misty air carrying the smell of wet earth filled her lungs as she took a deep breath.

'Whoa. Less of the hooray, I think. Chimney must be blocked. Let's just share the other room tonight.

You can't possibly sleep in this smoke and cold air.'

Bill opened her eyes with a jolt to the sound of someone snoring in her room. Audrey. She knew that snore. A wall between them was certainly a benefit. A blackbird sang in the darkness. It took a moment of muddled thought before Bill remembered where she was and as soon as she did, she simply had to get up. Inch by inch she eased herself out of bed to avoid waking the snoring Audrey, grabbed what appeared to be her pile of clothes in the dark and padded out to get dressed in the positively arctic bathroom.

She had no idea of the time but it felt vaguely like morning. Outside was still dark. Never mind, she couldn't possibly stay in bed any longer. Feeling the banister, she carefully made her way downstairs. A soft thudding sound startled her and she stood still, listening intently. It was only Lucy the cat, who appeared and rubbed herself around her legs. Lucy herded her in the direction of the kitchen, which was helpful as she was not entirely sure how to find it in the dark.

'Good girl,' whispered Bill and suppressed a sneeze.

'Yowl,' agreed Lucy.

Bill fumbled around the kitchen doorway for a light switch. Warm yellow light flooded the room and she put the kettle on. Lucy twined herself around Bill's legs until she found the cat food and put a few spoonfuls in a dish on the floor. Cat duty done, she drank a hot cup of tea at the kitchen table, warming her hands and her stomach at the same time.

Joy bubbled up inside her. Life was exciting. Sometimes it was good, and sometimes bad, but it was always interesting. Hastily she scribbled a note and propped it on the bench where Audrey would be sure to see it. Audrey had the keys and Bill wasn't willing to risk waking her by going back upstairs so she left through the back door, leaving it unlocked. The creaky gate was an obstacle, but she hoped Audrey wouldn't hear it as she sneaked out to the street.

It was a fine morning, chilly, clear and completely still. Daylesford was sparingly lit. Just outside Stewart House was a rare streetlamp, and Bill headed for the next pool of light around the corner. The blackbird's song accompanied her as she made her way on the short walk to the collection of shops that made up the little centre. The streets were deserted. This was certainly no bustling metropolis at this time in the morning, if ever.

Bill's attention was caught by the window of a chocolate shop. The gold-flecked antique glass showed a shimmering reflection of the town hall opposite. The window itself was framed by fairy lights. Peering into the shop, Bill could see a long glass counter, and dark wood walls lined with shelves laden with jars and little boxes. In the centre was a collection of comfortable-looking seats. She felt as if the entire shop was a rich chocolate to savour as a whole. The artfully painted plaster ceiling appeared to be glittering with a hundred faint pinpricks of starry light. Reluctantly she tore herself away and moved on down the street.

Ignoring the real estate windows, she paused at a shop selling antiques and curiosities. It was only marginally tidier than the spare rooms she had glimpsed in Inez's house, with their so-far unexplored collections. A current of warm baking smells distracted her, and she followed the trail to a bakery. Through the window she could see bakers busily carrying trays of fresh bread, sliding loaves onto racks. One of them saw her and waved in a cheerful morning salute. She waved back and walked on.

One shop seemed to specialise exclusively in cookware, and another had a most exquisite window display of handmade pottery on an old wooden table. Woven cloths spilled out of a basket surrounded by balls of artfully arranged candy-striped twine. Slowly Bill worked her way up and down the street. Her only company, apart from the blackbird, was a fat orange cat. It padded briskly across the road, ignoring her. She hoped it would ignore the blackbird too.

When Bill eventually returned home, she found Audrey in the kitchen making breakfast.

'Nice walk? Looks like a fine day.'

'I couldn't sleep any longer. The village is just lovely.' Bill sighed with pleasure and cradled the proffered mug of steaming coffee.

'Let's eat breakfast with Inez, it'll be warm in her room.'

Inez was sitting reading in bed with Lucy purring in her lap. She smiled at them as they entered.

'Good morning! I was quite excited when I woke up and remembered that you were here. Sit down, make yourselves comfortable. Did you sleep alright up there?'

'Yes, thank you. Bill has been for a walk already.'

'Oh yes, they certainly are common this time of year,' nodded Inez.

'I'm sorry?' Bill looked confused.

'Never mind,' said Audrey quietly to her, and turned to Inez.

'Do you know a chimney sweep?' she said loudly to her aunt. 'The fireplace upstairs is blocked.'

'Locked? It can't be, there's no lock, dear.' Inez arranged her already wrinkled forehead into deeper folds of concentration.

'Blocked! Chimney!'

'Why didn't you say so? The boys can deal with it. They come today for a couple of hours. Now that it's light you must see the garden. My grandmother planted much of it, you know. James and Simon do a wonderful job keeping it up. Just let me finish breakfast and get ready. I'll come with you.'

Standing on the back terrace, Audrey and Bill marvelled at how you could fit such a large garden in the heart of the village. Paths invited you to take short walks into areas partially concealed by trees and shrubs, stone-walled garden beds promising flowers with warmer weather. Even now in winter there was plenty in bloom. Camellias and jonquils were busily flowering and hellebores fought for space among clump irises and scented winter sweet. Large trees were silhouetted starkly against the milky winter clouds. They could only imagine how glorious it would be in spring. At the bottom of the garden was a garage tucked in under an enormous old chestnut.

'I love your garden, Inez,' shouted Bill.

'I don't know what you are making such a racket for. I put the hearing things in. A damned nuisance, they are, but I can at least hear you so don't say anything stupid. I can't stand stupidity and I will take them straight out again if you do. Let's go and see about the car.'

They walked along a herringbone brick path framed by neatly trimmed hedges.

'There's a trick to opening the door,' said Inez, jiggling the handle. 'You have to push it like so, a quick turn. Here we are.'

Inside was a car covered in protective blankets.

'Go on then, pull them off,' Inez needed the support of her cane and only had one hand free. Audrey did as she was told. Underneath the blankets was a shiny 1947 Austin Sheerline, two-tone in green and cream.

'Isn't she a stunner?' asked Inez. 'Good acceleration but a bit heavy on the fuel. Just look at the detailing. Mahogany, you see. Walnut too. One can just oil the wood a little, polishes up a treat.' She stroked her car lovingly. 'She has valve radio too, of course. Speakers both back and front. The seats are the original ones, so a little wear is to be expected. A bit bouncy on the springs and quite roomy.' She brayed and bumped Bill with her shoulder again but this time she half expected it and failed to drop a single thing.

'It's gorgeous. Is it registered?'

'She, not it. Certainly she is. She hasn't missed a year since I got her. I'll just get the boys to check her over and you'll be all set to go.'

'It's generous of you,' said Bill, a little nervous of driving such an imposing car.

'Oh, rubbish! Like a horse, you see.'

'Horse?'

'You need to exercise them. She needs a good run. Just the ticket, you're doing me a favour. There's a good girl.'

Audrey busied herself in the kitchen, finding recipe books and ingredients for biscuit-making. Lucy sat by the stove, her eyes following every move.

'What did you have to offer to bake for?' said Bill. 'You don't bake.'

'He is pretty charming, isn't he? Beautiful accent, the way he rolls his r's. Our first friend here deserves a batch of biscuits.'

'So he might do, but does he deserve yours? You told him you could bake...'

'I never lied, I just said I'd make him some, which I am. It'll be alright. It's easy. See, here's a good recipe. All I have to do is follow it, and we'll deliver a batch of freshly made lemon cream biscuits as promised.' She started humming as she stirred butter and sugar, grated lemon and cracked eggs. 'I see no flaw in that plan at all. Let's return the rental car on the way there. We can walk to the lake – there are umbrellas in the hallstand.'

The lumpy-looking biscuits soon went into the oven.

'You know, I should bake more often,' said Audrey. 'That was so easy. Maybe I can even make a little money at it, have a market stall perhaps. This could be my new direction. I just need a catchy name.'

'Plum's Peculiars, perhaps. They smell funny. Are they supposed to look like that?'

The biscuits had floated out to a thin yellow single biscuit that was starting to bubble and burn at the edges, rapidly charring the entire tray.

'Double damn,' exclaimed Audrey. 'It'll just have to do. Maybe the filling isn't supposed to go in until after the biscuits are done. Oh hello, Aunt.'

'What's that horrible smell? Are the neighbours burning tyres?'

'Audrey is making a treat for Hugo.'

'How splendid, a burnt offering. Serves him right for being over-familiar, what with all that hand kissing. It's unhygienic. What is it?' Inez peered at the tray and wrinkled up her nose.

'Lemon biscuits. They're only a bit burnt. I can break them into smaller bits,' Audrey said, feeling a little hurt. 'Gourmet pieces, see?'

'Mmm, yes, I do unfortunately. This is a gift, is it? I am sure he will be delighted.'

CHAPTER 2

Audrey and Bill's first stop was the newsagent. It also served, they noted, as a shoe repairer, dry cleaners and – the reason for their visit – a car rental drop-off point. They parked the car at the rear of the shop and handed in the keys. Now the village was wide awake. Added to the smell of baking was the aroma of coffees being made by hissing machines in every coffee shop, of which there were plenty. There was a gentle din of people starting their day. Chairs and tables had been set up on the wide pavements under awnings, and the florist was arranging his display of sweetly scented flowers in galvanised buckets on the pavement.

Bill was keen to return to the chocolatier, which was now open for business. She was excited to find the long glass counter brimming with pralines, truffles and creams – filled and unfilled – clusters, marzipans and nougats. It was hard to make a choice.

The friendly young shop assistant smiled cheerfully

at them, showing dimpled cheeks.

'May I assist you?' She was dressed in a crisply ironed shirt and striped apron, embroidered with her name. Her long nutbrown hair was tied with a matching ribbon.

'Oh, it's so hard. They all look fantastic. Do you have a favourite, Alice?' asked Audrey, reading the tag.

'It would have to be the espresso creams. Or the orange creams... All of them, probably.'

They deliberated at length before finally settling on dark chocolate whisky truffles, a few orange logs and a couple of pistachio clusters which Alice boxed and wrapped, finishing with an expertly tied ribbon.

'Just as well,' said Audrey. 'They're a gift and we might be tempted otherwise.'

They set off towards Hugo's place, carrying Audrey's special biscuits and the chocolate box.

'I've never seen so many people holding hands,' said Bill as they made their way through the weekend visitors. 'It's like a Siamese twin convention.'

'Daylesford is a popular location for a bit of romance,' explained Audrey. 'Later, the successful hand-holders come back for their weddings. Take note of the church opposite us. It gets a lot of trade because it's so attractive. Then, they don't want to leave and so they buy a weekender. Before you know it they're locals, grumbling at the lack of parking due to all the new hand-holders rolling into town.'

To get to Hugo's place, Audrey decided on a meandering shortcut through some forest. They paused occasionally to catch views of the lake through the tall pines. It was a pretty walk even in the intermittent drizzle.

Hugo's old timber cottage sat by itself on the waterfront, reflected in the water. A sign on the wall read 'Le Bouquiniste'. Book boxes were displayed along the outside walls, protected by a wide veranda. Swans, geese and ducks were busy in the reeds around the deck overlooking the water. Above the door hung a hand-painted sign saying *Audentes Fortuna Iuvat*.

'Ah,' said Audrey. 'He's not one to believe that the meek shall inherit, then.'

'You're the Latin expert, what does it mean?'

'Fortune favours the bold.'

A bell jingled above the door as they opened it to reveal a pleasant room divided into smaller spaces by timber bookshelves. Audrey sniffed the air approvingly. 'Coffee and books. There's nothing like it.'

In front of the counter was a potbelly stove with a fire burning merrily, adding to the mild yet distinctive papery scent. There were plenty of comfortable-looking chairs. The only thing missing seemed to be customers.

'How marvellous to see you both so soon,' said Hugo. 'Let me make you a drink. Coffee? I see that you made biscuits, I can't wait.' He peeked inside the bag, barely able to conceal his disappointment at the flat black broken bits.

'Very unusual colour for lemon, but I am sure they are *superbes*.'

'Actually these didn't turn out so well, so we brought you some chocolates too,' said Audrey and handed over the beautifully wrapped box. 'It's quiet, isn't it?' she added as they sat down by the crackling fire.

'Sadly, yes. It hasn't always been like this. I guess there are not enough customers for all the coffee shops to be equally busy. There is only a little money in used books, regrettably.' Hugo sighed and shifted uncomfortably in his chair. 'A short while ago a coffee shop with an aggressive strategy opened up. I'm sure the owner is staging fake complaints about his competition. Me *especiallement* I think, but others too. It is bad, but what can I do? Just wait it out until he grows bored with praising himself to the detriment of others, no?'

'But Inez told us that you were a revolutionary,' said Audrey. 'Fortune favours the bold, and all that. The bold don't sit back and wait.'

'Inez exaggerates and alas, that was a long time ago. One does not want to make so much trouble. A leetle, maybe...' He gave them a crooked smirk and showed with a well-manicured thumb and index finger just how little trouble was enough. 'Business changes all the time, it is to be expected. But if you wait a few minutes, there are lots of people due to arrive. I am a member of the local choir and it is my turn to host the weekly practice. Will you do me the pleasure of staying to listen and meet some people?'

'A choir, how exciting. Is there room for two more singers? Bill and I have sung in choirs forever.'

'Bill? Oh, I thought her name was Jill.'

'Just call her Bill, as in Electricity.'

Soon the doorbell started tinkling and kept going for quite a while as singers of various ages and sizes poured in.

The conductor, a tall man with mutton-chop whiskers and signal-red braces holding up his ample trousers, stood up and called for attention. Bill thought he was standing on a chair before she realised he was actually that tall. She would have needed a ladder to look him in the eye.

'Listen up, everybody,' he said and a hush fell over the group. 'As you all know, we are performing on Tuesday at The Bean near Gloria's Gardens. Today we'll run through the songs. Hugo tells me that we have two brand new singers joining us today: Bill, soprano and Audrey, alto.' Everyone clapped and cheered, making the two women feel very welcome. 'Someone share their sheet music please. Let's start with some exercises. Is everyone ready?'

After practice, coffee and tea were served, along with a basket of fresh scones that Hugo brought from his kitchen.

'Did you make these, Hugo? They are truly excell-ent.' Bill considered herself an expert on the eating and judging of scones. She was also an expert in knowing the tipping point for exactly how big the mound of cream could be before it toppled into a lap. She licked some stray sticky jam from her hand.

'I make them with a leetle bit of sparkling water from one of the local springs, it's the trick.'

'Delicious. May I have another?'

'It is nice to see a woman with the big appetite.'

A lean 40-something brunette exquisitely clad in a Sonia Rykiel intarsia knit coat joined them, trailing a cloud of perfume. She did not have a scone in her bejewelled hand and did not plan to eat one either.

'I'm Fiona.' She stretched out her hand in greeting, gold bracelets jingling.

'How do you do,' said Bill and clasped her hand. Fiona's smooth hand felt cool to the touch. Bill tried to infuse some warmth into it.

'I'm a soprano too,' said Fiona. 'I do most of the solos. Great to see new members.' She critically eyed them up and down. 'Will you come to the performance? You'll need to wear something black, any old thing will do. Here, take my score sheets home, I don't need them. You can learn the rep over the weekend.' She flashed a smile at the two women but Bill thought it looked more like a snarl, a baring of white teeth.

'But what if I don't want to wear black?' grumbled Bill as they left.

'I guess you won't be singing then.'

'I guess not – ah well, black it will have to be. I can't help feeling that blacks, greys and browns are so last week,' Bill sighed. 'A tiny hint of colour is all I ask.'

'You don't even have any colourful clothes. Stop being awkward.'

'Not yet I don't. But I might want some. Did you see the dress thing that woman was wearing? Gorgeous. People have so many clothes, don't they?'

'Far too many. I do agree though, we need something. For now we'll just have to wear what we've got. Let's go to this coffee shop and see what all the fuss is about.'

It wasn't hard to find. You just had to follow the trail of posters advertising events at the Best Bean: Have you been to The Bean? Be seen at The Bean! I've Bean! All the posters featured a photo of a suave-looking man of possible Mediterranean origin. Kitted out to look like an explorer, albeit a rather under-dressed one, he wore a skimpy singlet showing his rippling torso. To top it off he pointed at the viewer with a finger like a cocked gun and one eye squeezed closed as if he was either flirting or taking aim.

'What's wrong with him? Looks like he poked himself in the eye with his own finger gun,' said Audrey.

'He certainly seems to have a high opinion of himself. Look, there's the nursery.' Bill was happy to find it, as she was keen to plant some herbs in Inez's garden. She hoped it would be well stocked. The nursery, however, would have to keep for another time. Next to it stood a deep and fairly narrow house with chairs and tables in its gravelled front garden. From a pole in the garden hung a long banner which simply said 'The Bean' above a life-sized image of the same man.

'Talk about overkill,' said Audrey.

The house had windows all along the front and down one side, upbeat music spilling out into the street along with the tempting smells of roasting coffee.

'Great music. If only I didn't have my knee... ' Audrey sighed. She had ongoing problems with her knees, particularly the left one. She placed the blame squarely on all the kneeling she had done.

'If you didn't have knees you wouldn't be bending at all,' said Bill. 'Care for a shimmy?' The two women did an impromptu little dance with each other on the gravel, catching the attention of the man from the posters, who came out in greeting.

'Welcome to The Bean! Beautiful ladies! What can I make for you two groovy babes?' He smiled at them broadly, showing a blindingly white set of even teeth.

'You are a flatterer,' giggled Bill and slapped him gently on the arm. 'Two coffees please.'

He beckoned them to come closer until they were near enough to smell the faint woody hints of cedar from his aftershave. 'I am not one to boast, but it will be the best you have ever had,' he said and winked.

'Sounds intriguing, Mr...' ventured Audrey.

'Surely you know who I am? Don't you watch television? I'm Fabiano to my friends, or even just plain Fab. As I said, it will be the very best or I will keep trying. I have some Costa Rican Tarazu, or some supremo Colombian. Whatever you want.'

'Surprise us. And some of those little biscuits please,' added Bill.

'I shall make you my own signature brew, a Fabulous Fabiano's Vertigo. It's a high altitude single origin which will send your hearts a-flutter.' He winked at them and started deftly preparing their drinks.

'What's wrong with him? Looks like he has a twitch,' whispered Audrey.

'It's an unusual looking place you have here, Mr Fabiano,' said Bill, ignoring her. 'You must have put in a lot of work.'

'I have indeed. I'm glad you like it.'

Bill, who hadn't said she actually liked it, looked around properly. There truly was an extraordinary number of coffee shops in Daylesford. Some were country cosy, some stylishly modern and one or two were themed. This one had a style all its own. The space was made up like an outback gorge, or perhaps an indoor exhibit in a zoo.

'Look at that,' exclaimed Bill and pointed towards the back, where a small waterfall streamed endlessly near two stuffed kangaroos wearing boxing gloves who appeared to be guarding a door.

'I noticed,' said Audrey. 'Did you see the deer? It's like being on the set of a budget '60s film.'

The taxidermy deer was positioned to graze on a patch of plastic grass near the front window. Assorted stuffed birds perched on lamps, shelves and fake cliffs, and a small round-eyed possum supervised the tips jar. Not even the ceiling was spared, with a canoe suspended from large hooks. In the centre of the room was a small canvas tent next to a gas campfire vented straight through the ceiling and surrounded by logs to sit on. There were a lot of canvas camp chairs and a couple of hammocks. A pretty waitress wearing a safari suit rushed around carrying cups. All the seats apart from some of the log space were taken, so Audrey and Bill stayed leaning on the counter.

'I'll have a bag of that coffee to take home, please.' Audrey didn't feel disloyal to Hugo, as he didn't sell coffee in bags. 'You'll see us again soon – we're performing here next week with the choir,' she added.

'Fantastic. I've been told you're pretty good,' said Fabiano, who had argued with his wife Anna after she organised it without asking him first. It wasn't quite the image he wanted. These women were no hip chicks, in their dowdy skirts and sensible shoes.

'Thnk you, we've only just joined. The acoustics here are good, nice natural amplification. We shall try to put a little snap and bip into it.'

'Bip? Erm, fine, sure.' *God help us, a geriatric choir*, he thought. What would Anna book in next, the vicar and a sewing circle perhaps?

'These biscuits are delicious,' said Bill, taking the last one. 'Did you make them? We must have a bag. No, make it two.'

Bill opened one of the bags of biscuits and walked over to a couple of young men sitting in a hammock. 'These are homemade, darlings. Have some.' The men looked surprised but accepted.

An elderly man trying to read a paper in the far corner tried not to engage in eye contact. He had met this sort before. Before you knew it you'd have joined something that you had to pretend to be sick to get out of attending. He shook his head resolutely. 'No thank you, they are too hard for me.'

'Rubbish, just dip it,' said Bill, demonstrating with a vigorous repeated dunking of the biscuit, which immediately started to dissolve in his cup. 'Here, eat,' she commanded, bits of wet biscuit dripping on the unfortunate man's shirtfront.

'Not on a diet, are you?' A couple of women having a conversation looked up to find a bag of biscuits waving in front of them. 'Try one, go on.'

Soon the bag was empty, though admittedly quite a few had gone into Bill herself. 'We must be off, goodbye everyone,' she called out cheerily. 'See you next week. Come and see the choir here on Tuesday. Divine coffee, thank you ever so much.'

After they swept out, carrying the remaining biscuit bag and some coffee, an inexplicable feeling of emptiness briefly descended in their wake. It was as if Bill and Audrey had made everyone feel noticed and somehow bereft when they were gone.

On their walk home they dropped into the chocolatier again for a box of assorted treats as well as the bakery for a big, handsome apple flan, varnished with a shiny apricot glaze.

'I'm going to get fat,' said Audrey.

'Oh, tosh! You never put on weight. Anyway, we've walked for hours, the exercise will compensate. Inez will have some too, won't she? She eats heartily, I noticed.' Bill tried hard to forget just how many biscuits she had just eaten. They were probably not very fattening though – they didn't taste overly sweet.

'Inez said the boys who work for her come today. No doubt they'll help with the eating.'

'Who are they again? James and something?'

'Simon and James. We probably need to get more just to feed all these people.' They found another bakery – this one specialising in gourmet vegan goods – and bought some fragrant cinnamon buns, just to be on the safe side.

They returned home with their bagfuls of treats to find a woman with brilliant red hair and dangling turquoise earrings in the kitchen unpacking tins from a basket. Her shoes matched the earrings perfectly.

'Capital,' said Inez, seated at the table with a cup in hand. 'Here you are at last. I want you to meet Ballentine. A dear friend and a half-decent baker, she's here to road-test some newfangled biscuits. My niece Plum is the one who looks like a startled stork, and the short round one is her friend Bill.'

'Inez tells me that you bake a little yourself,' said Ballentine. 'Try some of mine, see what you think.'

'We just had some biscuits at The Bean,' replied Audrey. 'Brought a few things from the shops too.' They unpacked the buns, flan, chocolates and biscuit bag onto the bench.

'I see you're already familiar with Ballentine's brand,' said Inez.

'Oh, these ones?' asked Bill. 'We've already had some, they were great. Cooking is such a drag, all that shopping and stirring and cleaning. Only the eating part is pleasant, and that is all too brief.'

'I know what you mean. But when you do it for a living, it's different.'

'Don't get any ideas, Audrey. I know that look,'

said Bill. 'Next thing we know we'll be knee-deep in flour and sugar.'

'Save us all,' said Inez. 'The world is not ready for Plum's cooking.'

Ballentine handed them some pale green biscuits. 'I like to test anything new on Inez first. There is no one more certain to tell me what's what. Have one of these.'

'Pistachio?' asked Bill, and bit into it. 'No. Savoury, salty. What is it?'

'They're horrible, dear. It's green tea, isn't it? Are you following fads, now?' Inez frowned. 'Give me something else.'

'Oh well, I will try again,' said Ballentine. 'The oat and rosemary biscuits are such a hit I thought I needed more savouries. The colour is attractive though, isn't it? Try these instead.' She passed around some red biscuits speckled with white sea-salt crystals.

'Now that is something else altogether,' said Inez and looked at them closely. 'They look like toadstools. Delicious. What do you think, girls?'

'The texture, the flavour, so good. What makes them red?' asked Bill.

'It'll be beetroot juice, am I right? Or did your hair colour run?' Inez took a second biscuit. 'They really are good. Anyway, how's business?'

'Oh, you know. Slowly developing. I have a couple of new stockists, which is exciting. It's just a matter of getting enough people to try them, really.'

'I think I know someone who would sell your biscuits,' said Audrey. 'Hugo at the bookshop by the lake. You wouldn't happen to do lemon creams by any chance?'

'But of course. My Citron Cuthberts. I have some stock in the car, if you want to give him a sample. There's just one more sort for you to try: Gold Nuggets.' She passed round a tin of irregularly shaped golden biscuits, befitting their name.

'Instant winner, my dear,' announced Inez. 'A bit of marmalade in there?'

'Truly there is no one like your aunt, a palate as keen as her hearing.'

'What's that?'

'Just kidding, Inez.'

The front door banged shut, startling Lucy, who had been busy pretending to nap under the kitchen table. She skittered off to the hallway in happy greeting at the sound of the new arrivals.

'Hello Sugar Plum,' two male voices called loudly from the hallway. 'We're here!'

'Sugar plum?' mouthed Bill to Audrey.

'Inez,' whispered Audrey and shrugged. 'Because she is so sweet, perhaps?'

Two young men breezed into the kitchen, followed by a wire-haired little dog with a bristly beard and a short squashed face trotting along. 'Hi, Ballentine, yum. I see we're just in time for a bickie before work. Love the hair.'

'Hello boys. Just had it done.' Ballentine ran her hand through her long fringe, the colour of a fire engine. It fell asymmetrically back in place across her face. 'Astrid did it. She's a genius.'

'Boys, I want you to meet my niece, Plum, and her friend, Bill. Girls, this is Simon and James,' said Inez.

'Another Plum, how fruity. Inez has been looking forward to you both arriving,' smiled Simon. The two men could have been brothers at a glance. They were both slim with neatly groomed sleek dark beards and dazzling smiles. The dog stuck close to its owners, and peered indignantly at Audrey and Bill from behind James's legs.

'This is Mister Wolf. He's a bit shy. Ignore him and he will settle. Oh, Ballentine, green biscuits. That's unusual,' said James and bit into one. 'Interesting. Kind of weirdly medicinal. A new health flavour?'

'Well, they're off the menu. They failed the Inez test so I don't think they're going to be a hit.'

'I don't know. Name them Yoginis or something and make them fibre rich.'

'Not a bad idea, I'll tweak the recipe. Stand by for the next tasting. I've got to be off now, I'll just bring those Cuthberts from the car.'

'Is there anything in particular that you want us to do today, Inez?' asked James.

'Actually there is, if you don't mind. The chimney upstairs needs a clean. It might have a bird's nest in it. It smokes worse than my old uncle Wesley and he practically had a personal cloud following him around. Also, the motorcar is wanting a check over. I am letting the girls drive her.'

'Simon can pop over tomorrow morning and do the chimney if you can wait until then. The equipment's at home, although we could go and collect it now if you'd rather.'

'No, that's fine. As long as the girls are happy with that.' They nodded agreement.

'Right then. Do you want us to make you something for dinner or are you cooking tonight?' asked James, looking at Audrey and Bill.

'Those two? They consider tea and toast a balanced meal,' snorted Inez. 'Please make something. A stew perhaps, something hot in a pot.'

'We bought some things for afternoon tea later. Please join us, we couldn't possibly eat all of it by ourselves,' said Audrey. 'Well, maybe Bill could.'

'At least you bought it from an actual baker. I just couldn't face any of those biscuits you made for Hugo. Did he enjoy them?' asked Inez.

'I doubt it,' Audrey sighed. 'But since he is more polite than you are, he didn't actually say so. Now, please tell us, who is this Fabiano at the new coffee shop? He seemed to think we should know him from television, but as we don't watch any, we have no idea who he is.'

'You would be in the minority,' said James. 'He was in one of those long-running soapies for around ten years until his character moved away or died or something. He's what is known as a heart throb. He's done a few ads too. Stick his face on a product and it sells.'

'Now here he is in our little village, running a coffee shop,' said Bill. 'A sort of early retirement plan, the quiet life?'

'Maybe. I don't think he is a fan of peace and quiet so much, rather the opposite,' James replied.

Inez had a little lie-down with the paper while the boys went about their jobs. Audrey and Bill, proud new members of the Daylesford Choir, decided to practise their singing. A chipped old August Forster upright piano graced the unheated room flanking the garden terrace, and they spent a couple of cold hours going over the songs they had to learn before Tuesday. Every now and then they nipped into the kitchen so Bill could heat up her icy fingers at the wood stove. Not just nice and warm, it had a slowly simmering pot of something that smelt delicious. The culinary repertoire was certainly an enormous change from what they were used to.

'Simon is making Italian beef and porcini stew for

dinner,' said James, coming in from the garden with a handful of parsley.

'Hmm, we're hungry already,' answered Bill.

They managed to run through another four songs before they were parched, joining Simon in the kitchen where he was just setting the table for afternoon tea.

'Could you ask Inez if she will join us or if she prefers me to bring a tray?' Simon asked Audrey.

Inez always enjoyed spending time with the boys and unless she felt too tired was certainly not going to have afternoon tea by herself in her room. She had a vigorous appetite for her build and age. Bill looked down at her own figure. It wasn't fair, really it wasn't. She had been watching what she ate (which was too much, too often) all her life but nothing changed her slightly-too-generous middle dimensions.

'The pair of you have the most dreadful wardrobe,' said Inez.

'As the wardrobe belongs to you, that is entirely your fault,' said Bill.

Inez simply looked at her. 'Huh. Especially that hideous Peter Pan collar, Audrey, it does you no favours,' she continued, cutting a bun into quarters and giving a piece to Mister Wolf, who wasn't shy of her at all. 'It makes me think I'm back at school or something, which is confusing. At my age one should aim to limit the opportunities for confusion. You simply have to go shopping. At the very least, you will need boots.

Those shoes, apart from being hideous, are simply not good enough for our wet spells. There might actually be some useful winter clothing in the trunks in one of the rooms upstairs. Have a rummage. I seem to remember a lot of clothes, tweeds and such left behind by my brothers – should keep you nice and warm and in some kind of style. They might fit you, Plum. You are as much of a wire coat hanger as they were. As for you Bill, I'm not sure there will be anything in your size. Our family are mainly built like storks, not corks, but there are a couple of car coats that might fit either of you. Grab them, you'll need them for motoring as there is no heating in the old girl.'

Since there was no functioning light in the upstairs storage rooms, they waited for daylight the next day before searching for clothes. In one room were several old trunks that revealed an entire country gentleman's wardrobe, somewhat dated but still good. Audrey pulled out a stack of ironed and folded shirts in different stripes and checks, slipovers, vests and jumpers, all smelling faintly of cedar.

'If all this fits me, I shall never need to buy clothes again,' she said. 'Look!' She held up a pair of tweed trousers. 'These would fit me reasonably well, and they don't even need hemming. There are braces too. I can actually remember my uncle wearing this.' She lifted up a FairIsle jumper knitted in a pattern of

44

muted grass greens, blues and reds. 'Oh goody, no moths. Will there be anything here for you, do you think? By the way, don't worry about Inez's rudeness. She likes you.'

'How can you possibly tell?'

'Wait until you see her with someone she doesn't like and you'll know. Here's something, is this any good for you?' Audrey held up a beautiful indigo woollen dress that had been hidden underneath a pile of shirts. 'I don't know who this belonged to.'

'I'll never be able to do the waist up,' Bill said, patting her middle.

'Such nonsense. Everybody wore corsets back when this was in fashion. Look at the label, it's Dior.'

'It is wonderful, but it won't fit. I'll just wear one of your uncle's jumpers on top of what I have. Hang on, there's a kilt. I'll wrap it to my size and pin it. These old golfing trousers are hilarious. If I can button them up, at least they won't be too long.'

'They might actually look rather smart. You can wear them with this.' Audrey threw her a woollen slipover. 'So unfashionable that we'll be style-setters. I'm going to layer up with one of these singlets first, should keep me warm.'

Decked out like 1940s men's fashion icons they regretfully put their own worn but comfortable black shoes back on.

When they got back to Bill's room, Simon was just

coming out with a bucket full of soot. 'Look at you. You look amazing. Off somewhere special?' He put down the bucket and wiped his hands on a towel tucked into his belt. 'Wait, let me do something...' He took the green scarf Audrey was wearing and rearranged it, studying her critically. 'That's better. Gorgeous.'

'We might take those biscuits down to Hugo now, and try out the car,' Audrey said. 'We found the car coats, they're super.'

'James has serviced it. He fuelled up too, so you're all good to go if you want. Give the car a little run around the countryside while you are out. Shout if you have any problems starting, I'll be around for another half hour.'

Inez had been right about her car. It started as soon as Audrey pushed the button on the walnut dashboard. She had also been right about the worn out seats.

'I need something to sit on,' Audrey said to Bill. 'These springs are murder. We'll have to get some cushions. Would you be a darling and run in and fetch a couple while I warm up the engine?'

'There'll be no running while I'm wearing this,' said Bill and flapped her arms like a penguin, the sleeves of her coat extending way below her hands. 'It's hard to move, but nice and toasty.'

The car featured plenty of exciting little compartments to explore. The glove box was true to its name, holding several pairs of still-good driving gloves in it, as well as a couple of well-worn roadmaps, showing the area as it had been many years ago.

'That's fine as long as we don't decide to head down to Melbourne. It's probably doubled in size since that map was printed,' said Audrey.

They cautiously set off down the road. The engine ran smoothly, but the famous valve radio didn't work. Bill twiddled the dials but nothing happened.

'Never mind, the main thing is that we have brakes.' Audrey gently pumped the brakes, which responded reassuringly. 'We can always sing.'

As they took a left into the main street, people turned their heads to see the magnificent car glide past.

'Fun, isn't it? I feel like I should be doing a regal wave,' said Bill.

'I could wear a cap and you could sit in the backseat, nodding gracefully at people.'

They drove past the lake, towards Sailor's Falls. The village itself petered out with a couple of new houses on the fringes, then the road wound through bushland which in turn became open rolling farmland. They took a left and another left, figuring they would return to Daylesford if they drove in a wide circle. They sped through a couple of tiny villages on the way, promising a later visit.

'I feel like Toad of Toad Hall in this car. Toot toot!' said Audrey and put her foot down harder. 'Here's a long straight, let's see what speeds we can do.' The car leapt to the task, surging forward as though it had been waiting for this moment for sixty years. The landscape blurred past, and all too soon a sign flashed by: Welcome to Daylesford – Please drive carefully...

'Let's head to Hugo's now,' said Audrey, easing her foot off the pedal regretfully.

Hugo was standing outside the bookshop with a bucket in his hand, surrounded by a herd of swans all clamouring to get to the feed first.

'*Mesdames*, how special. So soon to return. Such clothes! They go well with Inez's old car, don't they? Oh la la, turn around and let me admire you.'

Bill giggled and gve a spin in her check golfing pants and oversized car coat.

'Here, we found you the best lemon creams in the world,' said Audrey.

'Found or baked? Ah, they look like the very thing. They will be nice with a strong coffee. Let's go in, I'll just finish feeding this lot. They get hungry in winter.'

Hugo busied himself with the machine while they took off their heavy coats.

'A tiny dash for Bill and very milky for me please. Could you teach me how to do that?' asked Audrey. 'I've always wanted to know how the frothing happens.'

'*Mais bien sur.* Come around here and I'll show you.' Hugo demonstrated the art of foaming the milk just so. It didn't look too difficult.

'Maybe we could get Inez to buy a small machine for home. What do you think, Bill?' said Audrey enthusiastically. The doorbell tinkled.

'We're closed,' called Hugo.

'Nonsense,' Audrey told Hugo, 'you want the custom, don't you? Come in,' she called. 'Let us make you a drink. Or sell you a book, if you'd rather.'

'Maybe we could open a coffee shop. This is fun,' she said to Bill.

'Now we've gone from wanting a coffee machine to wanting a coffee shop in the space of a few short minutes. Let's just drink our coffee, shall we? Anyway, we're here on a biscuit mission. Hugo, Inez's friend Ballentine has a company that makes these and many others. Her details are on the label if you want to stock some.'

CHAPTER 3

Lying in her bed, the woman stirred from deep sleep. The windows shook to an insanely fast rhythm. Boom boomboomboom.

'What the hell?' She reached out for her alarm clock on the bedside table and promptly knocked it to the floor. 'Arrgh!' She swatted at the floor until she connected with the clock. Squinting at the numbers she eventually managed to read 01.15. Sick and dizzy with interrupted sleep she turned over and pulled the blankets over her ears. Impossible. The bed itself seemed to vibrate in response to the sound. Was it machinery? Giant earthmovers?

As she slowly came to, she realised it was music, if it could be labelled as such. She turned on her light and tried to read. Surely it would stop soon. But it didn't. The beats grew in frenzy as well as volume and she gave up trying to relax. Fred, her old black Labrador, had woken up too and sat whining softly at her side.

'Might as well get up and make a hot drink.' Fred followed her into the kitchen where she made herself some tea and gave him a snack. She stayed up reading until the kitchen clock struck four. 'It's just not stopping. What do you think? Call the police or is that silly?' Fred thumped his tail a couple of times on the floor in apparent agreement with whatever she would choose.

'You have reached Daylesford and District Police,' said an answering machine. 'In the case of emergency, press 1. For all other business, press 2 to leave a message.' A message? How would that help her? She tried another number, that of the nearest town. They were bound to be open at night. It was a 45-minute drive, but if she was lucky they might just have a patrol on the road that could put a stop to this.

'Brickwell Police.'

'Oh hello, I'd like to make a noise complaint.' She felt a little stupid, calling the police for something so trivial. They would have many more urgent things to deal with. As Brickwell was a town, there would likely be drug syndicates to squash and international head-quarters to raid.

'Do you know the source of the noise?' The voice at the other end sounded bored.

'No, sorry.' Now she felt worse. She should have gone for a walk or drive and found out first. 'But it must be nearby,' she continued. 'Surely you can hear it through the phone?' She waved the phone about in the air. 'I'm in Daylesford. I realise it's out of your way but in case someone is patrolling in the vicinity... Oh they're not? Okay, I'm sorry. Yes, I'll call the council in the morning. Thank you Officer.' She put the phone down and sighed.

Still in her pyjamas, she threw her coat on and eased her feet into rubber boots. Fred was happy to have an early walk, tugging on his lead with excitement. Outside the sound was worse, and she noticed several of the neighbours' lights on. It was now 4.30am and still getting louder. She followed the sound up the road. When she turned the corner the source became obvious, as groups of laughing and talking people milled around the entrance to The Bean.

'A coffee shop? Indeed,' she said to Fred, who wagged his tail obligingly. 'Stop wagging, it's not funny. I don't care how famous he is. Come on, Freddie boy.' She walked around the block before returning home. It was 6.00am before the mercy of silence came. No point going to bed now. She was due to work in an hour no matter what.

On her way home in the afternoon she met a neighbour.

'Did you hear that awful racket last night?'

'Oh, it wasn't so bad, brings a little life,' he said, getting into his car.

A little life? Was he insane? She knew they had

been awake too, as she had noticed their lights on. Maybe they didn't want to make a fuss. Not her, though. She would go to The Bean and find out for herself what the story was.

But The Bean was closed. *They should have been bloody closed last night*, she thought crossly. The large plant pots outside the nursery had empty bottles nestled among the winter flowers, and more still were scattered in the front garden. The stuffed deer grazed on its plastic lawn, impervious to any goings-on, but wearing a tasselled party hat. She told herself that if she was still as angry after a good rest she would call the council in the morning.

'We haven't had any complaints,' said the council officer. 'You're the only one. He's such a lovely man. Charming. Surely he means no harm? Have you spoken to him? His coffee is the best and I would know, I drink it every day.'

'How can there not be complaints? I can't possibly be the only one upset.'

'Frankly there isn't a lot we can do unless you give us your name.'

'Which I will not do and I fail to see how that matters.'

'I can't help you. You need to bring it up with him, but do it gently. He's a sensitive man and I know that it would upset him greatly to know you're upset.'

That afternoon she returned, still as annoyed, to

The Bean. It was now open and full of coffee drinkers. The owner was standing at the bar counter. He breathed a huff of steam into a glass and polished it with a cloth.

'Welcome. Ah, a beautiful lady, first class, and on her own.' He looked up and smiled at her. 'Are you meeting a lucky someone, or will you give me the pleasure of your company at the bar counter? Let me give you your first coffee experience here on the house. You have not been before, am I right?'

'That's nice of you, but no, thank you. I was just wondering about the other night, there was some loud music. Were you having a special party?'

'Oh no, not at all. It's our weekly Saturday Nite Late. We'll be doing Fridays too, soon. You should come one night, it's great fun.'

'No, no, that can't happen,' she pleaded. 'You are too loud. You might as well have the speakers outside, or maybe that's what you did? And so late, too.'

'No one has complained, rather the opposite. Everyone likes it. You'll get used to it.' His smile was no longer as broad.

'What do you mean, no one has complained? I just did, do I not count?'

'Of course you do, you count as *one*, and *one* doesn't rate. Now if you don't mind, I would like to finish polishing these glasses.' He turned his back to her and held another glass up to the light to check for marks.

What an infuriating man, she seethed as she trudged home in the rain, which had begun again. Nothing but a smarmy loathsome git. Never would she drink from the poisoned cup he had spat in. She hunched into her turned-up collar but miserable rivulets of water still managed to find their way down her neck.

***

It was true to say that Fabiano loved his wife. He loved being seen with her, as her beauty made heads turn. It enhanced his success and made him look even better. It was also true to say that he liked Rick, his business partner. They had been friends for years and Rick was useful.

On Monday night he had a meal with Anna at their favourite pub before walking back home down the hill. It was nice being able to walk everywhere, a benefit of this country lark. He wasn't entirely sober, not at all. A different benefit was the apartment above The Bean, which came with the lease. Anna wanted an early night and he excused himself and went downstairs to meet Rick. They had some business to get through, mainly consisting of having a couple of glasses of after-dinner grappa. Fabiano was alone and just about to lock up when he received another visitor, but this one wasn't anywhere near as pleasant.

By Tuesday morning the rains had stopped. As the day

progressed the sun shone brightly, which was good news for performing. Rain could mean that people preferred to stay at home, and the choir loved nothing better than a good crowd. Just before two o'clock Bill and Audrey arrived at The Bean, slightly ahead of the rest. Fabiano's wife, Anna, met them at the door. She was almost as attractive as her husband, slightly built with the grace of a dancer and a thick mane of dark curly hair that reached well below her waist. Across the bridge of her little button nose was a smattering of freckles. Her tight-fitting explorer outfit did nothing to diminish her figure.

Hair like Medusa, thought Bill, who had quite plain hair herself. She had kept the same cut for her entire convent life. It was simple, short and practical, and she had never given it a thought before. There seemed to be a million styles available. How did you go about getting one?

'I was hoping Fabiano would be here before you arrived,' said Anna.

'He isn't here?' Audrey thought Anna looked tired. There were faint dark shadows under her eyes.

'I don't actually know where he is. His mobile is going straight to messages.'

It shocked them to realise that Anna looked like she might start crying.

'Whatever's the matter? Are you alright?' The warmth in Audrey's voice had a certain magic. She had a gift for focusing on the individual, making people feel they mattered. It worked so well because they genuinely did matter to her.

'No, I'm not.' Anna pressed a slender hand to her eyes. 'I haven't seen him since yesterday. Rick and I moved the furniture around to make a space for you, check if it's okay. I think there will be quite a lot of people coming.'

Overall, there was nothing really left to do so they decided to have a cup of tea at the counter while waiting to start.

'He definitely knew the choir was coming,' said Bill to Anna. 'He said he was looking forward to it when we met him. Could he have been in an accident?'

'I rang the hospital and the police. If he had an accident I would know.' Anna lowered her voice to a whisper. 'He could be having an affair. There are always so many women around him, they can't help themselves. We usually laugh about it but he has never not come home before. The other day he hid something from me too.'

'What?'

'Don't know, some piece of paper. We've never had secrets before, I don't know what to think.' She twirled a long strand of hair around her slender fingers.

'There'll be another reason,' Bill assured her. Maybe he's planning a surprise?'

'Maybe.' Anna sighed and moved away to serve a

another customer.

Bill wondered what it would be like to have hair like Anna's. Would the hair itself be enough to make you beautiful no matter what you looked like, or would it just be annoying? She tried to imagine summer heat. It would be like carrying around a giant cat perched on your head. No, she would probably prefer it short, though one could try on wigs to see how it looked...

'Bill? Are you in there?' Audrey bumped her, nearly upsetting her teacup.

'Hair. I mean I am here. I was just thinking about hair.'

'Never mind about hair, I think Fabiano is being really rude. He books the choir, confirms it, then doesn't come himself. The show must go on and all that, but it's rather naughty. Ah, the choir is starting to arrive now.'

In an effort to look cohesive on a budget, the choir wore black but in any style they chose. At best, Audrey felt they looked like a colony of bats lining up. Bill and Audrey just wore their dark skirts, jumpers and stockings.

'Ve are ze vampire sink-a-lonks here to zuck your blud,' hissed Bill.

'Shush. Buck up and look lively. Where's Hugo?' Audrey turned to Georgina, one of the altos.

'Sore throat. So have Ros and Fiona. It's a good

thing we have Bill to strengthen the sopranos.'

They performed two sets with a brief break. Still no Fabiano.

'I enjoyed that,' said Anna when they finished. 'Truly funny, especially the bits where you had to start from the beginning again. I've never seen a choir do a comedy routine before, Fabiano will be upset that he missed it. Perhaps we can arrange for you to do a repeat sometime?'

'We'll see. Speaking of arranging, let us help you put the furniture back. There are so many of us it will only take a minute.' Audrey was hurt on behalf of the choir. Comedy routine?

The choir deftly rearranged the chairs and tables, taking the customers with them. 'Lift your cup please. Mind your legs.'

'We'll move this last chair and we must be off too,' Audrey said to Anna. 'Thanks for having us.'

'Before you two leave as well, let me give you a sample collection of our coffees as thanks,' said Anna. 'I just have to finish making these drinks first. It's pretty hectic without Fab. If you don't mind collecting them yourselves, there's a box of samples in the storeroom back there.' She nodded towards the rear of the building, where the two kangaroos guarded the entry to the toilets and storage area.

'We'd love some. We can have it at choir practice.'

They walked to the storeroom door. Audrey grabbed the handle and opened it. She quickly shut it and turned to Bill, all the blood drained from her face.

'Bill,' she said, voice quivering slightly. 'Promise you won't show any reaction to what I am about to say, okay?'

'Okay,' Bill nodded.

'Fabiano. In there. I'm pretty sure he's dead. You have first aid training, you look.'

Fabiano sat slumped against the shelves of the little storeroom surrounded by a sea of coffee beans spilt across the floor. He was gagged with what looked like plastic food wrap, and his hands and feet were tied up with wide clear sticky tape and some orange nylon string for good measure. He was well and truly trussed.

'Jesus, Mary and Joseph,' gasped Bill and put her hands to her face.

'Just check if he's still alive. I know it's unlikely, but just check anyway.'

Bill stepped gingerly over the beans as they crunched underfoot and made her unsteady, and bent down to feel for a pulse. Up close she could see coffee beans stuck under the plastic, distorting his chiselled features. She turned to Audrey, wide-eyed.

'We must call the police. He's cold. I'll go and talk to Anna.' She stepped out of the storeroom and closed the door.

Audrey went up to the nearest person. 'Do you

have a mobile phone? I need to borrow it. It's urgent, sorry,' she said.

'You look terrible. Are you ill?' said the man, handing her his phone.

'I'm fine, thank you,' said Audrey and went back to guard the door as she dialled the emergency number. This was definitely a crime scene and she had to make sure no one else opened the door.

'Can't you find them?' said Anna to Bill. She was busy with another round of coffees. 'I'll be over to help in a minute.'

'Anna, I need to talk to you. It's important.' Bill looked serious in her black garb. 'Come and sit down.'

'But the customers...'

'They can wait.'

'What's up? You're making me nervous.' Anna abandoned her coffee making and followed Bill to some seats.

'You need stay calm now.' Bill's voice was low and insistent. 'I have some bad news for you. I am so very sorry. It's Fabiano. I think he might be dead.'

Anna looked up, eyes widening. 'Dead? Where is he? He can't be, that's rubbish!'

'He's in the storeroom. The police will be here in a minute.'

Anna stood up hastily and sat back down again as her legs gave way.

'Go to the front door and stop anyone who's leaving,'

said Audrey to the man whose phone she was still using.

'What? Why?'

'Because I have the police on the phone, and that's what has to happen. Please don't make a fuss. I can't stop them from back here and I can't leave this door. The police won't be long.' They were giving her instructions over the phone until they were able to put officers on the scene.

Bill was trying to stay calm in the hope of her own state reaching Anna. 'I believe he has been murdered, though the police will have to tell you that for sure after they get here.'

Anna swayed, her face white. Bill patted her arm firmly.

'Who would want to kill him? Why?' The 'why' turned into a keening wail and her voice rose. 'If only we had never come here.'

'Has anything strange happened lately? Anything at all?'

Anna just groaned and gripped the arms of her chair tight.

'Anyone who doesn't like him, any problems?'

'There are always problems with business, lots. People are jealous of him – just look at how busy we are. Someone made a noise complaint too. There has even been some people carrying on about the stuffed animals. I can't believe it. Is he really dead?'

'We'll know more once the police arrive.'

'He didn't come home last night,' she said in a small voice. 'He simply didn't come home. I was so worried and angry when I woke up. He was here all along. I can't believe it. Now he'll never come home.'

The first police car pulled up, and two uniformed officers stepped out.

'He's in the back room. We haven't told anyone apart from his wife,' said Bill.

'Stay where you are, please.' The police went in as if nothing particularly untoward was happening. Music played, coffee was drunk, and at the back door to the storeroom Audrey was having an argument with Rick, Fabiano's business partner.

'I need to get in there now, I have to fetch supplies. Stand aside, you crazy woman. This is our storeroom and you're trespassing.'

'I will not. Get your hands off me.' Audrey, unflappable, looked over his shoulder. 'Thank God, here are the police now. Over here, officers.' Rick turned around.

'We'll take it from here.' They opened the door briefly to take a look and started talking on their radio. They had just come from a property in Glenlyon where a lawnmower had been stolen. In this region, that was considered a serious enough crime to warrant an investigation.

The Major Crimes Unit from Brickwell would no

doubt come over for this one. In Brickwell, missing garden equipment did not merit anything further than a report over the phone and often not even that. For now though, this was their crime scene. One of the officers started moving protesting people out of the cafe, corralling them into Gloria's Gardens next door, much to the surprise of Gloria herself.

'Sorry about this, Gloria. We need to put this lot somewhere before we can get their details and let them go. It shouldn't be too long.'

'What's happened?'

'We need to seal off next door for a while. There's been an incident. You'll find out the details soon enough,' the officer said before turning to the crowd, which was starting to complain.

'I left my handbag in there, I need to get it,' said a woman plaintively.

'Nobody goes in there or out of here yet.' He closed the gates to the garden shop and stood, oblivious to complaints, awaiting instructions from the team, which couldn't be too far away now.

Soon more cars pulled up, as did the ambulance. Anna, Rick and the waitress were driven to the police station, along with Audrey and Bill, as they were the first on the scene. After having their statements taken the two women were ushered out, despite wanting to stay. It was mesmerising to watch the general bustle.

'Go on, go home now. Someone will be over to see

65

you tomorrow,' said the police officer at the front desk.

'Oh Bill, this is just terribly tragic. Poor man. And Anna, what a dreadful thing to happen. She's so young.'

'I know. Devastating. I don't want to go home yet, do you? I'm too wound up.' Both Bill and Audrey thought guiltily that if it wasn't all so awful this would easily be the most exciting thing that had ever happened to them.

'Let's go see Hugo and give him the news.'

They walked from the station to their car, which was parked outside The Bean. The fresh air did them good. All the same, it was comforting to sit in the enclosed and private space of the car. Audrey put the car in gear and they drove in silence to Hugo's. Today the lake mirrored the trees blackly on its smooth surface. Audrey sighed. It was so beautiful that it hurt, especially when she thought that for one particular man, the beauty of this world was forever gone.

'It's horrible, isn't it?' said Bill, not seeing the lovely scene but turning inwards. 'I'm cold, feeling shaky. Delayed shock, probably. Let's go in.'

The day had started out cool and had now settled into a bitter chill with a leaden purple sky showing promise of snow. At Le Bouquiniste, smoke was curling from the chimney. Warm yellow light shone from the windows. It cast an inviting spell, drawing Bill and Audrey in.

'How was the gig?' asked Hugo. 'Your noses are

white, it must be cold.' He was sitting by the fire nursing his cold, a tumbler of neat whisky in one hand and a book in the other. 'Do you want a hot drink, or would you rather whisky?'

'In a minute,' said Audrey, 'we must tell you some news first. You'll never guess what's happened.'

'Don't tell me. You burnt more biscuits?'

'No, no. This is serious. There's been a murder.'

'What? Who?'

'Fabiano.'

Hugo exhaled sharply. 'That's incredible. Terrible. Who did it?'

'No idea.'

'He has only been here for a few weeks,' said Hugo, shaking his head.

'No time to make enemies, you'd think,' said Bill. 'I think I'll make us some tea. Don't bother getting up, Hugo. I'll have a slug of that whisky with mine.'

'You can make enemies as fast as you like,' said Hugo. 'That one, he was doing a fine job of it from what I can tell. *Fils de salope!* A right bastard actually, with his arrogance and his *stupide* reviews.'

'What makes you think they were from him?' asked Audrey.

'Well, it started when The Bean opened. They weren't all just about my place, you understand. Other cafes got them too. But they were all similar, saying things like "worst coffee ever, don't go there", "waited an hour for service", "rancid beans", no? *Casse couille!* I need the coffee income. I can't possibly make a living on selling books alone. The rent here is *très, très cher*.'

Hugo was speaking rapidly, slipping in and out of French and waving his arms around. 'I confronted him and he just leered at me. *Quel bâtard suffisant! L'idiot laid!* Winning because you are the best is one thing, but winning because you are *un lézard dégoûtant* is quite another. We'll see if the reviews continue now. I will be keeping the eye, no?'

'Anna said that someone complained about noise,' said Bill. 'Do you know anything about that?'

'Only one? I'm surprised there weren't more. He had a permit to have "a little light music" in the evenings. But after the police and council close their doors at the end of the day, what can you do? I could hear it from here. Sound travels well across water.' He took a sip of whisky. 'I can't say I'm that sorry, really. I don't mean to sound heartless, he didn't have to die or anything but I am glad he is no longer able to act the saboteur. I need more business or I am out.'

'Can we help you?' asked Audrey. 'There has to be something we can do. What about the choir performing here?'

'Look around, there is no room. Once the choir is in, there's no space left.'

'We'll think of something. We can write positive reviews ourselves.'

'Don't. It makes us as bad as him.'

'But we adore it here,' Bill swept her arm out broadly, encompassing the space and managing to knock over a pile of neatly stacked novels. 'Of course we can write a good review.'

***

As a small village, Daylesford never contained a secret for long and by the next day the rumours had spread far and wide. The grocery shop was a hothouse for gossip and subsequently the best source for local information.

'Have you heard about The Bean? They're closed, of course. I bet it was that business partner. Seems he had a thing for the wife.'

'You're making that up.'

'No, it's true. Gloria told me. She should know, she sees them every day.'

'He had a lot of women hanging round.'

'But he was a lovely man. What a loss, his poor wife. I saw them together for dinner on Sunday. They looked so in love, so glamorous together. Like movie stars.'

'He was leaving her, that's what I heard.'

'Never.'

'The awful racket the other night. Pah! I had a good mind to go down and pull the plugs out.'

Meanwhile, a woman in her thirties was being dropped

off outside Inez's house.

'Sure you don't need me with you?' asked the driver, a local constable.

'I'll manage, thank you,' said Detective Sergeant Rosie Lloyd, brought in from Brickwell.

'I'll go and get some food while you talk to them. There's an old woman living there too, she's scary. Rather you than me. What do you want for lunch?'

'Nothing for me, thanks. I'll be bound to get full to the hilt with tea and scones.'

Audrey and Bill were sitting with Inez in the kitchen, discussing the extraordinarily sad events. They were interrupted by the sound of knocking on the back door. A woman with the face of a Botticelli angel stood outside, if you could imagine an angel wearing a dark trouser suit. The angel was holding up a police ID.

'I'm Detective Sergeant Rosie Lloyd. May I come in? The front doorbell seems to be out of order.'

'Not at all,' said Inez. 'You just have to remember to push, not pull. Or the other way. Whatever it says, do the opposite anyway. Do sit down. No, not here, you should go into the library. Much nicer. How interesting it must be to be a Detective Sergeant. But such a tragic thing. You must have a cup of tea, the kettle's hot.'

'Alright, I will, thank you. Just black, please. Call me Rosie.' Having grown up in a small community,

70

Rosie Lloyd knew that it was easier to agree than argue or you would spend an hour protesting at the endless proffered choices until you gave in anyway.

'This way, please.' The two younger women led her into a book-lined room of beautiful proportions and told her to sit while they fetched the tea. The massive fireplace was unlit and she shivered involuntarily, glad of her jacket. Through a couple of windows she caught glimpses of the gardens outside. She walked closer to one in order to get a better view. Draughts blew through unsealed cracks and missing glazing putty. *It would be impossible to heat this house, even with the fire on*, she thought. Her own place was tiny, comfortable and practical. It may not be very attractive but at least it was warm. The rattling of teaspoons on saucers heralded the return of the women, carrying a large tray.

'That looks nice. Now, I'd like a chat about yesterday. Tell me what happened.'

Bill began. 'We just joined the local choir. Have you heard the choir before? No? Oh, but it's good, very good. Shall we give you a sample? No? Well, another time. Maybe it's not appropriate. Though we do a beautiful Requiem. Not with this choir, that was another one. Never mind. Milk? Sugar? And look, there's apple flan. Do have some, it's excellent. Made with local apples I think. So special. There is a little clotted cream too. Anyway, we finished the singing and then we were going to fetch a small gift for the choir from the storeroom. Gifts are so nice, I think. We never did get this one though, did we?'

'No, because when I opened the door, there he was,' said Audrey.

'Yes, you just closed the door straight away and called me. We used to be nuns you see. I was in charge of convent first aid. Audrey never did any nursing. The sick and the lame get no help from her. Just joking. You're in a caring profession yourself though, aren't you?'

'I suppose you could call it that. It must have been shocking for you. What happened next?' These women needed a little tugging on the reins to get them back on track. Rosie would let them talk as much as they wanted as long as there was a result at the end. She took a sip from her tea, which was served in almost translucent bone china cups, a miniature silver teaspoon resting on each saucer. It was like drinking from eggshells.

Bill went on. 'I simply walked in, felt for a pulse just to make sure. He felt cool, you know. What did he die from? Suffocation?'

'I'm not able to discuss that. Did you move anything, touch anything?'

'Oh yes, absolutely. The poor man himself, the light switch, and the shelves all along for balance. There were so many coffee beans on the floor, you see. Didn't want to slip and fall over on the man. The door

72

handle too, of course.'

'You're young for a Detective Sergeant,' interrupted Audrey, smiling at her. 'Do you have a young man somewhere? Apart from in your lock-up I mean?'

Rosie felt her strength sapping. 'If we could just return to the question...?'

'Are you quite comfortable there, Rosie?' Bill replied. 'I think this chair's better. Here, let me move you.' Rosie bemusedly allowed them to propel her into a different chair, which looked quite similar.

Bill lifted Rosie's feet onto a low stool. 'Would you like a blanket?'

'No thank you, I'll be absolutely fine.'

'This room is as chilly as outside, nearly. We should have stayed in the kitchen really, but it isn't a good room. This one is much more welcoming. Just not in temperature. Have some more hot tea, that'll make you feel better. Now where were we?'

'You were in the storeroom. I understand it's unpleasant for you to recall, but let's go through what happened, what you saw.' She had somehow acquired a grey cat in her lap, which was busily pushing its claws through the fabric of her trousers.

'Certainly.' Bill repeated what she had seen, down to the beans under the gag. 'Do you have cats, Rosie?'

'No, I don't.' The cat had a soft underbelly, like a warm cloud. She lifted it off, as gently as she could manage considering that all its claws were stuck. Fine hairs clung to her trousers, making her regret not accepting the blanket.

'This is Lucy. She really likes you,' said Bill.

'Having animals can be so therapeutic when you are in a stressful job like yours,' said Audrey. 'If you ever want a cat, let us know. There are so many animals needing new homes, I'm sure we could find you one. I once knew a woman who volunteered at an animal shelter. She would walk them and feed them and clean out their cages.'

'Just think of it. Cages. All locked up. A bit like your station perhaps,' added Bill and sneezed.

'Yes, well, maybe not quite like that. We don't walk them much. Now, if we can just stick to yesterday. Did you know the deceased?'

'We only met him once. We've only just moved to Daylesford. Do you live here yourself?'

'Can you think of a reason why anyone would want him out of the way?'

'We have heard a few things. Apparently,' Bill leant over the table in a conspiring manner and lowered her voice, 'he had been spreading malicious reviews on the internet about other businesses. Hugo at the bookshop by the lake told us about things that were done to him. And there was a noise complaint too. Anna said so. Also, she was worried that he was having an affair. Or maybe he had to leave the city because of trouble there, but the trouble followed him up here.

What do you think about that?'

'It's always possible, I suppose. Now, if you have nothing further to add, I shall go. Thank you for your time. Here's my card if you think of anything useful. One last question: Who do you think did it?'

'We have no idea, we don't know anyone here really. We'll tell you if we find out anything useful,' said Bill, hastily wrapping up some apple flan. 'Here, take some with you for your colleagues at the station. You can warm it before serving, makes it even nicer. Better in the oven, do you have an oven there? So nice to have met you, Rosie. Goodbye and thank you for visiting.'

Rosie, carrying the gift of cake, walked out to the waiting car. Something about this pair made you feel all soft inside, as if there was really nothing wrong with the world despite all the evidence pointing to the contrary. Finding a murdered man seemed like nothing more than an exciting game. She planned to return again fairly soon. They certainly could talk. If they listened as well as they talked, they would be sure to give her more leads. They already had – the bookshop by the lake for a start, not to mention a possible affair and a noise complaint. She decided to go to the bookshop straight away.

'That took you a while,' said Susanna, her driver. 'What's in the bag?'

'Apple flan. Very nice, actually. I will share. Couldn't refuse them.'

'Did you meet the scary woman? She shouted at me and my brother so much when we were small that he widdled his pants. I'm still afraid.'

'She was sitting in the kitchen. Seemed harmless. How old were you?' said Rosie, amused.

'Five. I never got over it. Next stop on our list is the director of the choir. He has the biggest moustache I have ever seen.'

'Actually, I think we'll start with the bookshop by the lake. Do you know where it is?'

'Of course, but he's not on my list.'

'He is now. The women in there are ex-nuns but it couldn't have been a silent order. They can talk the leg off a table. We have a couple of new leads and I intend to pop back for more in a few days. They'll listen to all the gossip better than we can.'

At Le Bouquiniste a handsome man with dark hair, greying at the temples, sat reading by the fire. He looked up at the two women entering his shop and smiled. Most people did on seeing Rosie for the first time. This was seldom the case once she introduced herself. Since there was no one else about that they could see, this must be Hugo.

'Detective Sergeant Rosie Lloyd and Constable Susanna Edwards,' said Rosie and held up her ID. 'Are you the owner of this business?' She wasn't sure about how to pronounce Le Bouquiniste.

'I am he, yes. Hugo Dubois. How may I help you?' He put the book down and stood up. Rosie noticed that although he was no longer young, he had an impressive physique, moving with effortless ease. He looked capable of holding his own in a fight.

'I'm making enquiries about recent events in Daylesford and I understand you might have some information.'

'Always delighted to help the law. I take it this is about the death at The Bean? You wouldn't come this way just to follow up on the latest swan taunting,' he said, raising an elegant eyebrow.

'No indeed,' Rosie replied, not knowing what on earth a 'swan taunting' was and not being inclined to ask. 'Let's talk about Fabiano Battista, shall we? What can you tell me about him? I understand you knew him.'

'No, I didn't exactly know him. I had met him once or twice, of course. I think most people had, it's a small place. He was an active man, wasn't he? Popular with *les femmes. Aïe, aïe!*' He shook his hand in a Gallic gesture.

'How long had you known him?'

'As I said, I didn't really know him. A few weeks only. Can't be more exact than that. I bumped into him on Friday afternoon, I think, at the shops.'

Rosie was having trouble envisioning this man actually bumping into anything. He seemed far too graceful for that.

'I believe that you're a member of the choir. Why was it that you didn't go to the performance?'

'I was here with the cold and the sore throat. As you can hear, he still plagues me.' He pointed to his nose as if to illustrate his point.

'Can you tell me where you were on Monday night between nine and midnight?'

'Am I a suspect?'

'I don't know. You tell me. Where were you between nine and midnight?'

'Monday night I was preparing for an early bed as near as I can remember. I wasn't feeling well so I had a bath and a shot of whisky. My sister rang from France, and we spoke briefly. I went to bed with my book.'

'Did she ring on your mobile or landline?'

'Landline. It was around 9.30 I think. She got me just as I was nodding off.'

'Ever have a disagreement with Mr Battista? Any quarrels?'

'What do you mean?'

'We've heard rumours about negative internet reviews. What can you tell me about those?'

'Mmm. Yes, I have been concerned. Someone started writing crank reviews just after he started his business. It might not have been him, of course, but I was suspicious. I noticed that his own place had great write-ups. So many of them too, so soon after opening. Seemed, how you say, fishy. You can read them for yourself. I was furious. The cheek of the man. Competition is welcome *naturellement*, but play fair. If it all ends here, I was right, but the damage, he is done, no?'

'He is done? Oh, yes I see. We'll need the contact details for your sister, please. We'll be speaking to you again, Mr Dubois. Meanwhile, if you think of anything, give me a call.'

CHAPTER 4

'A surprise visitor! Do come in.' Audrey smiled at
Fiona, who was standing at the door carrying a bunch
of tulips and a bottle of wine.

'I had the marvellous idea to come and visit. When
you've just moved to a new place it's nice to make
friends. Here's a token gift to properly welcome you.'

'How thoughtful, thank you.'

Fiona removed her muddy boots and pulled out a
delicate pair of ballet flats from her handbag.

'So handy,' she trilled, and showed a slender ankle
to Bill, who grunted in response, looking down at her
own feet, shod in woollen socks and worn slippers that
had been made with love by a dear friend a long time
ago. They were as comfortable as old slippers ought to
be but they were no competition for the simple
elegance of these dainty slip-ons. Fiona's long hair was
perfectly smooth, and her black-and-white ensemble
was both classic and fashionable. All in all, she set

Bill's teeth on an uncharitable edge.

'This house is in a great location, isn't it? Shame it's so run down. It must be expensive to restore. I can understand why Inez never has. Perhaps she could sell it to someone with money and taste who would care for it properly. It wouldn't do to run it into the ground, now would it? Isn't there any heating? It's freezing in here.'

'Let's go to the library and sit down. The fire's laid, I'll light it. We won't be cold for long. There's sherry or whiskey, or tea and coffee if you'd rather?' Audrey was very polite. Well brought up and nicely mannered despite the Pretty gene for abruptness, it would take more than this annoying woman to ruffle her. She mentally let the two valuable words Kindness and Compassion flood her mind until she felt better.

'Thank you, I will. A cup of herbal please and a thimble of whiskey.' Fiona eased herself elegantly into the dilapidated leather Chesterfield nearest the fireplace and arranged her slender legs just so. 'The word is that you used to live in a convent. How interesting! Is it true?'

'Yes.'

'As nuns? Tell all. That sounds so exciting.'

'Does it?' Audrey tightened her lips and poked at the fire, willing it to blaze up. This was a definite no-go zone.

'Certainly does. Go on then, share. From the inside out.' Fiona wasn't going to give in that easily. She had never met a nun who had left the order before. This was prime gossip fodder. Fortunately for her, Bill returned with a tray from the kitchen before Audrey bit her head off – politely, of course.

'Tea and whiskey for you, and some for us too. Here we are.' Bill put the tray down on the low coffee table in front of the fire.

'We're loving the choir,' said Audrey, changing the topic smoothly. 'It was Hugo's idea for us to join. We really look forward to all the new music we'll learn, the people we'll get to know... Everyone has been most welcoming. Especially Hugo. He's lovely, isn't he?'

'Oh, he certainly is. I've known Hugo since I moved up here from Melbourne four years ago. I met him in the first week that I was here, much like you did. We recently went to Port Fairy together. It's so pretty on the coast. The boats, the houses. Have you been?' asked Fiona, failing to mention that the entire choir had come too as it was a performance outing. 'Such a dear man. He likes to recommend things for me to read. I write the tiniest bit of poetry myself. Sometimes we sit on the deck on a summer's evening, reading poetry to each other.'

She continued, smiling serenely. 'He can recite some of mine by heart. As soon as spring comes, he gets his canoe ready. Living where he does, he just has to pop it in the water whenever he feels like a little dreamy drifting. Maybe he will take you out one day? I can ask for you, if you like. Did you know he fossicks, too?'

'What does that involve?' asked Audrey.

'Oh, you scout around for gold, gemstones, things left behind in the gold rush like bottles and stuff. Ask him to show you his collection some time.' She reached for a tissue in her handbag and dabbed at her nose.

'You till sound a little croaky. How's your cold going?'

'Lingering on. You know when you no longer feel sick enough to lie down but it won't leave your system? That's how I feel. My nose has been like a tap but it's better now.' She coughed delicately. 'This herbal tea is soothing. What is it?'

'Fresh borage, ginger, a squeeze of lemon and a spoonful of honey. Great for coughs and colds,' said Bill. 'If you don't have any borage, the other things are good on their own. We have plenty growing right here in the garden.'

'I must bring some to Hugo, he's struggling with the same cold. You could say we're sharing it.' She gave a tinkling little laugh. 'May I have a little to take with me?'

'I'm sure we could get you some. Do tell us more about the fossicking, it sounds fascinating.' Audrey was struggling with feelings of resentment. It was their tea – they should be the ones bringing the healing. 'Borage is also useful against hot flushes. That might be handy for you to know at your time of life, or have you finished already?' she added innocently.

The conversation, which had been rather one-sided, now stopped completely.

'I have a perfect remedy for your chesty cough and blocked nose,' said Bill, who was also well schooled in the gentle art of conversing. She took a sip from her whiskey, happy that she hadn't diluted it by pouring it into her tea. It burned its way down her throat, followed by an irresistible tickle of naughtiness that she tried to suppress. But it was like trying to hold back a sneeze: sometimes it is simply too late.

'Do you? What is it?'

A drip had found its way to the tip of Fiona's nose. She dabbed at gingerly.

'It's a secret recipe. We used it in the convent a lot. Let me get you some. Being burdened with the sniffles is so tedious, isn't it? That red nose must be sore.' Bill went into the kitchen and returned with a laden spoonful of some kind of paste. It had a strange faint odour that got stronger as she rubbed it on Fiona's throat and earlobes, and as far down her chest as she felt was decent. Fiona wrinkled up her nose as Bill dabbed some on there as well, and a little on her temples.

'More here, and here. Silky, isn't it?'

'But the smell!'

'You'll improve no end. Oops, got some on your shirt dear, that's too bad, maybe we can fix that. Oh no, some here as well. Audrey, could you get something for it? Quickly!'

'Oh, definitely. I have just the thing for all stains.' Audrey left the room and came back with a wet cloth and a bowl with a powdery substance. 'Let me just paste this on like so.' She dabbed the wet cloth in the powder and rubbed it on Fiona's shirt. 'Now that's better, isn't it? We used this at the convent, too.'

Fiona looked down in horror at her white shirt. It was greasy, smelly and wet, covered in soggy powder.

'My shirt, it's ruined! Stop, no more!' She held her hand out as a barrier and stood up quickly, grabbing her bag. 'I must go.'

'Your cold sounds better already. See you at choir.' Bill walked her to the front door. 'Thank you for the flowers. Bye, bye now.' She closed the door and flipped the lock catch.

'There, she's gone,' she said to Audrey. 'I thought she'd never stop bragging.'

'You are very naughty.'

'I tried to stop it, I really did. It just happened. What was it you rubbed on her?'

'Some powdered chicken stock I found in the cupboard. I felt it would work well with your goose fat. She is quite a dish.'

'Yes, she is now. Let's go put the tulips in water, Inez might like them in her room.'

***

Audrey and Bill were having lunch the next day in the kitchen with Inez and the boys. Lucy was twining herself around Bill. No matter how much she tried to politely nudge her away, the cat stayed close, rubbing her sweet hairy little face on her calves. Bill sneezed and reached for a tissue.

'You two have to do something about your hair. No excuses, it's dreadful.' Inez sighed and stirred her coffee. 'It shows a lack of judgement. Is that really the image you wish to portray to the world? I have taken the liberty to book you both in with my hairdresser this afternoon. Don't protest. When was the last time you had a proper cut?'

'All haircuts are proper cuts,' stated Audrey matter-of-factly, and touched her hair, which was shortish and rounded with a fringe. Bill's cut was identical.

'Don't be obtuse, Plum! You are having haircuts, and what's more, you will enjoy them. You look pos-itively dreary. Come here Lucy, Bill doesn't like you.'

'I do, she's lovely,' said Bill and sneezed again. 'I just prefer to love her from a distance.' She hoped Audrey would agree to haircuts. She wouldn't be able to accept Inez's offer on her own.

'Well, I suppose the biscuit woman has amazing hair,' said Audrey. 'Dramatic. So does Anna at The Bean. Fiona's hair looks so perfect it could be a wig. And that beautiful detective, such shine. I thought good hair was something you were born with, and if you weren't, you restrained it with an Alice band.'

'Alice band!' snorted Simon, choking on a crumb. 'Oh Audrey, you're just adorable. If you're not given great hair naturally, you make sure you use a great hairdresser. Fiona will be ironing her hair smooth every day, and how do you think Ballentine's hair would look if she didn't put some effort into it? Plain as plain as plain.'

Audrey had a vision of leaning Bill's head on the ironing board, smoothing her curls with the steam iron. 'Crazy. Are you sure about that? Seems impossible. I have no time to spend on that sort of idiocy. It seems unfair. How long do men spend on fixing theirs?'

'Some men, quite a long time, actually.' The boys exchanged a look. 'But if you have a good, simple cut it's just a matter of adding a little product for perfection.'

'I agree with Inez. It's a wonderful idea.' James put down his cup, focusing on Audrey. 'I see you with hair like Jamie Lee Curtis.'

'Who's that?'

'A stunning woman, daughter of Tony Curtis and Vivien Leigh. You've heard of them, surely?'

'Oh yes. Films.'

'Keep it grey – it's a great shade, silvery.' He teased her hair a little with his hands. 'You'll look great. How about you, Bill?'

'I might grow it out some more. Long hair is nice.

Maybe I'll just even it out a bit, a little trim.' Bill usually cut her own curly hair, using sewing scissors to trim the bits that stuck out.

'Trim? Pah!' replied James. 'I'd lighten it up. Were you a natural blonde once? Become a lemon cream. Astrid's stupendous, she'll bring out the dazzle in you. Just let her do what she does best.'

Astrid's salon was a yellow weatherboard cottage set back from the street with a small front garden. A neatly trimmed privet hedge flanked the street, and equally neat box hedges bordered the stone path. A sign shaped like a pair of pruning shears hung off the veranda awning. Inside, the salon smelt deliciously of hair products. Astrid was blow-drying the springy tresses of a customer. Warm air swirled hair around, spreading scent. She looked at her new arrivals in the mirror and smiled.

'With you in a minute, take a seat! Make yourselves a drink if you wish.'

Along the window was an upholstered bench, from where you had a good view of the salon. It was bright and airy for such a small space, with art for sale lining the walls. There was a pile of handouts lying on a low table, detailing the works. Though there was nothing special about either the furniture, the art, the music or any individual feature, when you put it all together into a single impression there was only one word Bill could think of that summarised it.

'Cool,' she breathed. She had not had much experience with cool, but if there was a tangible feel of cool, this was surely it. A lot of it was contributed by Astrid herself. In her fifties, she could pass for much younger as long as you didn't look too closely. Her hair had not changed in her entire life. It was waist length and blonde, today slicked back and wrapped in a Spanish bun at the nape of her neck. She wore a startling combination of flat black men's lace-up shoes, yellow socks, and too-short black pants held up with black braces over a shirt as yellow as the socks. Around her hips was a leather belt with handy pockets for scissors and other things.

'Now, what can I do for Inez's protégés? Who's first? You? Hmm.' She looked hard at Audrey and circled her critically. 'Did you have anything in mind?'

'I want to look like Jamie Lee Curtis.'

'Don't we all, sweetie. Actually, I can sort of see it in you. The cheekbones are pretty much there. Smile for me!' Audrey, who had never smiled on command in her life, obeyed despite her desire to get out and run.

'Mm, not bad.' Astrid moved Audrey's head this way and that. 'Nice chin, good strong nose, excellent profile. I love the outfit. Yes, I can do it. Be still and keep your eyes closed.'

'Why?'

'It's not good for women to look at their reflection

when they have a haircut. It takes so long, and in the bright light they have lots of time to become overly critical of themselves. Self-criticism does not make a woman beautiful. I am the only one allowed to look so that I can see what I am doing.'

Bill watched from the waiting area. Astrid chopped theatrically with big rapid hand movements. She stopped and paused, then dove in with the scissors some more. She preferred to work in concentrated silence, leaving the talking to her customers, should they wish. Audrey was perfectly content to be quiet too. Keeping her eyes closed was harder, but she only looked at the floorboards so it wasn't really cheating.

'There we are, you can open your eyes now.'

Audrey looked in the mirror and failed to suppress a smile, unprompted this time. It was like looking at someone else.

'You look good, huh?' Astrid angled a mirror at the back of Audrey's head for a full inspection.

'I do, I certainly do. Thank you.' She had never noticed her cheekbones before, and she had always found her nose too large and sharp. Now she would think of it as 'strong'. She tilted her head this way and that, trying to see properly what she had done. It was amazing. She looked so different, all for a few snips of hair.

'Now you, the little one. Come, sit.' Astrid patted the old leather chair invitingly. 'Have you thought about what you want?'

'Yes. I want to look like a lemon cream biscuit.'

Astrid gave a little laugh, concealing it as a cough. 'I think I see. Sweet, yet with tang. Blonde, perhaps? Scrumptiously moreish?'

Bill blushed. 'Actually, I think I just meant blonde.'

'That's alright. Close your eyes please. Audrey, I'll need a couple of hours if you want to leave and come back later.'

'Get some cat treats while you're out,' said Bill. 'Whatever cats like best.'

'Sure. I thought the last thing you needed was to encourage her.'

'It's to keep her away.' Bill closed her eyes in anticipation of what was to come. Would she look anywhere near as good as Audrey? The feeling of Astrid handling her hair and head was utterly delicious. She was perfectly happy to surrender to her skills.

Audrey went out with a spring in her step. She couldn't help furtively admiring her new self in the shopwindows. Just a little glance. Not that she was vain, not at all. It was just such a change that she had to get familiar with how she now looked.

The pet shop was her first stop. If their range was anything to go by, cats ate well around here. She chose a bag of dried fish that looked revolting but perhaps not if you were a cat. Also some chicken-filled little cushions, like rubbery tortellini, which the assistant vowed were irresistible. There was a yellow cat sleeping on a cushion on the counter ready to test the theory if she was in doubt.

Outside, the sun had appeared, showing off the rain-washed village in a new light. Water had gathered in puddles and she walked around them, unwilling to soak her shoes. Wellies, she thought. We must buy some wellies. She found a window displaying a range of rubber boots – black, red, green and patterned. She was just considering going in to look at the green ones when she heard an enraged shout, followed by a scream.

Cautiously Audrey peered around the corner. Two women were having a sort of standoff outside The Bean. She listened for a minute, then walked towards them with determination.

'You bitch! I loved him, he was mine! Don't come here with your poxy flowers,' wailed a young brunette, trying to grab hold of a bunch of cellophane wrapped roses.

Her opponent was pulling back, petals scattering on the pavement. 'I hate you, you slut!' she shouted back. 'He didn't love you, he laughed about your pathetic whining. Ooh Fabiano, I love you so much, Fabiano... He loved *me*, you stupid cow!'

A mound of flowers, cards and wreaths were piled in front of the café door. Still gripping the flowers with one hand, the brunette latched onto the hair of her rival with the other, dragging her to the ground with surprising strength and enterprise.

'Ow! Let me go, you're hurting me!' The woman lunged out at the brunette wildly.

'Girls, girls. Settle down! This is not the way to behave.' Audrey stood with her arms open in a pose of no threat.

The women paused and looked at her.

'It really isn't,' continued Audrey. 'Show some respect. I'm sure you can work this out in a better way.'

They didn't seem to think so. The brunette, spotting her enemy's lapse of attention, landed a punch. The fight continued with renewed vigour. Audrey wondered what on earth she could do. What if she physically tried to get between them? She took a deep breath and stepped resolutely into the fray. Fortunately, this was the moment when the butcher from down the street appeared and grabbed the brunette, holding her firmly in strong arms.

'That's enough, Mimi. Quiet now,' he said crossly. 'It's the third time I've had to do this,' he said to Audrey and raised his bushy eyebrows incredulously. Mimi was kicking him and shouting abuse but not getting much swing as he held her close.

Audrey crouched down in front of the other one, who was sitting on the pavement, holding her head and moaning.

'She tore out a chunk, look!' She held out a mass of

long curly hairs. 'And just look at my clothes.' She got up and brushed some gravel off her knees. 'What a mess.'

'Yes,' said Audrey. 'There is no need for all of this, you know. You are both in grief, and everyone's upset. You should be united in your sorrow, not fighting each other.'

'He loved me.' The woman looked at Audrey, pleadingly. 'It's true, he did. He really loved me. She can't come here and stop me from paying my respects, telling lies. I bet she killed him herself, because he didn't love her!' A fresh outburst of abuse came from Mimi, who was being led away by the butcher, whose grip she had no hope of escaping.

'Come round the back, Mimi,' he said patiently. 'You'll say things you'll regret. You and Josie are friends, aren't you? Well, there you are. Shush now. We'll have a cuppa and you can tell me all about it.' The small crowd that had gathered dispersed as Mimi disappeared from sight. Josie gently arranged the torn flowers on the ground, tears rolling down her face.

'Do you want to talk about it?' asked Audrey, digging in her pocket for a handkerchief. 'Here, wipe your eyes. Josie, isn't it? We could go for coffee.' Josie nodded, and they walked to the nearest coffee shop which, being Daylesford, wasn't far.

'He was about to leave his wife for me,' said Josie sadly. 'He was the most beautiful, charming, loving man I have ever met. We were going to Florence together. I gave him the deposit for the tickets. That's where he's from, did you know?'

'No, I don't really know much at all. But he has been here such a short time, how on earth did he find time for romance?'

'You know when it's right. You just know. We both did.' Josie sighed. 'As soon as I saw him it felt like I had known him forever, instantly.' Fresh tears welled up in her eyes, which were red and streaked with the sooty black of mascara.

'Hmm,' said Audrey. 'Please don't fight. It's not going to bring him back. Mimi is a friend of yours, is that right?'

Josie shook her head. 'She was. Not anymore.'

'Well, you used to be friends, and you will be again. The way I see it, neither of you is going to get Fabiano now, but both of you are upset about him. Is it not better to be upset together? It's possible that he did love you, but it's also possible that she loved him. If that's the case, you could try to show compassion for her, not anger. Also, have you thought about how hard this is for the woman he was actually married to? You need to be better than this. I don't know you, Josie, but it doesn't matter. Trust me, you will not look back on this with pride later.'

Josie toyed with a drip of spilled coffee on the table, swirling it into an abstract pattern on the surface. 'You're right. You really are. I will call Mimi. But she's a bitch all the same.'

Bill's hair was wrapped in plastic when Audrey returned, laden with cat treats and interesting news.

'Won't be too long now,' said Astrid. 'You can try the massage chair while I finish.'

Audrey didn't need prompting. The chair groaned and rumbled, hitting spots in her body that sent tingles all the way out to her toes. It was turning out to be a most interesting and rewarding day.

'Ok, I'm done.' Astrid snipped a final strand and brushed the hair off the nape of Bill's neck. Her short hair was now a shiny natural-looking blonde. The curls were more unruly than ever but in exactly the right places.

'Now off you go, shoo! Inez will fix payment later.' She ushered them out.

As soon as they were on the street Audrey shared her news.

'Is it possible that he was using his charms for monetary gain? Maybe he's winkled more cash from other women,' said Bill, who could not stop touching her new hairstyle. 'We look different, don't we?'

'We do, but never mind about that. He was a fast mover, that's for certain. What a rascal. Seemingly, women fell headlong, straight into his arms. He reduced *you* to a giggling wreck,' she reminded Bill sternly. 'If he could do that to you on a first meeting, imagine what can be accomplished in a few weeks with someone more susceptible. He must have been a magnificent campaigner. You look great, by the way.'

Inez was reading in her room when they returned home, with Lucy draped decoratively across the headrest of her chair. She looked up over her reading glasses and frowned at them.

'That's better I suppose,' she said. 'Are you still convinced that all cuts are proper cuts?'

'My hair would still be shorter by any other means, even if I chose to file it off with a rasp. But okay, I admit that I had no idea we could look like this. You were right. I humbly accept defeat,' said Audrey. 'Thank you.'

'Yes, thank you very much,' echoed Bill. 'It is quite, quite wonderful.'

'Hmph! You no longer look like a mushroom and a chicken, and that is being charitable.' She returned to her reading. 'Now please pop out and get me today's paper.'

'She doesn't mean any harm. She's just a bit blunt in her approach,' said Audrey as they walked down the street towards the newsagent. 'She has always been infuriatingly frank but she is a good deal milder than her parents ever were. The sharp edges get softened as generations pass.'

'That'll be why you're such a softie, and not at all aloof, arrogant and stern,' said Bill. 'I can cope.'

'That's alright then. Oh look, a health food shop. I'm going to get some vitamins. Coming in? No? Won't be long.'

Bill stayed outside, admiring the window display. A cardboard cut-out of a radiantly happy woman wearing an oversized pair of pants stood next to a poster, which said in bold print 'I lost 36 kilos on the Total Support Diet! Be healthy, happy and confident – join today and let us provide all your meals.' Bill studied the ad intently. The Dior dress would fit her really well if she only lost a couple of paltry centimetres of girth. She could see the reflection of her face superimposed over the cardboard woman's. Bill was happy with her hair, but letting her eyes sweep downwards she was less than pleased. Her outline didn't match the cut-out at all, rounding off here and there. The last time she dieted she had actually managed to gain weight. So much agony, but for what? Another hole in her belt in the wrong direction. Maybe this was worth a go. The cardboard woman certainly seemed pleased with herself, top to toe. She went inside.

'Audrey, we are joining the diet thing.'

'Are we? Why?'

'You'll do it for support. I'll do it for the dress. Okay?'

'You can do it if you want, but I get too hungry. I have a large frame.'

Bill looked at her in silent reproach.

'Alright. I'll do it if it makes you happy,' said Audrey, 'but just for a short while.'

'What a good idea,' smiled the sales assistant. 'First we need to weigh and measure you, then we have a questionnaire to fill in and sign.' He took them to a little room at the back of the shop. After measuring their circumferences he frowned at Bill.

'Well done for signing up. I promise that we'll have you in shape very soon. What's your current exercise plan?'

'We don't really have one.' Audrey looked at Bill and shrugged. As far as she was concerned, planned exercise was something that happened to other people. Walking was good enough for her.

The man tutted. 'That won't do. You'll start at the basic level, on page 12 in your booklets. Each week, you'll increase your physical activity. As you can see, there are several fun options for exercise.'

'Fun!' Audrey looked at the pictures of people bending in an undignified manner.

'I'm glad you agree. Your body will become a machine, tuned and well maintained. You won't need to buy any food at all. A healthy and varied pre-cooked diet will be delivered every second day. Fresh fruit and vegetables are also included. Once a week we need you back here for a measure and weigh-in. There are also monthly meetings in Brickwell that are optional but I strongly recommend. You will find them marvellously inspiring. You can sign up month by month, which is the more expensive option, or for six months, which works out much better financially.

'Six months sounds good,' said Bill.

'No,' protested Audrey, 'let's try for a month first. It's all about healthy eating and exercise, isn't it? We already eat very healthily.'

'It's also about not overeating even on healthy food. This is important. You will train yourself into knowing when you have eaten enough. Learn moderation. You can never value yourself and your new healthy body too highly. The group session is one of our most valuable tools, but our most important one is the phone. You'll be paired up with a fully trained personal supporter who will ring you once a day. He or she will call you as soon as they have been allocated.'

***

Simon was preparing food in the kitchen when the first meals arrived the next day.

'What's this? You don't like my food?' He looked upset.

'There's a dress in one of the trunks that Bill has her eye on, hence the diet. I'll miss your cooking,' said Audrey. 'Better not to be tempted at all and just follow this diet plan. All our food comes delivered from now on. It's just for a month.'

'What kind of dress is it? Must be good.'

'Dior,' said Bill.

'Now I understand completely,' said Simon. 'Up to you, I guess. Does your diet pack come with a blindfold?' He poked at the foil carton. 'What's it supposed to be?'

'Lean Turkey Treat,' muttered Audrey, reading the accompanying sheet. 'But there's dessert.'

'Yes, there is!' said Bill brightly and clapped her hands with enthusiasm. 'Lo-fat Vanilla Fromage and some fresh fruit. It will be delicious.'

'You don't need to diet,' Simon scoffed. 'Just spend less time at the bakery if you're worried. Ditch the snacks.' He plated up Inez's dinner, adding a sprig of tarragon to the buttery Béarnaise sauce. 'Are you sure you're starting today?' He ducked as Audrey waved a spatula at him. 'Okay, okay, keep your amazing hair on.'

Lucy sauntered into the kitchen and homed in on Bill.

'There's a good girl,' cooed Bill. 'I have a surprise for you.' She opened one of the packets of cat treats and put the full packet on the pantry floor. 'She'll be busy, so I can eat in peace now.'

That evening they had a game of backgammon before bed. Audrey excused herself after losing badly. 'I'm not sure if I inadvertently locked Lucy in the pantry. Must go and check.' She was hungrily eyeing the contents of the fridge looking for possible snacks when the phone interrupted her search.

'Hello! My name's Margaret,' said the pleasant voice on the line. 'I'm your Phone Support. I'll ring every night and we can have a little chat about how much exercise you've done, what you've eaten and how you feel about it all. I'll give you my mobile number too, I'm at the end of the line all day and night. We'll have a chat again tomorrow.'

Audrey put the phone back in its cradle and sighed. She ate a bread roll and a wedge of cheese, washing it down with a glass of milk.

'Audrey! You're snacking!' Bill appeared in the door-way. 'I thought something had happened to Lucy.'

'Was hungry,' said Audrey, mouth full. 'Support thingy rang. You can answer the phone in the evenings in the future. It'll be her wanting to know how you feel about things.'

'You said you'd diet too.'

'I said I'd keep you company, I never said I wouldn't have supplementary meals or talk to anyone how I feel about it. Look at my height and frame! I need more calories than you just to maintain what flesh I have. But alright, I'll share your pain. Come on, back to bed.' She drained her glass and put it in the sink.

CHAPTER 5

Back at the station, Rosie and Susanna had been busily working their way through the list of interviews. People's opinions of Mr Battista varied greatly. It seemed to depend mainly on whether you were a woman or a man, in business or not. No one seemed to know him in any great depth, nor had they found any witnesses to the night in question. Alibis were loose, as people tended to go to bed early on a wintry Monday night.

Some leads, however, had appeared and they were looking at one now. Apparently a pair of handymen had done some work for The Bean and not been paid. Simon Addison and James Piper lived in a narrow old weatherboard turn-of-the-century cottage sandwiched between similar houses a couple of blocks from the lake. Rosie knocked on the front door. From within they could hear muffled yipping and little claws scrabbling excitedly on the floorboards.

'Yes?' An attractive man picked up the shaggy little dog, which gave Rosie a look of active dislike.

'Detective Sergeant Lloyd,' she said and held up her ID. 'May we come in? We're looking for Mr Piper and Mr Addison. We have some questions relating to Fabiano Battista.'

'Sure, come in, come in. I'm Simon, James is out the back. Through here, please. James! Police to see us.' He led her into the living room. 'Take a seat.'

Rosie sat down on the leather sofa and instantly sank deeply into it. It felt as if her knees were about to meet her chin. *Bad interview positioning, too late now*, she thought. She made an effort to lean forward and tensed up her thighs so she was half sitting, half crouching. Susanna remained standing, casually looking around the room.

'How can we help you?' James had appeared from a back room and sat down next to Simon. Rosie couldn't help noticing that they were sitting much more at ease on a firm sofa.

'I believe you had a financial conflict with the deceased,' she said. 'You did some work for him, is that correct?'

'That's right,' answered Simon. 'We didn't really know him, we just did a job. Some money was paid up-front, but not all. He was supposed to pay on completion but he actually refused, saying we hadn't completed it.'

'Did your opinion differ?'

'Absolutely. We'd finished the job but he said he had to do some work himself. Trying to get out of paying, really. Ask his wife, she was there when we finished it. Told us we'd done a great job.'

'I will. How much did he owe you?'

'A little under nine hundred.'

'Right. Where were you on Monday night between 9pm and midnight?'

'Surely you don't think we would kill someone for 890 dollars?'

'I hope not. But people have been killed for far less. Now, where were you on Monday night?'

'At home. We probably went to bed around ten. Mister Wolf was out for a quick wee just before that.'

'Mister Wolf?'

'This adorable little griffon.' Simon smiled at the shaggy thing in his lap, which glared nastily at her. Grey hairs bristled from its indignant little face. There seemed to be a lot of pointy teeth hiding in the undergrowth.

'I see. Can anyone collaborate your being at home? Any phone calls, visitors?'

'Don't think so,' said Simon. 'James, can you think of anything?'

James shook his head slowly. 'No, it was just a perfectly ordinary quiet night in. Sorry.'

'For Mr Battista, and for somebody else, it was not

ordinary at all. Thank you, that'll be all for now. Here is my card if you can think of anything.'

***

Though the garden at Inez's house was well stocked with trees, shrubs and flowers, it yielded little in the way of herbs apart from a plenitude of borage and some rosehips. The large linden tree would be harvested of its flowers later, and there was a sizeable bay tree with glossy aromatic leaves. Bill was accustomed to using a rather wider variety than that. Soon, she would plant some more herbs. Eventually she would like a well-stocked herbal pharmacy outside the back door. She had already picked a lot of the rosehips, which were drying in the kitchen, waiting to be powdered.

Determined to make her diet work, she felt she needed to add a suitable tea. The best she could think of was nettle and dandelion. No matter how hard she looked over the garden, she could not find any weeds whatsoever. The boys dealt with them so efficiently she had to go further afield. It could be today's exercise. She went inside and called to Audrey.

'But it's cold and horrible outside,' protested Audrey, who was playing cards with Inez in the kitchen.

'Rubbish! It will do you good. You're losing this hand anyway,' lied Inez.

'Hear the voice of reason,' said Bill. 'We'll go for

the tiniest of walkies, and see some of the countryside. Get your coat.'

Equipped with gloves, secateurs and baskets, they set off. Dandelions were popping up here and there, but nettles were a little harder to find. They kept walking until they struck nettle gold on the fringes of a small creek not too far from home, where tender shoots were poking up through piles of decaying leaves. Once the baskets were full, they returned home.

'Let's take some leaves to Anna as a pick-me-up tonic,' suggested Bill.

On their way to Anna's they dropped into the bakery and bought a bag of currant buns. They were rapidly getting to know their way around the baked goods of Daylesford. These were a very special treat baked only twice a week and were right now still warm from the oven. They smelt irresistible and would probably not stay uneaten for long. Being on a diet was going to be a sore trial.

The front of the coffee shop was dark. Bill imagined a desolate air had already set in around it, like a grey heaviness. She shrugged off the feeling and followed Audrey round the back, where an external metal staircase led to the upstairs flat.

'Should we have rung first, do you think? There are a lot of buns here that we're not allowed to eat if she isn't home,' Bill said ruefully, shaking the bakery bag.

'We don't have her number. She'll be in. I can hear

movement, listen!'

The door opened and Anna appeared, wrapped in a dressing gown. 'Well, hello there, what a surprise,' she said.

'We must apologise, were you resting?' asked Bill.

'I was just having a little lie down.'

Bill thought she could see the movement of a door slowly closing further down the dark hallway but Anna's springy hair blocked the view. She took a step forward, holding up the buns to show their offering.

'We thought we should come and see how you were coping. We brought you a little something for sustenance.' They walked in past Anna through the hallway to where a little kitchen could be seen.

'That's very nice of you,' said Anna, following them. 'Maybe the shock hasn't quite set in yet, but I feel pretty okay, really.'

'Let's have a hot cup of nettle tea, it'll be very good for you.' Bill was already filling the kettle. 'Can't have you getting run down. What you need is some care. Do you have any family nearby?'

They cleared away the dirty dishes from the table (two glasses, two plates) and arranged the buns on a fresh plate.

'Is there any butter?' Audrey opened the fridge, which didn't contain very much at all. A bottle of wine, some milk, something dried on a plate and yes, butter.

'It's not good to be alone at a time like this. Good

to see you have had friends over.' Bill nodded to the used wineglasses on the counter.

'Rick and I had a drink last night. He's been very good to me, taking care of everything.' Anna didn't look unhappy, nor did she appear sleep-deprived. In fact, she seemed rather chipper as she picked up a bun in her hand and took a bite. Her nettle tea sat untouched.

'You're so nice to me,' she said. 'Everyone is.'

'That's good to hear. You seem very well, in the circumstances,' said Bill.

'I'm okay, you know. He always had women climbing all over him, wherever we went. It's just how it was. Once I realised he hadn't been having an affair I felt so much better. He loved me after all.' She took a last bite of the bun and reached for another.

'Of course he did.' *I bet she never puts on weight*, thought Bill. *Maybe I will have just the one bun and eat it crumb by crumb.* 'Do you remember saying something to us about a note he hid from you?' she asked.

'I forgot all about that!' Anna looked up in surprise. 'I wonder where it could be. Maybe in a pocket. I haven't done anything about his clothes yet. I just can't. Rick said he would deal with that soon. Is it important?'

'Probably not. Do you mind if we take a look?'

'Go ahead. His clothes are in the wardrobe through there.' She pointed to a door off the hall.

Audrey went to have a feel in the pockets. She

found a handful of coins, three sweet wrappers, a yet-to-be-eaten piece of fudge wrapped in cellophane, a box of matches, a toothpick, two used tissues, a couple of screws, various receipts, and some scrunched up paper. She brought the bounty to the kitchen table.

'This is the lot from the wardrobe.' She smoothed out the paper. It was an ad for a local meditation retreat. In the top left corner was scrawled a number sequence, 553778. 'Nothing that seems significant here,' she said, pocketing the ad all the same. It was probably nothing, but you never knew. 'Could the note be anywhere else?'

'I have no idea,' said Anna, licking sugar from her fingers. 'I'll let you know if we find something when Rick clears things away. This tea is unusual, isn't it? I think I prefer coffee.'

'It's a great tonic, you must drink it all up,' replied Bill.

A crash came from behind one of the doors, as if something had been knocked over. Anna jumped.

Bill and Audrey looked at each other. So someone was there, after all.

'What was that?' asked Audrey.

'Rick has been staying for a bit. The noise startled me. I'm a bit jumpy at the moment. Nights are especially stressful and I had a bad night last night. He must have just woken up.'

'How kind of him. That must be such a relief to

you, some company,' said Bill.

'I don't know how I could manage without him.' Her sweet tone belied the glare she shot at Rick, who shuffled into the kitchen, hair on end.

He frowned at the assembled group and pointed at Audrey.

'You're the woman who was blocking my way. What are you doing here?'

'We just dropped by with some buns and tea. We didn't know that Anna had company. We are so sorry for your loss. Fabiano will be dearly missed.'

'Will you be reopening The Bean soon?' Bill noticed that Anna looked like she was about to start crying again and thought she'd change the subject slightly.

'I hope so,' said Rick. 'The police will let us know. I just want to get on with work, get busy.'

'Have you heard anything from them regarding the investigation?'

'What is this, the Spanish Inquisition? No, they're not good at sharing. From how they carry on you'd think we were suspects.' He moved to stand behind Anna's chair and placed a protective hand on her shoulder.

Audrey didn't want to say so, but they both seemed much too chummy and happy for a recently bereaved widow and a business partner left to pay the bills of a business that wasn't able to do any trade. The police would obviously include them in their investigations no matter how they behaved.

'I wouldn't worry about that,' she said. 'I'm sure they have to suspect everyone. The entire choir has been questioned but that doesn't make us murderers. You take care now, we'll be off.'

'I think Rick's moved in on the grieving widow,' Audrey said to Bill once they were a safe distance down the street from The Bean. 'The bedroom door was open when we left. I caught a glimpse of the bed and both sides had been used.'

'That was quick!'

'Either that or she sleeps on both sides. She must be frightened.'

'She wouldn't be frightened if it was them that did it. Did she seem scared to you?'

'Not one bit.'

When Margaret rang in the evening Bill was pleased to report on the nettle and dandelion tonic and the exercise involved in getting it, all the walking and bending. This led to a long discussion of herbal remedies and natural supplements to which Margaret could contribute little. No mention was made of buns. Yes, Bill had hugely enjoyed the cauliflower and vermicelli salad followed by low-fat yoghurt and half a sliced banana. She even claimed to feel very full. This was true, though the buns contributed to that.

The weather forecast for the next few days was for an unseasonal warm spell. Inez had encouraged them to do what they wanted with their rooms in order to make them feel more at home. It was a tempting thought to get some painting done while it was sunny. The east-facing walls were stained by damp, but Inez assured them the roof had been patched well enough and the gutters cleared, so hopefully no more water would come in.

Neither of them had done any painting before, but fortunately the boys were willing to give advice and lend them equipment. The paint sample charts at the hardware featured a lovely array of food names such as Butter Cream, Cinnamon Toast and Divine Apricot.

'When you're on a diet it's impossible not to be tempted by these. Imagine being inside an entire cinnamon toast room...' Bill closed her eyes, dreamily.

'That colour looks like plain brown, if you ignore the name. Call it Camel, and it will look the same but smell different. Stop reading with your stomach and choose. What do you want? Blue, yellow, what?'

'I think blue. A summer fresh sky, or forget-me-nots. Do you think it will be too cool? How about this Rich Vanilla tone?'

'There you are again, going on about food. I think any of those creamy yellows would be cheery. I'm going for a deep burgundy myself. I've seen a reddish rug rolled up in one of the store rooms, so I might go with that.'

'I might go for green, like the spring leaves of

a linden. Very soothing. Or this one. What do you think?' Bill turned to the sales assistant, who had waited patiently while they debated the various choices.

'They're both nice. You could take some samples home,' she offered.

'They can't both be as nice, one has to be nicer than the other, which is it?' pressed Bill.

'That one.' She pointed to one of the samples that looked virtually identical to the other.

Carrying tins of red and green for the walls and glossy white for the timberwork, they returned home. The boys had delivered a couple of ladders and some drop sheets. They started with the green room, and in no time at all the first coat was on the walls. Admittedly, there was some on the floors as well, and a little on the window. There seemed to be rather more than necessary on Bill's face and hair but that's what happens when you're the shorter of a pair of painters. The old wallpaper still showed through in patches but a second coat would fix that, surely.

'This is rather exciting, isn't it? So much better. We could do the whole house,' said Bill.

'Let's just stick to these rooms for now. We have a whole lot of work left, but I'm sure we have time for a first coat in my room too.'

The deep russet shade made the room quite dark, but it was certainly becoming cosier.

'I wonder how the lovely Rosie is getting on with

her investigations,' pondered Audrey.

'She'll catch the murderer in no time, I'm sure.'

'Are you? That's good. I think it's a bit creepy. It could be anyone, anywhere.

'Not exactly anyone,' replied Bill, thoughtfully. 'We know we didn't do it, nor did Inez. If you exclude people one by one, what you have left is the murderer.'

'That might work in a really small place, but what if he or she came from somewhere else? There's the whole world to choose from.'

'Could be so, but I think it will be closer to home. We should visit Anna again. I want some plants too, a few herbs. Maybe we could go to Gloria's Gardens. She might know something, being next door.'

'Wow! It's like a boudoir in here,' said Simon, who had popped in to see how they were doing. 'I like it. But where are you going to sleep tonight?'

Bill and Audrey looked at each other. They hadn't thought of that. Both bedrooms had the beds pushed out into the middle of the floor, but that was not the problem. The issue was the paint fumes, just as strong in both rooms.

'You won't be able to sleep here until you've finished. I would have done one room at a time,' said Simon. 'Never mind, you'll have to camp out on the sofas downstairs.'

The next morning Audrey had a hard time getting

started. She was stiff just about everywhere.

'Please let's just focus on one room,' she said to Bill. 'Not another night on the sofa. I kept getting myself stuck. I couldn't turn over without rolling into the wedge at the back. Your sofa creaks, it kept waking me up.'

'*My* sofa creaks? You should have heard yours. Every breath you took was another squeak for in, squeak for out. Squeak for in, squeak for out. Like sleeping next to a cage of mice.'

'That could actually have been mice, cavorting.'

Once Audrey had managed to unfold her creaking and protesting body they focused on the green room and added another coat, which stopped the wallpaper from showing through. They started on the timber woodwork but trying to stay inside the lines with a laden brush made for a slow job. The day passed quickly and before they knew it the boys were back, preparing a casserole for Inez's dinner. This time it was a slow-cooked lamb with capsicums, potatoes and onions. It simmered in the kitchen during the afternoon, taunting the women with its delicious aroma wafting up the stairs, mingling with the smell of paint.

'Are you sure you don't want any? Well, without you two eating, it will do Inez for a couple of days. It'll only get better as the flavours have time to sit and make friends with each other.' Simon spooned some into a container to take home for him and James.

'What are you having?'

Audrey looked at the microwave box. 'Cod with parsley. Not parsley sauce, mind you, just parsley. And cod. Looks nutritious, I can't wait. There are fresh pears for dessert to be served with a sprinkle of shredded coconut. Can we take some of your casserole to give to Anna?'

'There's plenty, take some. Speaking of Anna, the police came around to talk to us about Fabiano. The Bean owes us money for some work and apparently that's motive enough to kill for. Do you think they'll be able to pay us some time? It would be nice.'

'You didn't do it, did you?' asked Bill.

Simon gave her a baleful stare.

'Just checking! We're eliminating people to see who's left.'

'If you want to take some of my delicious casserole, don't be so stupid. Of course we didn't.'

After an early dinner Audrey and Bill packed up a generous portion of lamb casserole and set off to Anna's, hoping to catch her on her own. Casseroles were a good thing to give the stressed or bereaved. If they couldn't or wouldn't eat it straight away, they could slot it into the freezer for when it was needed. Fortunately, Anna was alone this time.

'You're so sweet. Thank you! So kind and thoughtful.' She pulled out a crumpled tissue from her pocket and dabbed at her eyes. 'Won't you come in?' They followed her into the kitchen.

'You shouldn't be alone,' said Audrey. 'Is there someone who can stay with you for a while?'

'Rick will be back soon and I have a friend from Melbourne coming up for a few days. It all seems unreal. It's hard to think of what I should do.'

'I can tell you what you're going to do. You're going to eat a wholesome filling meal cooked with love. It will strengthen you. Go on.' Audrey handed her a fork.

'This is good. You're so nice to me.' She chewed and swallowed obediently.

'Oh, tosh. It's no problem,' said Bill.

'This is similar to the dinner we had on Monday. The last supper for Fabiano.' Fresh tears streaked her cheeks. 'Sorry, I can't seem to stop crying. We went to the Crossed Goat in the evening. Fab had the lamb shanks, which were so tender they just melted away in your mouth. Fabiano said that he,' she cried some more, 'that he...'

'It's alright my dear.' Bill patted her arm. 'Shush now. Just try to be calm. Breathe in, and out. That's better. It doesn't matter.'

'He loved food but he loved coffee even more, of course.' Anna took another bite and pushed the plate away. 'No, I can't have any more.'

'That's alright, you're doing really well,' Audrey

said. 'Just put it in the fridge for later.'

Anna went on. 'He loved the shanks so much that he would have licked the plate if he could. Said that he might start adding food like it to The Bean. Slow cooking for winter, like a soup or a stew per day in a takeaway container for a few dollars. Cheap to make, good profit margin.' She blew her nose. 'I don't know what will happen to the business, now. Will the police let us reopen soon, do you think? I wish they would. Nobody tells me anything.'

'You'll have to wait and see,' replied Bill. 'I understand if it's hard, financially as well on top of everything else. Sometimes it's best to just keep working to engage your mind in things.'

'Oh, exactly! Fabiano worked so hard. When we returned from dinner he went back to The Bean to check on something, do some paperwork or whatever. Both Rick and Fabiano were keen to make it a success, they were always there. He never came back though.' She pressed the tissue to her face. 'I was fast asleep and woke the next morning to an empty bed. Now I keep waking up and feeling his side of the bed. I keep forgetting that he will never be there now.'

'There, there.' Bill patted her some more.

The front door opened and Rick came in, bringing a gust of wintry air.

'Anna, I'm back! Oh I see, visitors again.'

'Since you're here now, we'll leave,' said Audrey.

'We just dropped off a little bit of something to eat. She can't possibly get any thinner and she needs the energy.' She got up and picked up her coat.

'They've been so nice. Thank you very much for coming over.' Anna extended a graceful arm and held Audrey's hand. 'I don't know many people up here yet.'

Audrey and Bill buttoned up their coats and left.

'So now we know what he did on Monday night,' Audrey said thoughtfully as they walked home. 'Dinner followed by work. End of trail. All we need to figure out is who came to see him. Obviously someone did.'

'Is that all? Well, that should be easy then. There are no witnesses, are there?'

'There are always witnesses. People just don't realise what they've seen or heard, but suddenly they remember something. We'll just ask more questions of more people. It would be great if Rick was friendlier. I bet he has a lot to say.'

As they turned the key in the door they heard the phone ring. Bill rushed to answer and just made it, a little out of breath.

'Margaret, hello!'

'You sound out of breath, did I catch you at a bad time? You must have been doing your exercises.'

'Yes, you could say that,' Bill replied. She had run the length of the hallway after all. 'Loved the cod. A bit dry though, isn't it?'

'I find plain fish a wonderful addition to my nutritional needs, myself,' said Margaret.

'There are people who are starving. I will never complain about food on the table, no matter how dull,' said Bill.

'I will if you won't,' shouted Audrey in the background, overhearing the conversation.

'Shut up,' shouted Bill back.

'I beg your pardon?'

'Not you, Margaret, obviously. Audrey is becoming very cranky. Could it be a lack of food? Should I let her have something extra?'

'You can give her an item from the extras sheet. There are several things you can have as much of as you like. Carrots for sweetness is my favourite. Crunchy celery sticks are great, or even a glass of water. A piece of dried fruit, just the one piece mind you, is an excellent treat. Full of sweet goodness, it might make her happier and ease up on the symptoms.'

'Symptoms?' asked Bill.

'Such as feeling faint, unusual aggressiveness, etcetera. If the symptoms persist, give her something to smell such as oil of cinnamon or peppermint. She can imagine she has eaten the things she is smelling. Good in the bath too. Then a drink of water and she will feel better.'

'I'll tell her, she'll leap at the chance to eat something. Good night Margaret.' She hung up and went into the kitchen where Audrey stood eating Simon's lamb casserole with a big serving spoon straight from the pot.

'So what?' mumbled Audrey through a mouthful. 'I'm starving.'

'Say sorry.' Bill folded her arms and tapped her foot.

'Sorry. Sorry that you caught me. I'm going to bed. See you in the morning.'

When Audrey went down for breakfast she found Bill already there, having a piece of dry toast and some nettle tea.

'I apologise for letting you see me eat last night,' said Audrey. 'Forgive me?'

'Of course,' said Bill. 'I had already forgotten it. I think I've lost some weight already. The diet is definitely working. Can you tell?'

'No, not really. Maybe a little in the hair.'

'Just as well I have Margaret for encouragement.'

Inez came into the kitchen to have her breakfast. She usually liked to start her day with a little natural yoghurt drizzled with honey, a slice of fresh bread with some goats cheese and greens, followed by a pastry and a couple of coffees. Still she looked like a rake.

Not fair, thought Bill for the millionth time. *Maybe she has tapeworm.*

'Have you got any plans for today?' asked Inez,

spreading a generous layer of salty, yellow butter on her bread. 'This is the last of it. I could do with some fresh bread if you go out. The Sunday Market is on. You get the best bread from there.'

'We were going to paint some more. Market sounds like a good idea though for afterwards. I can always use a walk,' said Bill.

'Don't forget bread. Marmalade. Some pastries if you see any good ones. I have a friend visiting this afternoon.'

They brushed a final coat of red in Audrey's room. The white trims could wait for another day. Painting was harder work than expected, but it looked wonderful – rich and inviting and a vast improvement on the stained wallpaper.

'In my mind I see curtains, flowers, furniture... And that rug,' said Audrey, admiring their handiwork. 'It's a good start, anyway. Let's go and check out the market.'

They walked up the hill to the old railway station where market stalls had been set up since early morning. Stall holders stamped their feet and cradled hot drinks to ward off the chill. There were books and socks, car parts and movies. Home-grown artichokes, sprouts and parsnips snuggled up to organic apples, mandarins and pears. Potatoes were a big feature. Memorabilia, toys, curiosities and camping gear stalls displayed their wares, and found a buyer in Audrey, who decided that she needed a wind-up torch.

A hat stall with an outstanding array lured Bill in for a closer look. She tried on a bottle-green felt hat with a pheasant feather stuck in the leather trim.

'What do you think?' she asked Audrey, who was busy winding her torch.

'How much? Buy it. It suits you. This torch is a beauty.'

Keeping the hat on, Bill felt a bit warmer. They moved with the ambling tide through the stalls. She thought she spotted Anna in the distance, walking with Rick, but they were gone before she could be sure. A little further up was the bread stall. They bought a loaf of white sourdough. The marmalade caused some difficulty, primarily because there was such an abundance. In the end, after much deliberation and sampling, they settled on a jar of straight Seville orange marmalade and a jar of preserved pears. Muffins for Inez too.

When they got back home they found Inez drinking coffee with a friend.

'What an amazing piece,' she said, looking at Bill's headwear. 'Everybody needs a great hat, even people with good hair. Meet Jane, darlings. Jane is a very, very old, and a very good friend of mine. Jane, this is my niece Plum and her friend Bill.'

'I'm no older than Inez, thank you. I have heard so much about you already. Plum, you look so much like Inez when she was your age. Will you join us for a cup?'

'Did you get the things?' asked Inez. 'Oh good, pears too. Let's have them now.' Audrey had other, more private plans for the pears but never mind. They sat down with a drink. It was good to be back inside. The market was a wind tunnel and her cheeks had gone icy cold.

'I have a problem I've been discussing with Inez,' said Jane. 'We don't know what to do about it, and I wondered if you might have some idea.'

'What is it?' asked Audrey. She and Bill were always interested in what was in the hearts and minds of people.

'I have a granddaughter.'

'That is a wondrous thing to have, a grandchild,' put in Bill.

'And you, do you have any children? Oh of course, silly of me...' She cast down her brown eyes in embarrassment.

'Nieces and nephews,' said Bill briskly. 'We have nieces and nephews. Your grandchildren, are they well?'

'Oh yes. I have three. Two are boys; they're doing very well. One's studying accountancy and the other's a veterinary nurse in Melbourne.'

'Both admirable things, you must be proud,'

Audrey smiled encouragingly.

'Oh I am. But the last one, the youngest... She still lives here in Daylesford.' She shook her head. 'Her parents don't seem to be able to control her. She does some stupid things.'

'The young often do,' Audrey sad, remembering with a cringe some of her own silly things as a young woman. And more recently too, come to think of it.

'She's only fourteen. She's been out spray painting things on walls at night. Her parents don't know about it, but that's not the immediate problem here,' said the woman in an embarrassed tone. 'Penny, that's my granddaughter, told me something I need to share with someone, but I can't go to the police without getting her into trouble. Last Monday she was out very late, especially considering it was a school night. She was putting her special mark, as they do, on a wall behind the garden shop. A tag, they call it. There's an alleyway that leads to the bin area and so forth. As she had finished and was about to leave, she heard muffled shouting from inside The Bean, which is just next door.

'Rather than running away, she went closer to try to hear what was happening. She has no fear, that girl. There were two male voices. One of them she described as having a funny accent. Then, after the murder happened, she realised she had witnessed something that might be important but she doesn't want to go to

128

the police because she doesn't want to get caught out herself. She asked me what I thought she should do. What should she do? If I go to the police, they'll find out about her, and I promised that I wouldn't get her into trouble. I can't betray her trust, or she will never confide in me again. She might need to, at some time. And yet...'

The women sat quietly thinking for a minute, drinking their tea. Audrey spoke first.

'You can tell a lie, and pretend to be the witness yourself. Do you trust that she told you the exact truth about what she heard?'

'Yes, I do. She had to admit to me to why she was there, and she wouldn't have done that otherwise. I'm ashamed of what she has done and I wish she would just stop.'

'Well, you could always say you were walking past yourself and heard two males arguing. That leaves her out completely. But you would have to lie, and sign for the lie. Appear in court for a lie. This is not a good option. It is impossible. Also, taking her place doesn't help her on a personal level at all.'

'I agree,' said Bill. 'She has to give them the information herself. If she won't talk to the police, do you think she will talk to us?'

'I'll ask. I'll do it right away.'

Jane rang almost as soon as she got home.

'Penny's coming to see you at five this afternoon.

I said you'd be there. Will you?'

'Definitely. We look forward to seeing her.'

A few minutes past five o'clock Bill opened the door to let in a pale young girl wearing a hooded sweatshirt and jeans. Her hair, what little could be seen of it from under the hood, was greasy and lank with a long fringe partly concealing her face, further obscured by bad adolescent skin. Her posture was awkward too. She looked at them sideways from beneath her fringe, like a morose version of Princess Diana. She had not been given her grandmother's beautiful eyes but instead had slightly protruding ones that seemed to have difficulty settling on things for long. It was a bit unnerving to engage in eye contact with all the flickering.

All in all, she reminded Bill of an anxious little ferret with acne.' Come in, Penny. Welcome,' she said warmly and smiled. 'How good of you to come.'

They ushered the ferret into the kitchen, where candles were lit and the wood stove was going nicely. The Formica table was draped in a starched linen tablecloth and laid with Inez's best Royal Doulton bone china. Fresh camellias from the garden formed the centrepiece. Luckily there were still some muffins left, as well as a packet of Ballentine's best assortment. Bach's Air on a G-string flowed from Inez's portable CD player and set the mood.

'Sit down, my dear. What would you like to drink?

Tea, coffee, juice? Hot chocolate?'

'Hot chocolate, please.'

Audrey spooned some Dutch cocoa into a small pot. Then she added sugar and stirred briskly in order to eliminate the cocoa lumps.

'Strong or weak? Sweet or not?'

'Dunno.' She pulled a face.

'Then I shall make it the way we like it, and you can let me know what you think,' said Audrey. She added a small dash of full cream milk and stirred to form a paste. Gradually she added more milk and put the pot on the stove, stirring all the while. 'Soon be ready,' she said. 'I am very good at hot chocolate. You can make it with squares of dark chocolate too, but I find this the best. If I was to try to store chocolate at home Bill would eat it immediately. Cocoa lasts longer because it is less pleasant to spoon powder straight in your mouth than it is to eat a block.'

Bill looked away, embarrassed. 'But I do, pretty much,' she whispered to Penny. 'I mix it up with some butter, sugar and flour in a mug and eat it. Like raw biscuit dough.'

Penny smiled. 'I sometimes eat cocoa by the spoonful,' she said.

'Oh, me too,' said Bill. 'You have to be careful though, so you don't inhale. Coughing over that spoon soon advertises what you have done. Now, tell us what happened last Monday.'

'Grandma told you what I was doing, right?'

'She did.'

'Well, I heard shouting. Some guy with an accent and another one. They were really angry.'

'Did you hear them say anything specific, any words?'

'No,' she bit her lip pensively. 'I don't think so. It was just noise.'

'But you're sure that it was two men. Can you describe the accent?'

'Not really. It was just funny like...' She made a gargling sound. 'A bit like that. What should I do? Mum and Dad will go totally mental if they find out I've been tagging.'

'Maybe so. You do know that graffiti makes other people even madder than your parents, don't you? Have some more to eat.'

'People just paint it over, or scrub it off. It's not that bad,' said Penny and shrugged. She picked up another muffin.

'That's not how they see it,' said Bill. 'Anyway, that's not what we're here to talk about. Somehow, you will have to find the courage to go to the police. If you promise you will stop this tagging nonsense, we'll help you. But you do have to go. You know what is right, now act on it. You must let the police know straight away or they'll wonder what took you so long.'

'I can't. That's what Grandma said I had to do but

I won't and you can't make me. She said you would have some good ideas but you don't, do you?' said Penny truculently.

'We don't?' put in Audrey. 'We just gave you the best advice anybody could give – go to the police… If you won't speak to the police in person, why don't you write them a letter? We'll help, if you like.'

'Can we do that? That would be alright.' Her eyes settled on Audrey, just for a second or two.

'Strictly speaking, you should go in person. But they'll call your parents. I say, let's write a letter now. At least they'll have all the information then.'

Together they composed a letter in great detail, omitting only the tagging.

'What if they fingerprint it?' asked Penny.

Audrey looked at her. 'Have you been in trouble with the police before? Been caught tagging?'

'No!'

'Shoplifting?'

'Course not. You know, I don't have to be insulted like this. Just because I'm a teenager you assume I must be out drinking or shoplifting or doing drugs…'

'I'm making no assumption at all,' said Audrey. 'You asked about fingerprints. If you've never been in any sort of trouble, never had your fingerprints taken, why, they could dust your letter for prints until the cows come home, run them through every computer they have, and never get a match because they simply don't know what your fingerprints look like. You're under their radar.'

The Giaconda smile on Penny's face suggested she liked the idea of being under the radar.

'But we can keep you under the radar. We'll do it printless if it makes you feel better,' Audrey said, thinking also of the possibility that Penny might not be fully forthcoming on her interactions with the police. It would not be the first time a petulant teenager took refuge in a foolish lie, nor was it beyond the realm of possibility for the police to fingerprint a first offender as a way of scaring them back onto the straight and narrow. 'Get the rubber gloves from under the sink and a fresh sheet from the bottom of the pad, please. I'll write it with my left hand.'

Audrey wrote clumsily, misspelling words on purpose. 'There. Untraceable. Will you feel better now?' She slipped the note into an envelope and sealed it. 'We'll post it for you. The police aren't so scary, you know. The woman who came to see us was really nice.'

'To you, maybe.'

'I'd like to help you with something else,' said Bill. 'I am a bit of a wiz with herbs.'

'Like some kind of witch, you mean?' said Penny, sceptically.

'Just like that, but not at all,' said Bill. 'If you like, I can give you something to help with your skin.'

'Like what?' Penny shrunk back into her hoodie.

'Wait here.' Bill disappeared into the garden for a few minutes. She returned with a cut piece of aloe vera which she put in a plastic container. 'Put some of the liquid from this on your skin. It will stay fresh in the fridge for a week. Then come back for more.'

'Cool. What is it?'

'Toad flesh,' she said. 'No, not really, but it's top secret.'

'Yuk! What else can you do?'

'Many things. So very many things. This will do you for now, and I'll see you in a week. Take the rest of the muffins too please. And no more tagging.'

After Penny had gone, Bill and Audrey looked at each other and sighed. Things were not looking good for Hugo. A funny accent?

'Should we take her down to Hugo's to browse the books, do you think? She'll be able to hear if it was him,' said Bill.

'Maybe,' Audrey reluctantly agreed. 'That would make sense. I don't want to get him into trouble, but what if he did it?'

'This way we'll know for sure.'

CHAPTER 6

'What puzzles me,' Bill said to Audrey, 'is that since Fabiano and Anna lived in the apartment just above their coffee shop, why didn't Anna hear anything? Penny did, and she was outside. Do you feel like another visit to Anna? We can walk, get some exercise.'

'Can we go for an ordinary walk without a label on it? The mere word bores me. I hope we don't meet Rosie. I am not going to able to lie to her if she asks if we know anything new. She would spot a lie from a mile away.'

They found Anna alone again. After exchanging greetings, they sat down in the living room.

'We are just wondering about something that we can't work out,' Audrey said. 'Did you hear anything unusual during the night of the murder at all? A disturbance maybe?'

'The police asked me that too, but I sleep with earplugs. If I don't, the sound of a passing car or even footsteps wakes me up. Sometimes I even take sleeping pills. I wouldn't have heard a thing short of fireworks, maybe. Sorry.'

'I can give you some herbal tea to help you get a restful night if you like,' said Bill.

'Bill is great with herbs,' said Audrey helpfully.

'Sure. Just not the green thing you brought last time.'

'That green thing is a little miracle, but I'll try to give you something more to your taste. You've been through a lot and it's understandable if your sleep is disturbed. Have you seen a doctor?'

'Yes, she's helpful too. And yesterday someone dropped off a roast chicken and this morning I found a carrot cake on the doorstep. Would you like to take some with you? I can't possibly eat a whole cake.'

'We'd love to,' started Audrey but Bill interrupted her.

'You can give it to other visitors. We're on a diet. In fact, we're due for our weigh-in today. We'll drop by later with something to help you sleep.'

They had to wait for the customers to clear before they could weigh in undisturbed. Audrey said that she would prefer to skip the weighing, but this was apparently not allowed. Feeling it would be impolite to refuse, she stepped onto the scales to find they showed exactly the same weight as before.

'Don't worry about that, sometimes it can take a little while when you have no real excess weight. Why do you feel you need to lose weight?' The fit-looking staff member looked at her figure, and pinched her midriff critically. 'You could do with some more muscle tone perhaps. We have protein supplements that can help with that as you increase your exercises.'

'No thank you, I won't need any. I am more of a support dieter. Can we avoid the weighing in the future?'

Bill removed every bit of excess clothing before she stood on the scales, even her shoes.

'They're heavy shoes,' she explained. The scales showed an increase of half a kilo.

'Hmm. Have you been sticking to the diet?'

'Oh, yes,' said Bill. 'More or less, anyway. A little extra slips down occasionally, but nothing that really counts. Maybe it's just the body rearranging itself in readiness for a huge loss,' she said hopefully.

The assistant looked at her rounded shape. 'No, I don't think that's the case. We have some work to do here. I'll phone your support person. She'll have to monitor you more stringently. Do you feel she is doing a good job or would you prefer to try someone else?'

'Oh no, Margaret is just lovely. Very supportive. It is not her fault that my body is defective. It will be better soon.'

Back on the street, Bill gave Audrey a look of

reproach. 'It's all the things you eat that rub off on me. I refuse to go back there if I don't feel thinner.'

'Good,' said Audrey. 'They're much too energetic.'

When they got home they saw a business card on the doormat.

'Rosie's been,' said Audrey. 'Lucky we weren't home. I don't want to disappoint her with our lack of news. There might be some as soon as we've been to the bookshop with Penny.'

When Margaret rang in the evening, Bill was pleased to report she had given away a whole bag of muffins rather than eat them herself.

'I'm so proud of you. You'll succeed in time,' said Margaret. The call was cut short by Inez, who came in search of the leftover muffins. 'Got to go, talk tomorrow,' said Bill and hung up.

'Bill gave them away to an urchin,' Audrey explained.

'This diet of yours is not doing me any good. How annoying! I need a little morsel of something delicious. I'm working on an important Letter to the Editor,' said Inez and disappeared back into her quarters.

'What is she writing about?' asked Bill.

'She doesn't have enough opportunity at home to vent her boundless opinion on the shortcomings of our species. Needs to spread the word to the general population,' said Audrey.

'Do they get published?'

'The editor is too afraid of her not to. Heavily edited, of course, but that just serves to send her on another round of complaints. The editor's mother was in the Rural Women's Association with Inez. Thick as thieves. The letters are quite amusing at times, but don't tell her I said that. They're not intended to entertain.'

***

Bill woke up in her green room early on Wednesday morning to incessant yowling outside the door. Lucy was sitting outside, looking innocent and round-eyed up at her.

'Go away. Shoo! Hassle someone else, Audrey for instance, just one door up.'

Lucy had no intention of leaving. 'Yaouoay,' she said.

'You're not coming in. My room, not yours.'

'Yow,' said Lucy and started spinning vigorously, rubbing against Bill's legs.

'How about some breakfast, would that suit?' Bill slipped into her dressing gown and went to the kitchen. She put Lucy's bowl down in the pantry, making a loud clang as the bowl connected with the tiles.

'Is that you I can hear, Plum?' Inez called from her quarters. 'Who's there?'

'It's me, Bill. Just making tea if you want some.'

Inez apeared in the doorway. 'You have to stop

overfeeding the cat,' she said. 'I realise that you have a limited concept of acceptable eating patterns but don't expose my cat to your issues.'

'She was hungry.' Bill spread the thimbleful of daily allowable butter substitute on a piece of thin toast and took a bite. Maybe a blockade on the stairs would stop Lucy from going upstairs. She needed a cat-free zone.

It was amazing how your day ran away from you when you had no schedule to hang your time on, thought Bill. You did a bit of this, a little of that, stared into space for a while and suddenly your day was over. The intention today was to finish painting at least one room, but they didn't get that far. The patterns in the green room had started to show through the paint as if by magic and needed another coat, which would have been top priority if it hadn't been for Lucy.

'It's a good thing you left the tuba on the landing. A good start,' said Audrey. 'We can try looking in the spare rooms for cat barriers. Let's drag that rug out at the same time.'

Though heavy, the rug wasn't too awkward to get out. In the process Bill found a rather beautiful standard lamp with a tasselled silk shade.

'Do you think this still works? Might be worth a try. I have no bedside light.'

'Take it. We really should sort through everything

properly one day.'

As they looked for suitable things for a blockade they saw a wingchair in dire need of re-upholstery, with a matching footstool that they both wanted.

'You have it,' said Audrey magnanimously. 'I have the rug, which I am thrilled with.'

'And I have a lamp that I adore. You have the chair.'

'No, you have it. I think you are due something nice. Has Inez been vile again?'

'Could be worse, I guess. What do you think about that?' Bill pointed to an old fire screen.

'Not tall enough. Lucy will jump it. We'll take it anyway, and use it for one of our fireplaces. There's probably another one here, or in the attic. I can't imagine anything having been thrown out, ever. Maybe we can scare her with that.' Audrey pointed to a stuffed water buffalo head leaning in the far corner, cobwebs veiling the antlers like a chiffon scarf.

'Scare who, Inez?'

'The cat, of course.'

'You've met this cat, haven't you? Does she seem the kind to frighten easily? Let's just stack some boxes like a barricade.'

'And how do you propose we get up the stairs ourselves?'

'We'll have to move them, obviously. Until she learns to stay downstairs.'

'She's a cat, not a dog. Learning things to please

others is not high on her agenda.'

They added a pile of boxes to the tuba on the half way landing, leaving a gap large enough to squeeze through. They placed an empty large box as a gate.

'That should stop her,' said Bill.

They had enough time to put on another coat of paint before heading to pick up Penny after school. Bill had promised to buy her a book on herbal remedies at Le Bouquiniste, and Penny, in turn, promised to listen to Hugo's voice. The school car park was a flurry of cars and school buses, but Penny spotted them immediately and flung herself into the back seat, nearly crushing Bill's pheasant feather hat with her school bag.

'Hey! Ready for some undercover work?' Audrey revved the car, causing several heads to turn and Penny to sink lower into the seat.

Hugo was polishing the coffee machine when they arrived.

'*Mes amis*! What can I do for you today?'

'We've come for a book on herbals for Penny here. Do you have any?' Bill felt a simultaneous twinge of pain and excitement at the concealed truth, but how could they possibly tell him the real reason outright? Simon hadn't enjoyed being asked. It was better this way. Plus, she really did want to buy a gift for the girl.

They browsed the shelves, which held several useful titles. Bill selected one that seemed good, with enough text and good illustrations. They went to pay.

'Are you not staying for a coffee? Something sweet?'

'Why not?' agreed Bill. 'Choose what you like, Penny, we'll just have two black teas please.'

'Are they teaching you about herbs?' he asked Penny.

'I guess,' she muttered, and let her eyes roam over about ten things simultaneously.

'Well, that's good.' He slid in a bookmark. 'For the young *mademoiselle*,' he said, and put the book in a paper bag.

'I'm not a child,' said the nearly-not child.

'Of course not,' Hugo said. 'You are a young lady. Enjoy your new book.'

'Well, did you recognise the voice? The accent?' asked Audrey nervously as they drove Penny home.

'No. I might have if he shouted. What if I go back and start tearing pictures out of his books like some child – I bet he'd shout then.'

If they had lingered only a little longer outside, that is exactly what they would have heard, as the police were on their way to reinterview him. As it turned out, they had just received an anonymous note from someone claiming to have overheard a heated argument on the night of the murder.

'Yes, we argued!' shouted Hugo loud and clear, accent as strong as ever. 'That's not the same as killing him. I didn't bend so much as a single hair on his ugly head.'

'Why did you not say so before?' asked Rosie.

'Because I knew you would get yourselves in a twist, and I was correct.'

'First you claim to have been at home all night. Now we find that is not the case at all.'

'*Mon Dieu*, one can't admit to every tiny irrelevant thing which makes one look bad, *n'ést-ce pas?*'

'We can get you a police translator back at the station, if you keep doing that. You should lock up your shop – we're taking you in to the station. Let's go.'

'I can't just go, I have things on – coffee machine, till – impossible to just drop everything!'

The doorbell gave a merry tinkling and Fiona came in, a cloud of perfume preceding her.

'Can I give her my keys?' asked Hugo. 'Or is that an offense, as well?'

'What's going on, Hugo?' Fiona looked from Hugo to the police and back again, eyebrows arched, but not too much as everyone knew that it gave you wrinkles.

In response Hugo handed her the keys to the shop. He held on to her hand for a minute. 'You can do this. Switch off and lock up everything for me, please. I'll be back soon. I have a delivery in the morning if you can be here for that, in case I have not returned. It is a mistake, we will sort it out,' he said before leaving with the police.

Fiona, shocked, was at a loss for words until the car started its engine. 'Hugo!' she cried helplessly, stretching out her arms towards the departing car as if prolonging the touch of his hand.

Bill woke up to the absence of yowling the next morning and stretched out like a starfish in the wide bed. Good, the barricade must have worked. She opened the curtains to find daylight had arrived. She must have slept later than usual. She put her slippers on and opened the door to the hallway. A flash of silent movement and Lucy dashed into her room, a recently deceased mouse in her mouth. She dropped it on the floor and batted it with a dainty paw. 'Yow,' she said and purred.

'Oh no. Lucy, come on. Take your mouse and go. I'll feed you.' Lucy ignored the mouse and followed her down the stairs. When they reached the barricade Lucy simply jumped over it and sauntered, tail held high, ahead of her into the kitchen. Trying hard not to alert Inez in case she had her hearing aids in, Bill opened a tin of tuna and put it on the floor, closed the kitchen door behind her and went up to pick up the mouse with a stick and double layers of plastic bags on her hands. While she was out in the garden disposing of the mouse the phone rang inside.

'Bill! Telephone!' Audrey was still in bed, having

some quiet thinking time. Her thoughts were shattered into disjointed fragments as the phone kept ringing. 'Oh blast.' She grabbed her dressing gown and rushed to the old green telephone in the hallway.

'Hello? Hello? Audrey speaking!'

'Audrey, it's me, Fiona, from the choir. It's a disaster. Hugo has been taken away by the police.'

'What on earth?'

'I was just coming to see him yesterday and the police took him away. He gave me the keys so I could take care of the place. I thought I would be fine opening by myself but it has got very busy.'

'Well, that's something. He'll be pleased about that.'

'Can you come? I've tried to get hold of so many people. Sorry to ask for such a big favour, but we must keep the show on the road.'

'Absolutely.' A twinge of unease flickered through her mind. Maybe it was their fault. She suppressed the thought. 'We'll come straight over. Keep it up until we get there.'

She replaced the receiver thoughtfully. 'Bill! Where are you? Hugo has been arrested. We have a shop to run. Go and get dressed.'

'Really?' Bill came up the stairs, minus mouse. 'I was getting rid of a present from Lucy. The barricade had no effect at all. Oh dear me. That is very bad indeed. The police have too much imagination, or not enough, I can't think which. I'll be ready in a minute.'

Audrey went to choose a suitable coffee shop outfit for herself. Hugo himself was always smartly turned out. The job at hand, she felt, needed an intellectual and casual look so she chose a brown tweed three-piece suit, only slightly moth-eaten, a fine check shirt and a silk scarf knotted the debonair way the boys had shown her. A baggy green cricketing cap completed the look. Being able to wear whatever you wanted was rather a fun thing, but it put greater demands on you. There was a decision to be made every day.

'You look like a gentleman farmer. I don't know what to wear,' said Bill. 'I really like those long linen aprons bartenders wear. Do you think we can we get one on the way?

'There's no time. Just pick something.'

Bill disappeared into her room and returned a minute later in the kilt and a knitted grey jumper. 'This has to do. Let's tell Inez and go. We can have breakfast there.'

When they arrived at Le Bouquiniste they found an elderly couple drinking tea by a smoky fire. Fiona was kneeling in front of it, looking flustered. She poked and blew at the smouldering flames. A customer was waiting at the counter.

'Thank God you're here! There's been people in and out all morning.' Fiona stood up and wiped a smudge of soot from her otherwise well made-up cheek.

'I am not sure what He has to do with it, but can I have some service, please?' The man at the counter waved a book in the air. 'Or do I have to leave the correct amount?'

'As long as you don't order coffee,' said the couple by the fire. 'They don't know how to make it so there's only tea. Cold tea, if you can believe it. As cold as the fire. The reviews were right. It may be pretty but it's still pretty awful.'

'You need to be more forgiving,' said Audrey sternly and gave them a look of reprimand. 'Let us make you a new drink, free of charge of course. Hugo has been called away unexpectedly. The internet is full of rubbish. Bill, fix the fire. Fiona, go and have a break. Tidy yourself up a bit.' Audrey looked at the price of the book and deducted a third, figuring it would be worth it to Hugo. 'Sure you won't stay for a coffee?'

'Alright then, if you can drive that thing,' the man nodded towards the large machine, which was hissing menacingly on the counter.

'Of course I can. I've watched Hugo.' Audrey grabbed the handle of the sieve thingy and gave a firm twist, filled it with coffee, tamped it in what she felt was a professional style, returned it with another twist and put a cup underneath. Pressing a button hopefully, she was relieved to see coffee trickling into the cup. She poured milk in the steel jug and turned on the steam. 'Oops!' she cried as milk exploded all over the floor. 'I'll try again.' More careful this time, the steam and milk cooperated and a firm froth was soon building in the jug.

'There you go,' Audrey said, 'Please accept this as a small gift.'

'No need, you already gave me a book discount. Don't want to send the shop broke, do you?'

Audrey made two more coffees, put slices of orange and almond cake on a plate and delivered it to the cold tea drinkers. 'Please accept this as a gift. This is a most wonderful place, really. The fire, the books, the water just outside the windows.' Through the window they could see a swan emerging from the drifting mist. It paddled silently up to the shore by the cafe. 'Hugo feeds them, you know. This is one of our favourite places in Daylesford.'

'Pretty,' the woman agreed, eyes transfixed on the lake scene, where a couple of geese had joined the swan. 'Do you think that we could feed them, since he is away?'

'Of course. I'll give you something when you leave.'

The day passed and the till filled nicely without the need to give any more freebies away.

Fiona was already there when they returned to Le Bouquiniste the following morning. So was Hugo, slightly dishevelled.

'Thank you all for yesterday, I hear you have done

a fine job. They released me pending further questioning so it's not over yet. It is awful. I am very much the suspect.'

Bill bit at a cuticle nervously. *Oh dear*. Before she had time to make up her mind about whether to say anything or not, Audrey spoke up.

'Hugo, that might be because of us, one way or another.'

'You? How could that possibly be?'

'You see, we had a visit from Detective Rosie, you must have met her,' said Bill anxiously. 'We had a long talk and we sort of told her about you and the reviews. Sorry if we got you into trouble. We never meant it that way.' She realised how silly it sounded.

Hugo narrowed his eyes at her but said nothing.

'You told her? Bill, really. Why on earth would you do that?' Fiona shook her head. 'That wasn't very smart.'

'She was nice. We were just talking, and it wasn't like an interview at all. Don't worry, we'll fix it. No rock will be left unturned until we find the culprit.'

'Will you?' Hugo spoke up. 'Well, I feel so much better knowing that. I can't believe you would think I did it. Please leave.'

'But that's not how it was...'

'Out!' He pointed to the door.

'You can't blame him for getting angry,' said Audrey

as they made their way home. 'He spent the night at the station because of us. Did you see the smug look on Fiona's face?'

'I did. She's pleased, at least. Anyway, it only matters what the police think. It is possible that he did it, I just don't think so myself. He's hot tempered but that means nothing.'

'He's a man with passions. You can bet that's how Fiona feels, too. Come on, best foot forward. We have work to do.'

CHAPTER 7

When Audrey and Bill arrived at their front gate the mailman was there on his yellow moped, shoving a handful of mail mixed with advertising leaflets through the slot.

'You should get a sign saying "no junk mail". It'll save me from being obliged to deliver it all. Or just write it on the letterbox –I have to deliver it if you don't. You have no idea how much extra I have to drag around on my route. A load of rubbish.'

'Oh, no thank you, we want it. Thank you for doing your job so well.' Audrey smiled sweetly at the mailman, who gave a fully franked disapproving grunt and sped off.

'Inez loves the ads. Gives her something extra to get annoyed about.' She rifled through the mail, which contained a couple of bills among the usual hardware catalogues and offers from real estate agents. A pink flyer slipped out, advertising one of the many health centres in Daylesford. Super specials were on offer, including some two-for-one deals.

'You girls could do with some extra care. Let me give you a treatment,' said Inez after seeing the flyer. 'How about a massage? It's the thing to do here. You should go out and enjoy yourselves a little.'

Audrey agreed wholeheartedly. 'Why not? Thank you. Look at this list! I might have my eyebrows done. Or hands. Maybe my feet, that would be interesting. Let's ring and book.' After her successful encounter with Astrid she was not going to turn down further offers of treatments.

Thanks to the strident mailman, so few people received their junk mail – or if they did, bothered to read it – there were plenty of appointments free. Bill and Audrey were slightly awed when they arrived at the centre and were greeted by a tribe of young and healthy-looking staff clad in crisp all-white. A woman showed the way into a large room with cubicles off to one side and told them to get changed into white towelling robes and slippers, neatly laid out. Duly done, they sat on low rattan lounges filling out forms about any problems they might have (knees and aunts for Audrey, cat allergy and short-sightedness for Bill).

'We have other problems too numerous and hard to fit on this form,' muttered Bill. 'Such as: who complained about the noise and did the coffee beans mean anything? Does Hugo like Fiona as much as she likes him? Will Hugo ever forgive us? Plus the most important question: who did it?'

'Let's just relax. Ideas might come.'

'Ms Pretty? This way please.'

Audrey was made to disrobe and lie down under a sheet. She had never had a massage before and was happy to find it agreed with her immensely. The repetitive manipulation, warmth and scented oils had sent her to the point of dozing off when the masseuse stopped abruptly with a sharp intake of breath.

'What's happened? Do I have a bad mole on my back?'

'Forgive me, I'm also a clairvoyant. I felt something. Sorry.'

'Felt what?'

'I shouldn't interfere with your massage. Just relax.'

'I can hardly relax now, can I? Not after you frightened me like that. What did you feel?'

'It was probably nothing, but I had a fleeting image of a tall man.'

'Really...'

'He's strong. No, wait, there are two men. It's so dark, I can't see clearly... You're in danger! You must go far away. Oh, I do apologise. What am I thinking of, telling you these things?'

Her deft hands recommenced kneading and pressing on Audrey's back. Audrey was no longer the least bit relaxed or sleepy. Her brain was working in overdrive.

'Danger? Can you tell me anything more? Any details?'

'It was just a passing feeling. It's gone now. It's nothing. I really didn't mean to startle you.'

'Telling people covered by just a sheet that they are in danger from two men in the dark is not the most professional approach to your job, is it?'

'It just slipped out. Please don't say anything to my boss. It just came out. Let me see if I can see more.' She massaged in silence for a while. 'Yes, I see now, they're friendly men in the dark. Nothing to worry about.'

'What about the danger? You said I was in danger,' prompted Audrey.

'It's gone, can't see it. But be careful all the same. Danger is always around us whether we've been warned or not.'

'That's a bleak philosophy that I will refuse to adopt.'

'Up to you, but please be careful all the same.'

Meanwhile, Bill had suffered through a bitterly painful waxing of her eyebrows that had brought tears to her eyes. Now she was having her legs exfoliated with salt and oil. It was making her skin tingly and warm in a most refreshing way after the first treatment, which she regretted having. Her therapist was the chatty kind. So far, she had gone through the weather, her plans for the weekend and of course the talk of the town, murder.

'Jenny Jones, do you know Jenny at the grocery shop?'

'No, I don't know many people yet. We haven't been here very long.'

'You soon will. Everyone knows Jenny. She lives in the middle of Daylesford and said the night-time noise from his place was unbearable. She tried to make a complaint, said it was turning her head inside out. I live in Trentham, myself. There are some pubs and things there but never any noise. The neighbour's dog though, it's bloody noisy. As soon as its owners are out, there it goes, barking its head off.'

'So do you think he was killed because of the noise?' Bill tried to get her back on track.

'Had to be, the way Jenny went on about it. Deprive people of sleep for long enough and there's no telling what they'll do.'

'You don't mean to say that you think Jenny is a suspect?'

'Jenny? No, she talks too much about it. It'll be someone who hasn't said a word, you just wait. How do your legs feel now?'

'Red raw, but alive in every pore.'

'That's the way we like it. Your eyebrows came out well – you have beautiful eyes. Would you like a lash and brow tint while you're here? It would frame your eyes nicely, open them up.'

'As long as it doesn't hurt as much as the eyebrows.'

Bill found that tinting had no pain involved at all and was feeling rather pleased with herself. She was too impatient to sit down while waiting for Audrey to emerge and paced the white waiting room. She could hardly wait to tell Audrey that they had a new clue.

'Let's go and see this Jenny straight away,' said Bill, scratching at her eyes. 'Did you notice my new eyebrows? What do you think?' She brought her face close to Audrey, turning this way and that in order for her to admire the beautician's handiwork.

'Hmm. Is it supposed to be that red? You look like you walked into a shelf.'

'A little redness is normal. It'll go away soon, never mind about that.'

'Okay, apart from that I think your eyes look fantastic. Really. Now let's go to this Jenny.'

Jenny was bent over a garden bed, pulling out weeds. She wore muddy rubber boots, which reminded Audrey that they really should go and look at some. A chocolate-coloured Labrador sat chewing on a stick. He wagged his tail with doggy enthusiasm as they approached.

'What a beautiful garden.' They stopped by the white picket gate where a hand-painted sign declared that this was where Jenny and Fred lived.

'The weeds keep growing, anyway.' Jenny wiped her muddy hands on her trousers and adjusted her beanie. 'I don't really do much to it anymore, just a bit of weeding and pruning. It takes care of itself. You can have some cuttings if you like. Do you live in Daylesford?'

'We're new. I'm Bill and this is Audrey. We live just up there, at Stewart House,' said Bill, fighting the urge to scratch her eyes. No one had warned her how itchy it would be to be beautified.

'Pleased to meet you. I'm Jenny. I know Inez of course. How's her hip going? I haven't seen her around much lately.'

'The usual aches and pains. She feels the cold something terrible.'

'The cold isn't much. Soon spring will be here and everyone will complain about how warm it is. What's wrong with your face?'

'My face? Oh it's nothing, I just had my eyes dyed.' Bill pressed her hands gently on the sore spots, which were feeling hot.

'Actually, Bill, it's getting redder. You could do with a cold compress until it goes away,' said Audrey with concern.

'Have you looked in a mirror?' asked Jenny. 'I think you're allergic to the tint. I've seen that look before.'

'Allergic? Can you be allergic to tint? I do feel a bit tender. Do you mind if we ask you something?'

'Sure, what do you want to know?'

'Someone said that you made a noise complaint

about last Saturday's debacle at The Bean. We understand if you don't want to tell us anything, but you see, a friend of ours is a suspect. We don't think he did it and we're trying to find out as much as we can ourselves. A little investigative help is never wrong, is it?'

'Best leave all that to the police. I don't know much but it was an awful racket, that's for sure.' She told them all that had happened: how dismissive the police and the council had been of her complaint, and how Fabiano himself had told her that she 'didn't rate'.

'I always like to believe the best of people,' Jenny said, 'but he was not a nice man. He was punished immediately. I am sorry he had to die, but he just didn't listen. People make all the right noises now but it's easy to like someone when it's too late.'

'What did you make of that?' asked Audrey as they walked home. 'She seemed a little unhinged. It almost sounded as if she was pleased, with that line about being punished.'

'She made me a tiny bit uncomfortable,' admitted Bill.

When they arrived back home they found a potted hyacinth in full bloom and a chocolate sampler box waiting for them on the porch table.

'What a lovely smell, I adore hyacinths,' said Bill. 'Who can this be from? Maybe the choir.'

Scribbled on the ingredient label in marker pen were the words 'To Audrey and Bill'.

'Does that say... mmm... Martha? Mary? I can't make it out. It could be anyone,' said Audrey, peering closely at the name. She started to unwrap the box. 'We'll just thank whoever it is when we find out.'

'Hold it right there,' said Bill. 'No more chocolates for me for a while. I will look like a barrel on legs if I don't stick to my diet.'

'Oh dear, what a pity for you. You are to be admired for your discipline,' said Audrey, as she struggled with the foil wrapping. 'Inez and I will eat them.' Lucy arrived with a hurried step. 'None for you either. Because you are a cat, and this is not for cats. You can have a scratch between your pretty little ears.' She paused and stopped unwrapping. 'I'm being mean, sorry. Let's give these away to someone else and remove the temptation. I'll just peel the thank you note off first and fix up the wrapping.'

'Why don't we go back to Jenny and give them to her?' said Bill. 'As a friendly present. We can keep the hyacinth. Flowers don't make you fat. Margaret always tells me to smell nice things when I feel hungry as a non-fattening treat and she is really right about that. Then we can talk to Jenny some more. She didn't say very much. I'm sure we can pick up on some thread of information she doesn't realise is important, just as the police said.'

Jenny was still in out in the garden, sweeping the path.

'Did you lose something?'

'Not at all, we just wanted to offer you a treat as thanks for the offer of cuttings,' said Bill. They handed her the box. 'There are several things I'd love to propagate from your garden if I may, later on,' Bill added.

'Handmade chocolates', said Jenny, admiring the box. 'You shouldn't have.' She glanced up at Bill, her look changing from appreciative to horrified. 'Will you look at that! Now you really need an antihistamine. I have plenty. Come in for a cup of tea and I'll fix you up.'

'Antihistamines? I think I'll just wait, it's not that bad. It will soon go away I hope. A cup of tea would be lovely though.'

'Suit yourself. I'll get the kettle on and get you a cool wet face cloth you can hold on the sore spot.'

They sat down in her kitchen, which was painted a sunny yellow. The cups were yellow to match. Fred provided a brown contrast as he lay underneath the table, thumping his tail.

'When you think of everything that has happened,' asked Audrey, 'aren't you frightened to be on your own?'

'I'm not on my own. I have Fred.' He wagged his tail faster at the mention of his name. 'No matter where you live, you'll get what's coming your way.

I don't think I'm in any danger but I admit that I'm a little tense. You can't flee from fate. There is a murderer somewhere, maybe right here among us.'

'In this room?' gasped Bill.

'Can we be sure that there isn't?' said Jenny and leant in conspiratorially. 'Bad things are happening, that's for certain. First I was awake with the noise, and now I'm awake with the fear of what will happen next. The police should have paid attention when I rang. Just look what happened when they didn't.'

She opened the box and put a truffle dusted with cocoa into her mouth. She nudged the box towards the women.

'Have one yourselves.'

'We'll stick with the tea thanks.' Bill gripped her mug tightly so her hands wouldn't leap out and take a chocolate all by themselves.

'They're delicious, heavenly,' said Jenny. She reached out for a second one and froze, a look of panic on her face. Her mouth opened and closed, forcing out a strangled wheeze. She clutched her throat with her hands, tearing at her shirt collar.

'Are you alright?' cried Audrey. They stared in horror as Jenny staggered off her chair and collapsed on the floor. Bill bent down and unbuttoned the top buttons of Jenny's shirt.

'Help me get her on her side. I need to clear her airway.'

Fred joined in eagerly, licking and pawing. He loved it the best when people were playing on the floor with him.

'She's choking! Call an ambulance,' said Bill.

If you are in luck in Daylesford, the ambulance is very close at hand. If you are out of luck it will be in the countryside somewhere, which will make your wait considerably longer. Jenny was fortunate, and in no time at all two cheerful ambulance officers came in and took control. They bundled her into the ambulance and drove off, leaving Bill and Audrey on their own. Fred had been banished to the laundry.

'Now what do we do?' asked Bill, stunned at the speed with which her afternoon had changed. One minute you are having a relaxing time being treated to all kinds of attentions and the next you find yourself, resplendent with swollen face, abandoned in a stranger's yellow kitchen.

'We'll let Fred out,' said Audrey. 'Then I need to think. Let's have another cup of tea.'

Bill had another go at the cuticle she had started chewing earlier and picked some long brown dog hairs off her skirt. Her eyes really hurt and she was trying not to touch them.

'I don't think she was choking,' said Audrey eventually. 'I'm wondering if the chocolates were poisoned. They were meant for us, remember. I haven't had time to tell you yet but my masseuse told me I was in danger. Two men, strong, darkness. She had a vision, she's a clairvoyant apparently. All that close, focused contact with her client can bring it on.'

'Clairvoyant! How incredible,' said Bill. 'Yet... the chocolates! Do you really think that someone just tried to kill us? She can't have been that good though. I see no darkness, unless she was referring to darkness of the mind. Only the brightest of yellow.'

'She may have muddled things up. The ambulance men were certainly strong, but absolutely darling, not dangerous at all. I wish she had been more specific.'

'What, like stay away from chocolate? We have Margaret to warn us about that,' said Bill. 'Today started so well.' She thought for a moment. 'Fred will have to come home with us. We can't leave him here.'

They grabbed a plastic bag from under the sink and packed up Fred's blanket, his bowls and some dog food. Jenny's house keys were on the kitchen bench. Audrey found Fred's lead hanging on a hook in the hallway, and he sat nicely while waiting for them to clip it on.

'You're a good boy, Fred' said Bill, and gave him a pat on his velvety face.

They walked home with Fred in tow, deeply troubled. Had they inadvertently killed someone? Things were most definitely not going to plan.

'Let's go to the hospital later and see how she is.

And we have to be on our guard in case someone tries again. Those chocolates had our names on them,' said Bill. 'But first we'll go to the police. We'll give them the note and the rest of the box. It's crime evidence now.'

'Where's the note?'

'I put it in the kitchen bin.' Bill tied Fred up to the front fence. There was no need for him to meet Inez and Lucy just yet.

By now the note was smeared with coffee grounds and sticky from close contact with a broken egg, making it even less legible than before. They put it in the plastic bag with the chocolate box.

'Let's not mention the clairvoyant to the police,' said Audrey. 'They won't take it seriously.'

'I won't,' promised Bill. 'This is a matter of life and death.' Her hands trembled a little as she tied Fred up outside the police station doors.

The sergeant behind the desk looked at the two agitated women, one of whom had very odd-looking bright red eyebrows and puffy eyes, as they gave him a lurid tale of poisoned chocolates, strange notes and murderous intents. Only the brown dog waiting outside seemed sane.

'So let's see if I've got this right,' he sighed. 'Someone whose name begins with M or possibly W, maybe even NI, wants to kill you because you know too much. Now you have accidentally killed someone else because you don't want to put on weight.' He paused to look at their figures. 'And you want me to send these chocolates away to the lab to be tested. Perhaps you want some police protection to prevent any more danger by chocolate?'

'That is most kind, but I don't think they would try the same thing twice, do you, Officer?' replied one of the women, the skinny one. 'That would show a lack of imagination, and that is not the way of this person. Strikingly different each time. Coffee the last time, chocolate this time.'

'Could be ham the next, you mean,' said the sergeant.

'Exactly. It could be any method at all. And you forget that we don't actually eat chocolate, so we are perfectly safe,' said the woman with the eyebrows, looking at him through what he could only think of as coin slots.

'Yes, imagination... Plenty of that. Leave your details with me and we'll be in touch if we need you.' He kept the chocolates. They were making his mouth water. He might put a few in the staffroom too, since his own waistline could do with some attention.

The hospital in Daylesford was a beautiful old building in the grand Victorian style, paid for by the long-gone gold rush. It was not large but most impressive for a village. A cheerful-looking woman with rosy cheeks and a burr of frizzy chestnut hair sat working on a computer in the foyer.

'Can I help you?' she smiled, showing several dimples. One of the women in front of her had terribly swollen eyes and supraorbital arch. *Orbital cellulitis maybe?*

'Is it possible to find out some information about a patient who was admitted today?' asked Bill.

'What's the patient's name, please?'

'Jenny Jones. She arrived in an ambulance earlier.'

'Oh, of course, Jenny.'

'Is she dead?'

'Dead? Why would she be? She suffered an anaphylactic shock. Seems that she ate some chocolates that had traces of nuts. We'll keep her in overnight, just as a precaution. She should be alright to go home tomorrow. She's resting in a ward now.'

'So you're sure she wasn't poisoned?'

'Why would she be poisoned? It was just her allergy. She knows better. You should always read the ingredient list when you have allergies.'

'Can you give her a message? We'll keep Fred at Inez's house until she gets out of hospital. She knows Inez. Here are her keys, we've locked the house. She'll want to know that everything is alright.'

'I'll tell her. I thought you were here seeking emergency care for your own allergy. I can get a doctor to look at your face if you like. I think you should.'

'No thank you, I'll be alright.' Bill was so relieved

that they hadn't killed Jenny that she didn't care about a little reaction. It would soon be gone anyway.

'I feel stupid now,' said Audrey as they left the hospital. 'Do we go back to the police and say that we were wrong?'

'We can just ring, save on the humiliation. Let's take Fred for a walk around the lake before we go home.'

As they got close to the car park near Le Bouquiniste they saw Hugo by the water, feeding the swans.

'I'll stay here with Fred, you go,' said Bill, adjusting her collar to reach as high as she could although it would never reach her eye area. She bent down to pat Fred instead, turning her back on Hugo, who was waving at them.

'Audrey, Bill! Did you get the chocolates?' he asked, looking quizzically over at Bill's back.

'They were from *you*?' said Audrey.

'But of course they were from me. Is apology. I was shouting, it is not gentlemanly.' He raised his shoulders and shrugged. 'Is many people giving you chocolates?'

'Might be. We... Never mind. It's too complicated.'

'You have a dog now?'

'Only temporary, long story. Let's not even discuss it. We're so glad that you forgive us. We really do promise that we're doing all we can to help.'

When Bill woke up the next day she was very pleased to note her face was less swollen. As she thought, no need for medicine. She batted her new dark eyelashes at herself in the bathroom mirror and guided Fred through the barricaded stairs to let him out in the garden.

'Why is there a dog in the garden?' Inez asked Audrey.

'Jenny Jones is in hospital. We happened to be right there when the ambulance came so we took Fred home. I think she'll be home today.'

'Lucy will be pleased. She doesn't like him. Now that Hugo is back from the dungeons, why don't you invite the horrid old socialist for drinks tonight and cheer him up a bit?' suggested Inez. 'It can't be easy for him. First he has to pretend to like your biscuits and then you get him banged up in the slammer. What a sore trial you have proved to be as friends. We shall have cocktail hour and I'll teach you how to make a few. Good. That's settled. Ask the boys as well, it will dilute the company of the old goat.'

Stewart House had not entertained for a while. In years past, grand parties had swirled through the grand building and its grounds. The ancient bottle collection received a dusting and candlesticks were rounded up from the house and scattered around the library, throwing a warm soft light over the worn room, reflecting in the mottled and flaking mirrors.

Bill filled vases with camellias and japonicas while Audrey lit the fire, allowing the heat to settle and blend with the subtle fragrance of the flowers. Lucy approved of the extra comfort and made a nest for herself in front of the fire, but whenever Bill came in the room she got up to follow her favourite human around.

'She adores you, the precious poppet,' Inez cooed and swept up her cat, tickling her under the furry chin. 'So naughty, aren't you?' Lucy ran straight to Bill as soon as Inez put her down again. Bill, reluctant to touch the cat, went to the kitchen to entice Lucy away with some snacks.

'I've told you before about trying to turn the cat into a Behemoth,' said Inez as she appeared behind her. It was true, Bill realised. In the short time they had been there the cat seemed to have swelled a little.

'Not to worry. Just stop it,' Inez continued. 'We'll need some mint from the garden, quite a bit, and we also need to get these lemons squeezed. The eggnog can be prepared now so it's ready when they arrive. Good and wintry. My father used to let me beat the eggs when I was a young girl. I enjoyed the rotary whisk. Always tried to jam my little brother's fingers in it, but he grew wise unfortunately.'

Inez cracked a couple of eggs, deftly separating the yolks and the whites into two bowls. 'Start beating the egg whites. Add sugar as you go. Like making meringues, see?'

Bill and Audrey took turns as their arms got tired. 'Weaklings. Beat!' Inez poured in some sugar. 'Audrey can finish this if you nip up to your room,' she said to Bill. 'There's something for you up there. Go!'

Bill obediently went upstairs. She opened her door with some trepidation and was much surprised to find the coveted wingchair, complete with footstool, resprung and upholstered in a William Morris fabric so beautiful she wanted to cry. There was also a small side table with a vase full of daffodils. A rug in green tones covered the floor in front of the chair, and the lamp she had brought out from storage stood behind it, illuminating the scene. A woollen rug was folded on the footstool. She could only smile with joy and ran downstairs as fast as she could.

'Looks about right,' Inez was saying to Audrey. 'Beat the yolks separately now. More sugar. Fine.' She turned to Bill. 'Audrey told me you wanted the chair.' She brushed aside Bill's thanks and handed her another whisk. 'You can whip some cream, gently.' Soon there were three bowls lined up on the counter with whipped whites, yolks and cream.

'We'll mix brandy, rum, bourbon and milk into a bowl, then add the rest,' said Inez. 'Do we have any nutmeg? Never mind. It will have to do. Here's the doorbell now, just on time.'

Hugo had accepted his invitation with apparent delight and arrived dressed up in a suit with a badge on the lapel, which said 'Enemy of the State' in bold print on a yellow background. The boys arrived behind him bearing a platter of elaborate canapés.

'Love the eyebrows! Have you seen your surprise yet?' they asked Bill eagerly.

'It's wonderful,' she beamed and gave them each a kiss.

'Inez has had the Morris fabric since the dawn of time apparently, asked us to do a superfast job. Say that you like it.' They were almost as excited as Bill herself.

'Oh, it's all so beautiful. I'll have to thank you instead of Inez because she won't accept any gratitude.'

'Madame,' Hugo kissed Inez's hand, 'I beg of you to receive this leetle gift.' He gave her a bottle of red vermouth. 'Extra supplies for le cocktail.'

'Thank you, Hugo. Can I have my hand back now, please.'

'Such a *charmante* hand, one wishes to keep it forever, embraced in a tender hold.' Hugo grinned and held her hand tight. 'Beautiful rings, too. Would you like my badge, to add to the jewel collection?'

'You are dreadful, that's enough of that,' said Inez and thumped him hard on the shoulder. Her strength defied her apparent frailty. 'I accept the badge, thank you. We shall go into the library, there's a fire burning.' She pinned the badge to her dress and gave it a fond pat. 'Plum, fetch the eggnog. The first cocktail! Who wants a sample?'

Everyone did, except for Inez herself, who was content with neat whisky.

'Welcome. To our wives and sweethearts!' she raised her glass and downed the contents in one go.

'May they never meet,' replied Hugo.

'Yum,' said James, licking his lips. 'Perfect for tonight. How lucky we are to have such friends to share a cold winter's night. What are we sampling next? I usually only drink wine and cider.'

'Pah. Wine is all very well with your food but not for cocktail hour. Next is a special auntie drink, mint juleps. My own aunts, may they rest in peace, used to have this as a staple when we went to visit them in Elsternwick. I always called them Aunt Juleps. They would give me some with a little sugar water instead of bourbon and we would have summer drinks on the veranda. It was repulsive but a nice memory all the same. We, however, shall have it with bourbon as it was intended, and plenty of it.'

Audrey ground up the fresh mint leaves with some caster sugar in a bowl and put the mixture in tall glasses full of crushed ice. Bourbon was poured over the top.

'Give it a good stir,' directed Inez.

'It needs a toast. To all aunts!' said Bill. 'Even other people's.'

'Hear, hear. To all aunts,' chorused the guests and drank solemnly.

'Refreshing, I suppose, in its way,' said Audrey.

The juleps were followed by gin fizzes, martinis and sidecars.

'This one's my favourite, I think,' said Bill, slurring ever such a tiny bit. 'I'll have one more of these. Yummy lemony icy cold. But first a break. Let's go to the dining room, I'll play us a song.'

She rested her drink on top of the piano and played the intro to a song they had just learnt for the choir. As far as she could remember it was about a girl who had a cat with silky hair but she wanted a dog instead and cried a lot. Audrey accessorised with Lucy and joined in the refrain. It was a far cry from Gregorian chants and hymns.

Daddy wouldn't buy me a bow-wow! Bow wow!
I've got a little cat
And I'm very fond of that
But I'd rather have a bow-wow
Wow, wow, wow, wow.

'Fabulous,' said Simon and applauded. 'Hey, James, why don't you do your soft shoe shuffle?'

'It's been ages, I'm not sure...'

'Of course you can. Play something, Bill.'

James, whose mother preferred to take him to work rather than hire babysitters, had spent many hours of his childhood in the dancing school where his mother worked. He had no trouble dazzling his small audience despite lacking recent practice. Inez's green eyes glittered.

'Bravo,' she called and clapped. James took her hand and brought her onto the floor to do a few slow gentle steps.

'More, more!' requested the audience.

'That's enough.' James bowed from the waist. 'Thank you, but I think more drinks, not more dancing.' He kept his hold of Inez and escorted her back to the library and put another log on the fire.

It was well past one when the guests put their final drinks down and decided, slurrily, that it was best to go home, if only they could remember where that was.

Audrey got up much too early the next day after having had nowhere near enough sleep. She was thirsty and had been tossing and turning like a washing machine on spin cycle until her nightgown was a tightly twisted coil pinning her down. Eventually she gave up trying.

She squeezed past the now even higher box barricade and made a cup of tea in the kitchen. She brought the tea back upstairs and ran a hot bath. The chipped enamel tub may have been a bit rusty but the water was hot, clear and plentiful. She poured a handful of cooking salt in the bath, added a decent dash of Epsom for the magnesium and two drops of bergamot oil.

She dipped in an exploratory toe carefully. The bath had to be hot enough to nearly hurt, and shallow enough to allow topping up with more heat once she had acclimatised. Perfect. She sank into the water and inhaled the spicy floral vapour. She could see a square of starry winter sky through the window at the end of the room. The window was good for focusing on as it gave a path on which her mind could travel.

Next to the bath was a chair where one could put a drink, a book and a handtowel so one's book didn't get wet. This early morning was not one for books though, just thinking. Baths, in Audrey's view, were places of retreat and solitary contemplation. In this particular tub, as in most, she had to make the decision of whether she wanted her knees above water or her shoulders as both could not fit in simultaneously. She alternated the positions as each body part cooled, warm water gently sloshing over her in the process.

The soaking was making her feel much improved, but still she felt terribly stupid about rushing to conclusions. Really, they were grown women and ought to know better. They would be of little help to Hugo in finding the real murderer if they didn't get better at this investigating lark. They had to talk to people. That was something they were good at. Perhaps they could join a few more groups. It would be a good way to get to know locals, and knowing people would be helpful in investigating.

The bell rang shrilly in the corridor outside the bathroom. Inez.

'Oh blast,' muttered Audrey. 'Bill,' she called. 'Bill!' She heard the sound of Bill's door opening and running footsteps, followed by an almighty rumble and a scream.

Audrey pulled herself up in the bath, water sloshing everywhere. She could hear no further sounds, the silence ominous after such a commotion. As she tried to grab her dressing gown in her hurry to get dressed it fell in the tub. 'Bugger!' She really must learn some good profanities to use in case of emergency. Trying to avoid slipping on the water that had pooled on the floor, she wrung out her soaking dressing gown and put it on. Gingerly she made her barefoot way out of the bathroom.

'Bill? Where are you? Are you alright?' she called in the dark.

'Clearly not,' came a voice from the bottom of the stairs. 'Forgot the effing barricade. I might have broken my arm.' Bill gingerly cradled her arm.

Bill had alrady added to her vocabulary, Audrey noticed. At least she was alive. Who knew what state Inez was in. The bell rang again, a good sign of life in a patient. This was a morning to be thankful for small mercies.

'Must go, I'll be back as soon as I can,' she said to

Bill. 'Will you be alright for a minute? Good. I'm really sorry.' Not wanting to add to the casualties list, she went to Inez as carefully as possible, leaving a watery path behind. She switched on some downstairs lights as she went through.

'Inez, what's happened? Are you ill?'

'You'll have to take me to the doctor.' Audrey had never ever seen Inez look frightened before. Her face was white and she looked every inch her age. 'I'm not at all well, so dizzy and nauseous that I can hardly stand up. My heart.' Her hands were clasped to her chest. 'It's pounding and racing. Am I going to die now? Bring me Bill, she can tell me the truth. If I am, I need to say my last words to you. I have been practising.'

'Alrighty, don't worry. Stay calm and I'll call for an ambulance.'

'No ambulance.' She reached for her cane and started to haul herself up. 'I can do it, I can even drive myself. See?' She was standing, though a trifle unsteadily. 'What on earth are you wearing?'

'I was having a bath.'

'Dressed?'

'Fell in the bath. Look, you are either dying or you're not. Sit back down for a second. I have to go and check on Bill and get the car keys and something dry to wear.'

'Check on Bill? Why does she need checking?

Don't leave me!'

'Won't be a minute.'

Audrey skidded all the way back to the foot of the stairs where Bill still sat holding her arm.

'I'm convinced it's broken. I can't move my fingers. How's Inez?'

'Just keep holding it and go to the car. Can you mange? I am throwing a coat and shoes on. See you out there. Inez thinks she's dying but is refusing an ambulance. I don't know what's wrong with her but she looks pretty frail. I'll help her out to the car.'

Audrey pulled some clothes on and grabbed a coat for Bill to throw over her shoulders, figuring that a minute extra would make little difference. Coat, shoes, keys: ready to go. She wrapped a blanket around Inez and supported her as they shuffled out to the car where Bill was waiting. She had no trouble finding the hospital, having been here only just the other day. This time she pulled in just outside the big glass doors of the emergency entry and helped Inez out of the car.

'What's happened here?' said the nurse. 'How are we, Inez?' She spoke loudly and clearly, enunciating every syllable.

'I am not here for my hearing. Just a little unwell.' She glared at the nurse, her composure back at least temporarily.

'If you would like to take a seat I'll find someone to

take care of you.'

'I want some machinery hooking up, and my levels need checking. Can't you see that I am not well?' said Inez. 'You whippersnapper, I want someone senior who can do this properly! Look how weak I am.' She held out a trembling pale hand.

'Now, now, Inez, this hospital has a policy against abusive behaviour. And I am a fully qualified thirty-four years old.' The nurse rolled her eyes at Audrey, who made a gesture of helplessness in return.

'That's all very well, you have many years left in you but don't use all of them waiting to get me help.' Inez was talking to an empty space as the nurse had already left to get her new admission organised.

Soon Inez was in bed, tucked into crisp white sheets. There was enough free space in the hospital to give her a private room, just next to the nurses' station. 'So we can keep a really close eye on you, make sure you get better quickly!' she was told.

A doctor arrived and examined her. Inez didn't say a word about incompetence this time, but the doctor had grey hair and glasses, which served as more reassurance than a white coat and a stethoscope.

'There is nothing wrong with her that's immediately apparent,' she said. 'I'd like to keep her for a bit all the same, to make sure everything is alright. Has she been overdoing it? Anything unusual? She's supposed to take things easy. It's all the usual suspects at her age, heart etcetera.'

The cocktail party, thought Audrey, hit by the memory of a long and alcohol-drenched night full of dancing, singing and laughing. All the symptoms were those of a severe hangover. Martinis, way too many martinis. She was feeling under the weather herself. 'Maybe she's been a little more active than usual,' she said. She couldn't tell the doctor the embarrassing truth. 'We had guests last night and she stayed up later than usual.'

'Well, that might be a cause. Regular and healthy habits are the thing. We'll call you if anything changes, but for now she's happy here I think, isn't that so, Inez? Call us in the morning, or drop in and see how she is.'

'Happy? Pah. Hush now everyone,' whispered Inez. 'My everything hurts. Close those curtains and leave me alone.' She shut her eyes.

Audrey went to the waiting room where Bill was still sitting, waiting for help.

'This hospital is amazing. They may not have all the latest gear but they do help you before bones have had time to heal by themselves. They've already taken the x-ray, I just have to wait for someone to set it. It's definitely broken. How's Inez?'

'Resting. I think it's a hangover, nothing more, though I didn't say so to the doctor. All she needs is rest and fluids of the non-alcoholic kind. She'll be fine.'

Bill looked at her, then down at her arm. 'She has a hangover, so I get a broken arm. Well, it could be worse. She could have had the broken arm, and I the hangover. I can cope.'

Audrey was pleased that she had taken the time to get dressed as they had to wait for ages while Bill got plastered. Just her arm, this time.

***

Inez was sitting up in a chair entertaining a fellow patient when they came to pick her up the next day. Seemingly fully recovered, she was chirpy and not even slightly subdued.

'Nothing wrong with me at all, which is more than can be said about you,' she said to Bill, who had her arm encased in bright blue plaster. 'You poor thing. I know a good joke. Doctor, Doctor, I broke my arm in three places! Well, don't ever go to those places again.' She looked at Bill and Audrey. 'Why aren't you laughing?'

'We are supposed to look after you and we managed to put you in hospital, while trying to cheer someone else up who because of us is in trouble for a murder. Things are not going overly well,' replied Audrey.

'You've always shown talent for creating trouble, Plum. That is why I like you so much. Your father was very dull, as brothers go. He did well to breed someone as troublesome as you.'

'But to end up in hospital!'

'Such fun. Wasn't it a marvellous night?'

'It was. Glad you're better, Aunt.'

'Now take me to the pub. Just jesting. Home will be adequate.' She patted Bill's good arm. 'I hope you'll recover soon.'

CHAPTER 8

For many people, part of the process of moving to a new place is getting a library card. Audrey and Bill were both keen. It was an opportunity not only to get books, but to get to know people as well. Daylesford's library was not big. Consisting of one deep and narrow room only, it had a long counter behind which a woman was vigorously flicking through a book, looking at what appeared to be dried water damage.

'New membership? Certainly,' said the librarian and clicked a pen several times. 'I'll just need ID with a current address. Someone has read this book in the bath.'

'We only have driving licences with our old address,' said Bill. 'We live with Audrey's aunt Inez, do you know her?' So far, it seemed to Bill that everyone knew her one way or another.

'…know her?' the librarian chimed in to the end of Bill's question. 'Yes, of course. I can't join you up without proper ID, but why don't you use your aunt's card?' Her long brown ponytail swished from side to side and she clicked her pen again. She reminded Audrey a little of a tense dressage horse.

'Well, we don't have it.' Audrey was herself guilty of reading in the bath almost every day but to date had never actually got any books wet. Surely that was what books were for, reading in the bath? Good books should have assorted stains, smudges from a long and often-read life. The best review a book could receive was a marmalade stain, hurriedly wiped off. You knew that it was so good that the reader hadn't been able to put it down, even while eating their breakfast or, as in this case, having a bath.

'...have it,' said the librarian. 'That's no problem, I can look her up. Here it is, and look, a reserved book has come in for her. You can deliver it and save her sending you down later.' The librarian was like having your very own echo. Audrey felt like asking her something unpredictable just to see if she could guess the ending.

'May I borrow the book that has taken a bath? It looks mesmeric.'

'...eric,' came the prompt and correct echo. 'Here. Would you like a small tour of the library? It has to be small, due to the restricted size of the establishment.' She took them to one end of the room. 'You can plug into any of these points here,' she pointed open-handed like a flight attendant, 'and here, if you wish to bring along a laptop for the internet. Here is our large-print collection, and the magazines.'

'...zines,' chirped Audrey helpfully. Bill gave her a sideways glance, which Audrey pretended not to see.

'Here are our most recent acquisitions, and here are the recently returned.' Audrey opened her mouth, about to do the echo, but Bill kicked her hard and she yelped instead.

'Ordinary-sized print fiction is along here, non-fiction is here and large-print books there. DVDs, CDs and PCs for internet use here. You can book it for 30-minute timeslots, all free. Here is local history, young adult, and at the rear is the children's section.'

She pointed with her open hand to the back. A group of children and assorted caregivers sat in a semi-circle listening to a story. 'It's story time twice a week. There is live music once a week, too. We have some volunteers who are really good.'

'We might listen to this one right now, if you don't mind. Thank you for your time.'

The storyteller sat in the biggest chair, reading from an open book. 'On a rainy, squishy day,' he read, not missing a beat as he looked up to see his most recent listeners sit down somewhat gingerly on the low chairs at the back, 'all the worms come out to play...'

Bill and Audrey hoped the story wouldn't be too

long. These chairs were murder.

'...if we all pull together and help one another, everything will work out fine, what's mine is yours and yours is mine,' finished Hugo and closed the book with a snap. 'That's all, see you next time.'

Audrey and Bill eased themselves out of the little plastic bucket chairs, which was extra hard for Bill with only one arm free for balance.

'Did you get beaten up in the line of duty? That's a small price to pay for proving me innocent. Thank Inez for the other night. I shall send flowers, she will hate that.'

'Fell over on the stairs. Do you do this often?' asked Bill, rubbing the small of her back with her one arm.

'A couple of times a month. We have a roster.'

The librarian approached. 'I see you know Hugo already. He's a talented storyteller. Sometimes he does wonderful voices. Oh Hugo, do that one, you know? Icky! Icky!' she screeched. 'Sorry, everyone. This is a library, sssh!' she hissed. 'How did it go again?'

Hugo looked uncomfortable. 'I can't remember.'

'…member,' said the librarian. 'We're always looking for new volunteers if you wish to join us. There is visiting the aged and infirm too. Tempted?'

'Absolutely,' said Audrey with enthusiasm. Bill looked startled. 'Capital idea, hey Bill?'

'Capital,' said Bill weakly.

'…pital,' echoed the librarian. 'I shall add you to

the volunteer list. We meet the second Thursday of every month in the evening, which is tonight.' She clicked her pen in triumph.

A customer coughed loudly at the front counter.

'Ssh, I'm coming,' said the librarian and walked over to serve. 'Hush please.'

'Has it escaped your attention that I am an invalid and need rest?' said Bill.

'Rubbish. You still have one working arm left. Resting is not an option until we have solved the problem. We picked up a reserved book for you, Aunt,' said Audrey. 'We bumped into Hugo too. You'll never believe it, but he was storytelling.'

'Spreading his Bolshie message to the young and innocent, no doubt,' said Inez and snatched the book from Audrey's hand. 'Excellent, the biography on Menzies. He used to date the librarian, you know. That's how he gets away with it.'

'Who? Menzies? Really?' Audrey raised her eyebrows.

'Hugo, you simpleton. The librarian he dated is the one in charge over there, a rather attractive, chubby woman with a ponytail and an echo. Brings my books sometimes.'

'Yup, that's the one. We're going to try the library volunteering tonight.'

'What on earth for? You haven't fallen for handsome

Hugo, have you?'

'Don't be silly. We're getting to know people and the town. It will help with our investigation.'

At half past six in the evening Audrey and Bill presented themselves at the library. They had aimed to arrive early enough to use the library computer to write a helpful internet review on Le Bouquiniste but time had run away. Hugo was already there when they arrived, looking gorgeous and bookish in corduroy trousers and cable-knit sweater, a Byronesque lock of hair flopping over his forehead. He embraced them with three greeting kisses each. A faint scent of leather and cloves lingered briefly.

'I see you're wearing the jumper I made, so happy that you like it,' said the librarian and brushed off an invisible hair from his shoulder, straightening the wool in a proprietary fashion.

Audrey had always detested doing cable knit. A fellow nun had tried to teach her but she never mastered it. She could see there was a lot of love in the jumper. Objects took on the spirit and intention of the maker. If, as nuns, they made things to sell, they would pray their way through it, thereby infusing the object with prayers. A knitted jumper was no different; this sweater was an elaborate love note.

The volunteer crowd consisted of nine people plus the chief librarian, who welcomed everyone but especially Bill and Audrey. A couple of young women nodded at them encouragingly and an older man with a slight twitch gave them a nervous smile. There was a dapper little red-faced man wearing a cravat who smelt faintly of alcohol, a blonde efficient-looking woman in her mid-thirties, a woman in horsey clothes and Hugo. The roster was discussed and determined. The library provided a monthly run of visits to the homebound, which involved selecting and delivering library materials. There was a twice-weekly story time and occasional related craft activities.

'I'm one of the homebound deliverers,' said Alastair, the dapper man, to Audrey. 'Would you like to come with me on the next trip? We always go in pairs.'

'Why not?'

'The library doesn't have its own car so we use our own. Do you drive? You see, I don't and someone has to.'

'That's because you drink too much,' shouted the blonde woman from across the room.

'That's my wife, Monique. Ignore her, I usually do. She does a marvellous story time complete with puppets that she fashions at home from kitchen refuse. Some of them you can even eat after story time has finished. Most of the themed craft sessions in the school holidays are hers too. What was the last one, darling?' he called.

'Egg carton people.'

'She's a sculptor, a good one. Makes horses, mainly.'

Bill, who was neither familiar with small children nor keen on doing the homebound run, volunteered to do the selecting for the deliveries. She was paired up with Adele, a young woman whose face she finally managed to place. It was marvellous that even though they had been in the village for such a short time she was already starting to recognise people. Adele worked in the grocery shop and knew who they were, too.

'It takes a couple of hours to do, max. I'll show you. We prep the bags anytime during the week prior to delivery, which is monthly. I'm free tomorrow if that suits you.'

The librarian gave a short inspirational talk about the value of volunteering in libraries and they drank more tea. Hugo walked them home afterwards. Bill was crankily kicking small stones, scuffing her shoes.

'Is it really necessary to join volunteering groups? I'll do this one, but no more.'

'Of course it is,' said Audrey. 'Just look how many people you just met. It will be very helpful. There are plenty of more groups to join, but this one is enough for now, I agree. Can we ask you something serious, Hugo?'

He nodded. 'Of course you can. What?'

'Did you kill Fabiano? We don't think you did, you understand, but we need to ask.'

'Is this your idea of an interview? Do you think I

would say yes if I had done it?' Hugo was amused.

'We're investigating, trying to find out what happened,' said Audrey. 'We have to ask.'

'No, you don't. And no, I didn't. You had better work on your technique. You can't go around asking every local if they did it for elimination purposes.'

'The police asked us that. I think it's a good question. You can watch people when they answer to see how they react.'

'And how did I react?'

'Amused, not even slightly insulted. You didn't do it.'

'Thank you, I also know that I didn't. I only wish I knew who did.'

Adele was already at the library when Bill arrived, wearing a poncho. Getting dressed was tricky with the arm, but Audrey had helpfully unearthed an old poncho from the Pretty family stash. It was beautifully warm. It was also full length. Inez explained that it was a horse-riding poncho from Peru. Bill was thrilled that the Peruvians were not a taller group of people or she would not be able to move at all. In fact she could have gone camping in it, but she was warm and dry under it all.

'Adele, here I am!' She waved with her good arm, causing a lot of flapping of wool.

'Great, erm… coat?' tried Adele.

'Can't get my arm in the coat, hence the tent. What do we do?'

'Here are the selection sheets for our people. They get to tick what kind of things they like, and we pick things in the hope of striking something good. Most of them live at home – only Ms Heyerman is in care. We can start with Mrs Moody here. As you can see from the sheet, she likes operettas, not operas, nothing dark or heavy. Also anything with clarinet in it. She doesn't want movies. She can read any size print, but will only read things with a happy ending. Mrs Grimshaw, here's her sheet, can't tolerate any smut yet likes violent crime. Ms Heyerman mostly watches DVDs, but will read a book if it is good enough. Ms Heyerman is absolutely ancient and grades everything we give her so we can fine-tune our search for the perfect things.'

'How do I know they haven't borrowed it before?'

'We put their initials in the sheet in the back of the book, see? Then we check. Sometimes it doesn't matter, especially if it was a while ago.'

Bill enjoyed trying to get into the minds of the people she selected for. The easiest was Mr Tibbet who was a voracious reader of Westerns (large print only). He had to have books brought in from other libraries as there was never anything new for him otherwise. He didn't mind, and repeats were fine too.

Bill had plenty of things to tell Margaret when she

rang that evening. They didn't talk about food at all, just about library volunteering, the awkwardness of aunts and the challenges of poncho wearing.

Audrey drove the old Austin to the library, ready to start her job. Alastair was inside, reading *Vogue Living* and having a cup of tea. He drained his cup.

'Right, let's load up and go. It's a lovely old car, isn't it?' said Alastair. 'I'll drive if you like.'

'No, thank you. I thought you said you didn't drive?'

'Well, I do. Come on, let me.'

'Not your car, not your decision,' she said, trying not to get irritated. 'Get in and behave.'

He climbed in a bit awkwardly on the passenger side, just missing hitting his head on the metal frame of the car. He patted the dashboard.

'Nice. Very nice. My wife is a terrible driver. Doesn't even care who gives way in a roundabout. She thinks it's about who looks as if they need it the most. If you look impatient, she waves you through. Head towards the lake. Our first visit is Mr Rodriguez. How's your Spanish? *'Ole! Hasta mañana!'* Alastair leant in to her closely. 'Burrrrrito!'

'Paella,' she retorted. Was that alcohol she could smell? 'It's limited in the extreme. Doesn't Mr Rodriguez speak English?'

'Not a lot.'

Mr Rodriguez lived in a little unit on Miller Street. His delivery consisted of Spanish titles brought in from a central depot. He smiled and bowed a lot, and exchanged his last bag for a new one. They waved and left, exchanging more smiles and nods.

'He never takes any time. Not chatty like the next one. I hope you're hungry. There'll be tea and plenty of talk at the lovely Mrs Carlton's.'

Mrs Carlton, long since retired from housekeeping at the old Grande Imperial, lived in a cottage of dollhouse proportions at the end of a long gravel driveway. She preferred romances, crime and thrillers, and was excited over some of Bill's pickings. A perfect hostess, she had set a table for three in style. On the lace tablecloth was a tiered display of Chelsea buns, Florentines and éclairs. A steaming pot of tea and Wedgewood porcelain completed a setting that would have made Bill cry tears of joy.

Audrey enjoyed herself wholeheartedly, having seconds and thirds. Mrs Carlton was pleasant company, which couldn't be said for Alastair. Audrey suspected he was doctoring his tea with a hipflask. He was getting louder and more raucous by the minute.

'Are you feeling alright, young man?' Mrs Carlton looked at him disapprovingly over her glasses.

'Young man! Ha ha, thassagood'n!'

'We should be leaving. Thank you for the lovely tea. It was a pleasure to meet you.' Audrey shook Mrs

Carlton's hand as she firmly ushered Alastair out the door.

'See you next time!' Mrs Carlton waved and closed the door just as Alastair stumbled into her flowerbed.

'Buck up, are you drunk?' Audrey hissed at him as he picked a squashed flower from the ground.

'You're a blurry good driver, you are. Blurry good, f'r a wom'n. Hey up.' He handed her the flower with a bow and a flourish.

Audrey opened the passenger door and pushed him down on the seat, then drove off back in the direction of the library. The other deliveries would have to wait.

'Where do you live? I think we should go there instead of the next delivery.'

'Racy, woohoo. Wife's home. Jus' go to the forest. Park. You're a bit long in the tooth but a goer, hey?' He leant over to plant a smacking kiss on her shoulder. 'Gimme those tomatoes.'

'Mr Alastair,' said Audrey sternly, not remembering his family name. 'You are being offensive. Sit down, shut up and behave.'

But he didn't. Instead he let his hands roam free, trying clumsily to get inside her car coat.

'Stop it immediately!' roared Audrey. She swatted at his hand and the car veered off the road into a field, coming to a halt as she hit a large shrub. Alastair was thrown forward with a thud as his head connected with the windscreen. He mumbled something incoherent and went limp.

'Oh, the bloody, bloody man.' She blessed the car for agreeing to start and steered it gently over the ridged field back to the road. There seemed not to be any real damage to the car. At least it still ran. Back on the road, she headed straight for the hospital.

'You, back again so soon?' The same nurse was at the reception desk. 'What's happened this time?'

'I have someone in the car outside, Alastair whatshisname. He's drunk and hit his head on the windscreen. I can't get him in here by myself.'

'Alastair? A wee little thing? I know him. What's he been up to this time? He wasn't driving, was he?'

The staff buzzed into action and brought Alastair in. He alternated between holding his head and complaining and singing. 'Blurry good, eh? Eh? Whoopsadaisy. Hahaha.'

'He's sloshed. I know his wife Monique, I'll ring her straight away.' The nurse looked up a number and dialled. 'No answer. She's possibly at home, but she works from a shed next to the house.'

'Can you tell me where he lives? I might as well go myself. I can leave a message if she isn't home.'

'Certainly.' The nurse gave directions. 'Try not to bring us any more business, please. Drive carefully. Apart from you, there's only one other person I see here more frequently.'

'Who's that?'

'I can't say. Medical confidentiality.' She beckoned Audrey to lean in closer. 'Between you and me, the guy who died came in more than once with his wife. They said the coffee machine was faulty and gave steam burns, but I don't know, myself.'

Audrey drove, still loaded with library deliveries, a few kilometres out of the village to where Alastair and Monique lived on an acreage fringed by forest. Regular tapping could be heard from what looked like a large garage. Audrey followed the sound and found Monique in what turned out to be a studio, chiselling out the rough shape of a horse leg. Monique waved the mallet in friendly greeting.

'Hi! What are you doing here? I thought you were delivering with Alastair.'

'I am, I mean I was. Actually I just tried to ring you, but there was no answer.'

'Phone's in the house, I don't like to be disturbed out here. What can I do for you?'

'We had a tiny accident on the run. Alastair's alright, don't worry. I had to brake suddenly and he hit his head. Nothing serious I think, but he's at the hospital. I am so sorry, it's my fault for going off the road.'

'I doubt it. Silly man was drunk, wasn't he? He's impossible. Should have kept him at home today.

I drove him to the library and he seemed alright but you never know with him. He's as charming as you like but infuriating. I guess I'd better ring them and see what's what. Come into the house with me.'

The house would once have had several small rooms, but had been opened up to form a spacious central room, full of large paintings on the walls.

'Alastair used to paint a bit,' said Monique, nodding to the walls as she picked up the phone. 'Not much these days. Hello. Hi, Shona, this is Monique. Yes, I just heard. The idiot, he's totally hopeless. Yes, I will. Thanks, I'll see you later then.'

'How is he?' asked Audrey.

'No better than he deserves. He has a new lump on his head and will have a headache for a while. I can pick him up soon. I must apologise to you on his behalf, he has no sense at all. Right now he's being annoying in the hospital.' She sighed. 'Thank you for coming over. Not a great start to your volunteering.'

Audrey returned to the library with her bags.

'I will not be going out with him again.'

'...again,' chimed the librarian, sadly shaking her head. 'There's no one who can come out with you now, so the next team will have to deliver these as well. I'll ring the borrowers and tell them. They expect you to be there at a set time each month. Punctuality is important.'

'Well, right now there are other important things

to consider, like a drunken volunteer harassing another volunteer until she goes off the road. We could have been killed,' Audrey responded, slapping her palm down hard on the desk for emphasis. For once, the echo didn't come. Not used to displaying any aggression, Audrey looked at her hand in surprise. Her palm stung, giving her silent and instant reproach.

'Well. Sorry. I'll go now. Didn't mean to startle you.'

Bill was stoking the fire in the kitchen, which smelt like fresh bread.

'Didn't expect you back so soon,' said Bill. 'Bread's nearly ready. You just missed the boys, they put a loaf in the oven. I promised to take it out when the timer goes. Smells divine, doesn't it? How was the delivery run?'

'I had a horrible time. Alastair was drunk and I drove the car into a paddock.'

Bill looked suitably horrified. 'Inez's beautiful car?'

'That one, yes. The car is fine. It hit a bush, no dents. I'm fine too in case you were wondering. We had a little off-road adventure. Alastair is fine too, in case you were thinking of asking, but he's a creep who can't keep his hands to himself. I was enjoying the deliveries apart from that and I'll insist on a different partner next time.'

Though Audrey's initial reaction had been to quit the whole thing, she brushed that thought away as stupid. Of course she would continue, she was no quitter. Minus Alastair.

'I learnt something new that I will share with you if you at least pretend to be sympathetic. I have just had an accident and am probably in shock.'

'Tosh. Cup of tea? Shot of medicinal brandy?'

'Yes to both. Thank you. Could you take off my shoes and rub my toes?'

'That's pushing your luck. Get on with your discovery.'

'Okay. I had to take the lecherous sot to the hospital because he hit his head on the windscreen. The same receptionist we met before was on duty and we started chatting. She said that Fabiano and Anna came to the hospital several times with minor injuries, burns and things.'

'How indiscreet. Not that I am ungrateful, that's really interesting. We have to go and talk to Anna again. How can we ask if he was violent? It's not something we can just say, surely?'

'Let's bring her a tub of your calendula cream and some soothing tea. She said she wasn't sleeping well, didn't she?'

The next morning it was raining hard. Audrey wasn't sure but it seemed as if damp had crept back through the wallpaper in a couple of spots, raising the fresh paintwork in blisters. Maybe a couple of strategically placed pictures would do.

'There's a leak in the roof,' said Bill at breakfast. 'Or two. I've put pots underneath.' The hard sound of water dripping into metal containers echoed from upstairs.

'I thought Inez said it was fixed?'

'I think the word was patched. We'll have to watch the pots so we don't trip. Why doesn't she fix the roof?'

'I imagine that roofs are very expensive.'

They took the car to Anna's so they didn't have to get totally soaked. She had company again, a woman she introduced as Maria, a friend from Melbourne.

'We brought you some chamomile tea, useful for relaxing before bed. There's a bath sachet too, lavender and hops. If you like it I'll get some more. Try it, it's soothing.'

'Thank you.' Anna held the bath sachet to her nose and took a deep breath. 'Smells yummy.'

'I make a calendula cream too, have you ever used it before? No? Extremely good for your skin. Here, let me put some on your hand.' Bill took her hand and started rubbing in the cream, firmly massaging her hand and wrist.

'That feels great,' said Anna.

'Doesn't it?' Bill worked her way a little up her arm, pushing the sleeve up as she went. Anna's skin was pristine. Unless a miracle had occurred, there was no way this arm could have suffered any recent burns or bruises. 'Give me the other hand too, you need both done for balance.'

Anna willingly let Bill put on the cream, rolling up her sleeve herself. Nothing on that arm either.

'Can I try some too?' Maria put some on her hands and rubbed it in.

'You can keep the jar. Right, we won't disturb you since you have company already. Let us know if you need anything at all.'

'There was absolutely nothing there,' Bill said when they were back in the car. 'No scars or even discolouration. Skin like silk. Where would steam hit you, making coffee, if not on the arms?'

'Face? Throat? But we would have seen it. You didn't go all that high up her arms anyway. Also, maybe the injuries were from spilled things, in which case you have to get back there and massage her legs. Or chest. She has acres of chest but I don't think we could easily explore that. Alastair could though. Just a quick feel to see how loudly she screams.'

'Don't be stupid. What we'll do is book her a massage. She'll have to take her clothes off. Then, we ask the masseuse afterwards about injuries.'

'Oh yes, obviously any masseuse will happily tell us all about their customers.'

'We'll go to Ellen, in the choir,' suggested Bill. 'Then, at practice, we'll ask her in some good roundabout way. We'll work on it.'

'Well, the nurse was rather chatty. Maybe Ellen will be too. Let's do it.'

They went to Ellen's Massage and Wellbeing Centre and bought a one-hour massage, booked on a cancellation that day. It wasn't cheap and put a dent in their budget, but they got a good discount for covering the cancellation and also for being choir members. They returned to Anna straight away.

'Back again? Did you forget something?' Anna smiled.

'We brought you a little gift to cheer you up,' said Audrey. 'You look so much more relaxed with a friend visiting. Will she stay for long?'

'Just a couple more days, then she has to get back to work.'

'I see. We booked a massage for you this afternoon. If you can't use the appointment with Maria here, we can go back and see if it can be changed. Say that you will? It will be good for you.'

'You two really are generous. Thank you so much. Now I am crying again, sorry.'

'The seed is planted,' said Bill. 'Now we have to wait for choir practice and see if we get a result.'

'We can't just sit around and wait all that time. I want to do something cheerful. Let's visit Hugo.'

'Good idea. Can we look at wellies first? There's a possibility that we have to build an ark as well, but dry feet are a good start.'

Sporting their new wellies, they decided to walk to the lake. Mud or puddles held no fear now, and they splashed and stomped like a pair of toddlers. After feeling so invigorated, it was pleasant to relax by Hugo's fire with a pot of tea. The wellies were muddy so they left them by the door. They rested their feet on a stool, wriggling their toes with pleasure.

'I would ask you to make yourselves at home, but it seems you have already,' said Hugo, who had just finished wrapping up a sale. 'I'm about to close. May I join you?'

They convinced him to read them a story, which was better received now that they had comfortable chairs. In return they sang a song they just learnt about an ice cream cart vendor called Antonio who had ditched his love. They could really get into the spirit of the music hall.

'Fiona said that you look for gold,' said Bill. 'That sounds exciting.'

'No, not entirely correct. I hardly find any gold, just bits and pieces. It can be exciting, but I love being outdoors and it is a good reason to explore new areas. I'm heading to Beechworth with a small group of fossickers to look for topaz soon. Maybe you would like to join us?'

'Wonderful,' said Audrey. 'We'd love to come. How do you do it?'

'We have a little poke about, walk in the bush, have a picnic. Sometimes we go down old shafts. Because Beechworth is a little further off we'll stay the night.'

'Sounds like fun except for the mine shaft bit – that sounds dangerous. Maybe I'll skip that bit,' said Bill.

'It *is* dangerous,' Hugo grinned, 'but if you are with someone you will always be able to get help. We use ropes. Or you can just go along for the hike. Come, let me show you some of my finds.'

He led them through the connecting door to his residence, which was much smaller than the shop. In the combined kitchen and living room was glass cabinet with a display of coloured glass bottles, medicine jars, a pipe, some coins, a Chinese teapot and some rusty metal bits. The collection also included a plethora of pottery shards and other small things.

'It is my cabinet of curiosities. The exciting thing is not knowing if you will find an old toothbrush or a gold nugget.'

'An old toothbrush wouldn't be as exciting,' said Audrey.

'You are wrong there. Old toothbrushes are really rare, a good find. I haven't come across any myself but I might yet. I have some gems and other things too, but I don't keep them in this cabinet. This is only for oddments. Are you up for the Beechworth trip?'

'Wouldn't miss it. I'll pack my own toothbrush though,' said Audrey.

Margaret rang just as they were finishing washing up after dinner. It had been unusually tasty, consisting of a spicy red bean stew served with salad. She and Bill had a long and pleasant chat about why people were so nasty. It seemed unreasonable, when being nice was a preferable and easy option.

Bill did not admit to sampling the fresh bread with just the tiniest spread of butter, nor the double shot of brandy she shared with Audrey. You can't gain weight when you are stressed, she reasoned. No point in being consumed by guilt – surely there were calories in that, too. Margaret congratulated her on a successful day, assured her that she could do it and that the most difficult step in exercising was the first one. They rang off.

'I don't think I'll continue this diet after the month is up,' said Bill. 'Margaret will be disappointed.'

'She may be, but I'm happy to hear it. The boys can cook just ordinary low fat, can't they? Inez will never know as long as we heap the butter on her plate.'

'I was actually thinking of something more severe, like the Israeli Army Diet.'

'That's complete nonsense, I won't let you. Let's

just walk more. We can forage for wild plants, or borrow Fred for dog walks. There's forest everywhere, hills and dales.'

CHAPTER 9

The following few days were largely uneventful for Audrey and Bill. They both felt the beginnings of a cold and spent some time indoors resting up. Bill was itching to get out in the garden, but her arm and cold put a stop to it. She planned to dig up some of the lawn and plant valerian, thyme, lemon balm, sage, liquorice and Echinacea. Instead she used the time off to read her way through the many Agatha Christies in Inez's library.

She had quickly polished off *Peril at End House* and had started *A Caribbean mystery*, chiefly because there might be descriptions of the climate to make her feel warmer. There was so much to learn about investigative techniques that would come in handy. You could either know absolutely everyone involved, or you could know nobody and just think about it, hard.

The books had a musty smell, which was not a surprise considering they lived in a largely disused and unheated room. Bill tucked the blanket around her until only the hand holding the book stuck out. She felt her eyes getting heavier, and heavier, one eye closing, and then she was out for the count.

Audrey and Inez were playing a round of Egyptian Rat Slap using biscuits as stakes. The jury was out over who was the most competent cheat. Inez's audacity had already won her the title of Ruler of the World and Champion of Gin Rummy. She was now keen to prove herself in a less challenging game.

'Look,' said Audrey. 'There's a Body in the Library.'

Inez turned her head toward the sound of snoring behind her. Audrey used the distraction to pick up a few cards.

'Let her sleep, best thing for it,' said Inez. 'I might go for a nap myself, as soon as I have won this round.'

'You'll never beat me. Beauty before age!'

'Wisdom before it all. Slap!' Inez claimed the pile of cards and won the game. 'You will have to get up very early indeed to beat me, dear. I hereby claim the title of Imperial Rat Slapper, but you may call me Ruler of the World. Come on Lucy, we're having a lie down.'

Audrey sighed and picked up a random book from the shelves. She tried to get comfortable on the sprung sofa, which was not so easily done. The book she chose turned out to be an account of African exploration, helpfully titled *A journey into Africa's interior*. It had many notes scribbled in the margins. She looked at the title page in search of its original owner. Rupert Pretty, her grandfather.

Despite the riveting topic she felt herself joining in with the peaceful rhythm of Bill's sleeping and was soon fast asleep herself. It was twilight and the fire had burnt down to embers when they woke to the clatter of the doorbell.

'I'll get it,' said Bill and blew her nose noisily. She kept her blanket on and shuffled to the door. 'It's Penny,' she called to the others when she had opened the door.

Benny? thought Audrey for a second before she realised that Penny with a stuffed nose might just become someone else.

'I think it's a little better already, see? Grandma says to thank you with this.' Penny rattled a tin full of homemade shortbread. 'Can I have a fresh toad please?'

'Of course, let me give you some more.' Bill braced herself to step out into the garden. Coming back to Penny with aloe vera, she held out a lemon as well. 'You might want to try some of this too. Squeeze a little and dab on your face. Alternate with the toad, morning and night. Come back in another week. Thank your grandma for the biscuits.'

That night, Inez's emergency bell was given another workout. It rang out a couple of times before Bill's door opened and her sleepy figure emerged swathed in a dressing gown. She gingerly made her way in the dark to Aunt Inez, who sat up in her bed clutching Lucy. She pointed a gnarled finger at the window.

'There's someone outside,' she whispered excitedly. 'Keep quiet.'

Bill pulled the curtains open, revealing a round-eyed face staring in. It quickly turned around and darted up the tree.

'A possum. It's just a possum on a branch, Inez,' said Bill in a resigned voice. 'I'm going back to bed. We can prune the branch tomorrow so it can't sit so close to the house. Sleep tight.' She tiptoed back upstairs, having left her slippers under her bed. The floors were cold and she was grateful to be back under the covers.

A couple of hours later the bell rang again.

'Your turn, Audrey,' shouted Bill. 'I'm staying right here. It's just a possum.' She turned and bashed her pillow into submission. She heard Audrey's door creak open and steps fade away downstairs before sleep once again overtook her.

'There was someone in the garden, I swear,' said Inez. 'No possum. It was a tall shape moving slowly, nowhere near the tree.'

Audrey tweaked a corner of the drapes and peered out. 'I can't see anything.' Pale moonlight shone through bare branches, casting dappled shade on the ground with

216

deep dark patches around the solid blocks of hedges and conifers. 'It's almost impossible to see anything unless it makes a move. It's too dark.'

'You'll have to stay put until he moves, obviously. Unless he has already left. I heard the crunch of foot-steps on the gravel.'

'You? You're imagining things. You can't hear gravel crunching.'

'Can so. I know someone is there. Take a fire iron and go out, Plum,' she pleaded. 'Go on. I'll let you win next time we play.'

'Not if I let you win first. I have a better idea.' Audrey flicked the switch for the outside light, which shone weakly over the path outside. 'See? Nothing.'

'Silly girl, you scared them off. They'll be around the corner, or running already. Go, go, go,' she urged, clasping the blankets tightly under her chin. 'You're wasting time.'

Audrey grabbed the fire poker to make Inez happy. She turned the light off again to give herself cover, in case Inez actually turned out to be right, and eased the French doors open. She slipped into the garden and stood silently for a minute adjusting to the cold and dark. There was some rustling of small animals and birds turning in their nests or whatever they got up to at night, but little else.

Her breath gave her presence away and she figured that it would work the other way too. Anyone hiding would be made visible through their exhaled plumes unless they were holding their breath. Even a possum, she presumed. Fire poker raised high, she slowly walked around the corner. Nothing. She eased her way around the next corner as well, intending to do a full circle around the house.

On the third corner, she completely missed the metal ash bucket left out on the path, right where she was walking. She tripped and fell headlong into the garden bed. There was the sound of sped-up movement and a tree rustled as a big fat possum rushed up for safety.

'The bloody possum! Bugger, my knee!' She banged her fists on the path in pain. Her knee had taken a pounding and the pain was excruciating. She would have to sit here on the ground for a minute until she could get up again. The knee was throbbing. Throbbing so loudly it was audible, in fact sounding like footsteps ... She froze and grabbed the poker, raising it in the air.

'I'm armed! Stop right there.'

'Hey, hey, take it easy, don't hit me.' Bill appeared with a furled-up umbrella in her good hand. 'Did they get you? Where are they?' She spun around, searching for an attacker. 'You were gone so long Inez rang again, sure that something must have happened.'

'It did. I tripped on the bucket. I've hurt my knee. Help me up, gently.' They limped back to Inez's room.

'Did you get beaten up?' Inez's eyes glimmered with excitement. 'I was right, I knew it.'

'Sorry to disappoint you, but I fell over. That's all.'

They settled into the chairs in Inez's room with the glass doors firmly bolted and the curtains drawn. Lucy, perhaps feeling her owner's distress, was happy for once to stay curled up on Inez's lap, for which Bill was grateful.

'I'm going to give you a larger allowance to cover the incidental expenses for the investigation,' announced Inez. 'It must cost a bit in bribes, coffee and cake and so forth. You need to crack this. It's making me rattled to have a murderer on the loose.'

'Bribes? Who could we bribe? The possum? That one will do anything for an apple,' said Audrey.

'You'll find someone. A scab on the streets, or is it a snout? A fox? You know what I mean. Or you could try to bribe that young WPC who was here. She looked easy.'

'Aunt!' said Audrey, shocked. 'I'm not even going to try bribing the police, no matter how amusing you think it would be to see me in the docks. Anyway, they aren't WPCs anymore, those days are gone.'

'Can't see why you won't try bribery. You want results, you might have to pay.' She cackled. 'If you want to know how the police are going in their investigations, you will have to ask. She might not say, of course, which is where you will have to use alternative means. I seem to remember my father being competent at using an informal rewards system. Take a leaf from his book. Can't hurt.'

'It *can* hurt. I will not do anything illegal. I can ask her nicely though. We'll ask her over for a cup of tea tomorrow if she's free. Will that make you happy?'

'That's a good girl. This should cover your expenses to begin with. Let me know when you run out.' She handed Audrey a white envelope. It contained a small wad of 50-dollar bills.

'Don't worry, I can afford it. I'm having a good time. I want to know exactly what the WPC says, so come and speak to me after she's gone. Now off you go, back to bed.'

Inez woke full of energy. Dawn was just breaking, changing the magic of the moonlit night into something bleaker. She dressed warmly, picked up her cane and walked out into the garden with Lucy. There was no doubt in her mind whatsoever that someone had been outside last night, but she needed evidence of what, or who, that had been.

The trees looked the same, the frost on the grass perfectly ordinary. There was nothing out of place on the ground that she could see. She followed the path leading around the house and took the side trail leading down to the garage. A rustling in the bushes made her jump and take a couple of side steps, which made her trip on Lucy and fall backwards. Pain shot up her arm as she landed awkwardly on her elbow. Lucy ran up a tree in her hurry to get away.

'Help, help!' The pain radiated out to her fingers and up her shoulder. Lucy climbed a bit higher, ignoring the plight of her mistress. Inez's neck and head hurt too, and the frosty ground was not a good place to lie down. The chill rose up through her clothes. She tried to ease herself onto her side but the pain stopped her.

'Help!'

Bill and Audrey were asleep in their rooms at the front of the house and had no chance of hearing much through the thick stone walls. But the tall hedge surrounding the garden provided little in the way of a sound barrier and a man out for an early morning dog walk stopped.

'Hello? Did I hear someone calling?' He knocked on the high garden door.

'It's locked, open the gate round the front. Please help me.' The man and his dog soon appeared at her side, the dog enthusiastically licking her face.

Lucy, tail twitching, climbed higher up the tree and watched from above.

'Get away from her, sit! Sorry about the dog. Let me help you up.'

'No, don't touch me. Tie your dog up, there's a good man, and go into my room. Pull the bell cord by the bed. Help will come.'

He did as she asked and soon Bill and Audrey arrived. This time there was no debating whether an ambulance should come or not. They kept her warm until the ambulance crew arrived with a stretcher and carefully loaded her up.

'Not so rough,' shouted Inez. 'I'm not dead yet. You girls, finish what I started. Go through the entire garden, leaf by leaf.'

'But Aunt, I need to come with you.'

'Nonsense. What good could that possibly do? You're not a doctor, and besides, you need to earn your allowance. You'll be a nuisance, all that maudlin hanging around. Comb through the garden. They might have dropped something, left a trace, whatever. What did they want, that is the question. These people have been clomping around destroying evidence but there are plenty of untouched spaces. Do it.'

The ambulance doors closed behind her, muffling her ongoing commands, and sped off towards the hospital. Lucy ran down the tree and yowled demandingly. Audrey scooped her up and went back into the house to get dressed and make hot chocolate. She rang Rosie Lloyd and left a message.

Bill and Audrey were still out searching the garden when Rosie arrived. They told her that Inez had been frightened by a suspected intruder.

'Did you see or hear anything yourselves?'

'No, but Inez was certain there was someone there,' said Audrey. 'Most likely it was a possum. How is your investigation going? Moving on nicely with lots of suspects?'

'I really can't tell you anything, you know that.'

'We have something to tell you. You see, we've been asking around a bit ourselves. There are some questions that might interest you, such as: 'Is it possible that Fabiano was mistreating his wife?' Bill looked at Rosie eagerly.

'What makes you say that?' she frowned. It was news to her.

'It could just be gossip, it's a small place. We can't ask her, but you could.'

'I would prefer it if you didn't listen to too much gossip. Everyone likes to think that they know something no one else knows about. The investigation is progressing but it's not a quick thing. I hope your aunt recovers soon. You should install some strong and bright sensor lights in the garden, they're good for security.'

'With the possums running around, the lights would be on and off all night like a discotheque,' said Bill.

'If we don't listen to the gossip, what else is left to listen to? Until we've tried the pieces of information, we don't know if something is gossip or actual fact,' complained Audrey when they were alone again.

'I can't find a trace of anything apart from the footprints of the ambulance people. Let's go and see how Inez is treating the hospital staff this time.'

They were just opening the garage doors, ready to leave for the hospital, when an out-of-breath voice called to them.

'Hi, wait!' They looked in the direction of the sound and saw a woman running, waving urgently. 'It's me, Maria,' she called.

'Hello, what can we do for you?' asked Bill.

'I wanted to say thank you for looking after Anna. She's not herself, so worried and stressed. I wish I could stay longer but I have to get back to work. Will you drop in on her for me? Rick spends a lot of time there but I'm not sure that's a good idea. She says she's fine, says she doesn't need counselling.'

'You're a true friend. Of course we can,' said Bill and took her hand. Bill excelled in holding hands.

Maria let go reluctantly. 'You were on your way somewhere. I mustn't keep you. Thank you.'

'Why didn't you ask her about something we can use for clues?' said Audrey when they were in the car.

'Like what, exactly? Not so easy to think up, just like that. You didn't say anything either. Never mind, let's just do what she asked. Now we have a really good reason for popping in occasionally without feeling like a nuisance.'

'She's in good spirits,' said the nurse at the hospital. 'But she's full to the hilt with painkillers. The elbow is fractured and we're monitoring her general health. The doctor thinks she ought to stay on for a bit, given her age. She was only here the other day, so let's hope she gets better soon. Go and see her, she's down the corridor in room 9.'

They found Inez sleeping soundly and turned back to the nurses' station.

'Could you tell her that well be back later? Say that we'll bring her some news. That will cheer her up.'

They drove by The Bean on their way home and saw that the roller door was halfway open. 'Are they opening already, do you think?' said Audrey. 'Let's see what's happening.' They knocked on the roller door, making the iron rattle.

'We're closed,' said a voice from inside.

'Rick? Is that you in there?' called Audrey.

'Who wants to know?' Rick poked his head under the door to see who the legs belonged to. 'Oh. You again. What do you want?'

'We saw the door open and we've run out of coffee. Can we buy some, do you think?'

'Sure, come in.' He lifted the roller door a little further to let them in. The cool and dark space smelt faintly musty instead of the strong delicious coffee aromas from before. The waitress was sitting, red-eyed, at the bar counter. She blew her nose noisily.

'A poncho and wellies. How very... Daylesford.' Rick took a sidelong glance at Bill's peculiar floor-length wrappings. 'Do you remember what kind of beans you bought before?'

'High Altitude something or other. Ground, please,' she said.

'Which grind? Plunger, drip, Turkish, espresso?'

'Those Italian metal stovetop things that push the water up and gargle when they're done.'

'Right. Instead of buying ground, you should get beans and a grinder – grind what you need each time. You'll be amazed how much better the coffee is. I have a few for sale here.' He took one down from the shelves behind him. 'I can give you a special price. Need to free up some cash. A one-off deal.'

'How much are they?'

'We only stock one kind of electric. It grinds the beans well without shredding them. You'll be happy with it.'

'We'll take two,' said Audrey. Bill looked at her, surprised.

'That'll be 1200 dollars for the two,' said Rick.

'Oh, I didn't realise they were so expensive! Maybe not, let's just get the coffee.'

'We do sell a manual grinder. It does a fine job but takes a little longer.' He turned to the shelf and brought down a thing that looked like an oversized pepper grinder. 'I can sell two for 90 dollars.'

'Excellent,' said Audrey, 'We'll take them. And two kilos of beans in two bags please. It's good that you're caring for Anna. She'll be lonely now that Maria, the gorgeous girl, has gone. How are you coping?'

'I do what I can. I don't understand who would hate him enough to kill.'

'We're trying to understand it ourselves. There's at least one person who knows more than we do. What are your thoughts?' Audrey put on her most sympathetic face.

The waitress interrupted by blowing her nose noisily.

'Stop crying, Karmony,' said Rick. 'It won't change anything.' Karmony slipped off the barstool and ducked under the roller door without saying goodbye.

'Sorry about her. I can't give her a job anymore and that's upsetting for all of us. My thought, for what it's worth, is competition. You saw how busy we were. We were in the right place at the right time. A jealous man could get angry enough to kill, maybe.'

'If you were so busy, how come you didn't do better financially?' asked Audrey.

'It was early days. All the money going in was immediately going back out again, and then some. But it seems that Fabiano had more money than he told me and Anna. We have a bit of money owing here, and I'm down as a guarantor on a personal loan to Fabiano. I haven't heard from the bank about what will happen to that now that he's gone. I mean, whether I have to pay back the loan. Anna found some cash at home, did she tell you?'

'No, she didn't.'

'I shouldn't tell you, really. Don't tell anyone else.'

'Was it a lot, this cash?'

'Not sure.' He wriggled a bit, as if wriggling out of the question itself. 'Anyway, it's good to have a little bit of money because the police have frozen the accounts. Anna needs to live on something other than fresh air.'

Bill and Audrey left with their bags.

'Why did you buy two grinders? Can we afford that?' asked Bill.

'Inez's expense account is sufficiently plentiful, and we'll be grateful and use it all up to good purpose. Relax. For the price of a couple of grinders and some beans he voluntarily spent time talking to us, even theorised. And Inez will get a story when we go to see her – she wants some action.'

'We should write down what we spend, so we can present some decent accounts to Inez. As the sole provider of operating capital in this venture I think she is entitled to it,' said Bill, opening the glove compartment. 'Bound to be some paper here.'

She found a stubby pencil and an old invoice for

replacement tyres. She drew two columns and wrote Grinders, 2, $90; Coffee beans, 2 kg, $98. 'Coffee's expensive, isn't it? I need to add the massage as well. Should I add the price of ongoing minor items for Anna do you think?'

'If you like. Just add it as Anna – Misc.'

'The second grinder—what's that for?'

'It's for softening up Fiona, so the expense will work twice. Once in the getting, and once in the giving.'

'Fiona? Please tell me we're not going to visit. I couldn't stand it.'

'Yes you could,' said Audrey. 'She can have a kilo of coffee too. She knows Hugo well, and has a finger on the pulse of the town. We'll be nice and go for a social visit.'

'I'd like a word with that waitress too. She knows them all, and must have some information we don't know about.'

'Great lead,' agreed Audrey. 'How do we find her?'

'With a name like Karmony it should be easy. We'll ask around.'

Fiona lived in an airy modern sugar-cube house with walk-through access to the lake. A long redwood arbour covered in climbing roses led them to the front door. Bill took a deep breath and pressed the bell. Through the rippled pane of glass in the door she saw the distorted shape of Fiona approaching. She put on a beatific smile in readiness, hoping it wouldn't fade.

'What a surprise! You don't have to give me anything for that old shirt, I had forgotten it already,' lied Fiona. 'A coffee grinder, how lovely. I won't accept though. I already have one, see? Couldn't live without it. I have an electric version. But so sweet of you to want to give me a gift. The coffee is appreciated. From The Bean?' She looked at the label on the bag. 'I didn't know they were trading again.'

She embraced them both and gave some air kisses, Hugo style. They went into the living space where an elevated position gave expansive views of the lake through the bare branches. The grey tin roof of Le Bouquiniste could be seen in the distance.

'Put that electric grinder of yours to good use and let's have a cup,' said Audrey and made herself comfortable on a plump feather sofa. 'The Bean's not open yet, but we went to chat with Fabiano's partner. This is a lovely room. The deck must be nice in summer.'

'Once the leaves are out the view gets blocked. I'm thinking of having some of the trees cut down. The view is marvellous this time of year, isn't it?'

Audrey thought the trees helped make it beautiful, but was loath to disagree in case Fiona got upset and they couldn't ask any more questions.

'The trees rather make it, don't you find?' Bill had no such compunction. 'I wouldn't touch so much as a twig.'

'That just shows how little you know. Sprawling trees are all well and good in their place, which is in the forest.' Fiona brought a tray with a silver sugar bowl, cream jug and porcelain cups. There was also a plate with a handful of almond biscotti.

'Here we are. Please help yourselves.'

'Thank you,' said Bill and accepted a tea cup. 'No thanks, no biscotti for me. I'm watching my weight a little.'

'Really?' Fiona opened her eyes wide. 'I didn't realise you were bothered about appearances.' She saw Bill's eyes narrow and blacken. 'I'm sorry, I didn't mean it like that. I meant that you were free from vanity.'

Audrey interrupted before Bill could manage a reply.

'You see, we think Hugo is innocent but we need to find out who did it. Otherwise, we fear he will eventually be convicted of something he didn't do. We're talking to as many people as we can, scratching around for any information at all. You never know what little snippets can be cobbled together. That's partially why we're here. We wanted to apologise about your shirt, of course, but also to see if you had any information, anything about Hugo, for example. You know him really well, don't you?'

'I certainly do. We're so close, I doubt that anyone here knows him better. He couldn't possibly have done it.'

'Sure. But how, exactly, do you know that he didn't? Evidence is the only thing the police care about. He has no alibi, and he had motive. It would help immensely if the police could rule him out in a proof-positive way. He's being obnoxious with them and it's not helping.'

Fiona thought for a second. So that was their game. They wanted to ingratiate themselves with Hugo in order to get him to like them more. We'll see about that. She, and she alone, should be the one to save him.

'I don't know what I can say. He can be argument-ative, of course. He is a passionate man, but look at how he cares for those swans, for instance. That is the work of a gentle man. He wouldn't turn to violence unless you were to harm the swans, maybe.'

'You have nothing more concrete?' pressed Audrey. 'You can see Hugo's place from here. Would you notice if there were lights on in the evening, for instance?'

Fiona, who regularly looked at his distant lights, wistfully imagining herself wrapped in his arms in that lamplight, shook her head. 'Maybe I could, if I paid attention. It's a while ago now, obviously I can't remember every single night. I'm not always home in the evenings, social life can get busy. You know how it is.'

'We wouldn't know, sorry, our social life probably bears no resemblance to yours,' said Audrey, despite having recently spent a long evening with both alcohol and songs of dubious moral origin in the company of Hugo. 'If you see anything, remember anything, will you let us know?'

'Of course I will,' said Fiona who was planning to do nothing of the sort.

CHAPTER 10

Inez's arm was in a suspended cast, which looked exceedingly uncomfortable. She was lying down with her eyes closed, but her bright eyes opened when they entered.

'Did you bring me something? I'm dreadfully bored. How's Lucy? Getting fatter?'

'You've only been away for a few hours, I should think she's exactly the same.' Bill opened her bag and put a couple of magazines on the bedside table, along with the library book on Menzies and a box of chocolates.

'Grapes, it's supposed to be grapes. The nurses will steal the chocolate.'

'Stop shouting, Aunt.'

'I'm deaf, I'm allowed to shout. Quickly, hide box in the drawer before they see. Should have been flowers too. They say I'm lucky it wasn't my hip. Huh. Now tell me your results. Have you solved it?' She looked at them, eyes glittering. 'Well? I'm in a lot of pain, you know.'

'First, we went through the garden and found nothing,' said Audrey loud and clear.

'Not so loud, help me with the hearing thing.'

Audrey fiddled with Inez's hearing aid.

'Better now? Good. We found nothing in the garden.'

'Nothing? What am I paying you for? Do it again. There'll be a sweet wrapper, or at least a crushed plant where the perpetrator inadvertently stood, leaving boot prints. Sherlock Holmes could always be relied upon to find at least a bit of Trichinopoly ash. And we have nothing? How disappointing. So tell me: what exciting things did the policewoman say? How much did you pay her?'

'Ssh, Aunt, people will hear you.' Audrey looked towards the door nervously.

'Don't care. Well?'

'She didn't tell us anything, but we told her something to give her a new lead to explore.'

'So she paid you?'

'Aunt Inez! Do you want the story or not? Well, I knew she wouldn't say anything. She's a clam. If you press her, she just ends up getting you to tell her things. She recommended that you install security lights. Instead, we went to The Bean. Rick was there with the waitress. She was crying.'

'That's more like it. I'll take a crying waitress over some poxy cigar ash anytime.'

'We sort of bribed him,' put in Bill, 'bought a couple of grinders and a lot of coffee. Just wait, we'll make you some when you come home.'

'Never mind the coffee, what did he say? Forgive me if I am not as sharp as usual, they have me on the strong stuff. Comes with big warnings on the packet, so it must be good.'

'He spoke about money, how he was a guarantor on a loan that Fabiano had taken out,' said Audrey. 'Also, it seems Fabiano had more money than he let Rick know. Anna found money in their apartment though we're not allowed to talk about it. The police have frozen their assets but not the cash.'

'Why not freeze the cash?' asked Inez, loving the phrase 'freeze the cash'.

'I guess because they didn't know about it.'

'How much was it?'

'He didn't say. This is the first time we've spoken to him that he hasn't been totally hostile and we didn't want to push it. The way he spoke of it suggests it was a bit more than a couple of twenties. We need to talk to the waitress too. She's called Karmony.'

'Harmony? That'll be Regina Falconer's youngest. Unless there's two with the same name. Except Regina calls herself Rainbird now. I think Harmony lives with her sister somewhere in the forest.'

'I'm pretty sure her name is Karmony.'

'Yes, yes. That's what I said. Falconer. Her sister is Melamine, or something like that.'

'How can we track her down, now that she no longer works there?'

'That's for you to figure out, practise your detective skills. I'm just a sick aunt, bored in hospital, what would I know? Then what happened?'

Audrey continued the story. 'One of the grinders and half the coffee was for us. The second set was for Fiona as an apology of sorts for the ruined shirt. She's really annoying, but has known Hugo for years. We thought she might know something useful.'

'Good thinking. The woman is loathsome, but like so many other ultra-vain people she is easy to tease. Not much sport, but all the same... Go on, what did she say?'

'That he was kind to swans.'

'You gave a grinder and a kilo of coffee for an ounce of kindness? Poor exchange.'

'She didn't want the grinder so it was just the coffee. We'll give the grinder to the boys instead. Fiona must know more, she's totally smitten. Where Hugo, she goes.'

'What?'

'Joke, sorry. Never mind. We'll come back tomorrow. We all have to wait for choir practice to hear any results from the massage.'

'I want good news when you return. You just have to hope the masseuse blabs. You should tell the boys to lend you Mister Wolf. He'll bark his tiny little head off if you get another intruder. I'll feel safer knowing you have adequate protection. That trip hazard cat of mine is no use. Well done, all in all. It's a good start.'

Audrey and Bill failed to see how something so small and shy could be much help, but they agreed that Mister Wolf was possibly more useful in the defensive arts than Lucy. They dropped in on the boys after the hospital.

'A grinder, how amazing!' said James. 'Thank you, we'll truly cherish it.' Mister Wolf jumped up at Bill, wagging his tail.

'Good boy,' said Bill, bending down to give him a scratch, poncho billowing. Fortunately she was only allergic to cats. 'We came to tell you that Inez is in hospital and won't be home for a few days, not sure how long. Any duties she had lined up for you can wait.'

'How come? What's she done?'

'She thought there was an intruder and went into the garden, and slipped on the icy path. Her elbow is broken and she's a bit ruffled in general. If you fancy visiting, she's in the local. She's worried about us being in the house on our own and wondered if Mister Wolf wanted to come and stay.'

'An intruder? And was there one?'

'Don't know,' said Audrey. 'We saw nothing.'

James looked down at Mister Wolf, who met his gaze, tail wagging enthusiastically. 'Do you want to go for a holiday? Yes? Whoseagoodboythen?' Mister Wolf was in rapture, loving his master with his entire furry little being.

'I don't know. He would miss us, and we him. Why don't we all come and stay for a night or two? Would that make her happy?'

'Fun! Yes, let's do that,' agreed Audrey. 'You can take Inez's quarters, it's the most comfortable spot. Thank you.'

The boys came carrying a pumpkin lasagne and shared it with Audrey. Bill stuck with her readymade box meal, which today was a Lean Chicken Surprise.

'What's the surprise?' asked James, eating another mouthful of lasagne oozing with ricotta and cream.

'I don't think it is actually chicken at all,' said Bill morosely.

'I can see why that would be surprising,' said James.

'Usually the meals are labelled exactly for what they are, so Chicken Surprise would have to be as described. Maybe there is a missing "d" and it should have read "Chicken, Surprised".' Bill pushed the box away.

'Not as surprised as I'll be if we have an intruder,'

said Audrey. 'Though it would please Inez immensely to be right. Who's for coffee? The fire in the library is lit.'

Bill had made the boys carry downstairs an old gramophone along with some records that had belonged to Inez's parents. It seemed they had been fans of Josephine Baker, which suited Bill just fine. She made them all listen to a crackling rendition of *Ram-Pam-Pam* several times, joining in with the chorus.

No one heard the garden gate open, least of all Mister Wolf, who was enjoying a little snooze in Audrey's arms, while his ears got stroked. Lucy had retreated to the dining room and was perched on top of the old piano, safe from dog encounters. They were on a second repeat of *Breezin' along with the breeze* and idly contemplating how you made banana skirts when there was a crashing sound.

Instantly alert, Mister Wolf jumped down from Audrey's lap and ran into the dining room. Lucy stood with all hairs on end, hissing loudly at the glass doors. A vase had fallen off the piano and smashed.

'What's up, Mister Wolf?' Audrey opened the doors and they followed him outside. He ran to the front gate, eagerly following an invisible trail. Around the corner, a car engine started up and pulled away with squealing tyres.

'Well. How about that?' said Audrey, her heart

pounding. 'I wonder what they wanted.' They could see nothing untoward in the garden, and went back inside.

'This is interesting,' Audrey remarked. 'Let's rig up some sort of trap in the garden tomorrow night, just in case they come back. Inez will be pleased to hear she was correct.'

'But of course I was right,' spluttered Inez the following day. 'Did you doubt me? I am so disappointed in you, Bill. I expect a bit of silliness from Plum, but not from you. What are you going to do now?'

Bill wasn't quite sure how to take the compliment. She always felt that Audrey was more sensible.

'We're going to rig up a set of wires with tin cans tied on for tonight,' said Audrey.

'See what I mean, Bill? There she goes again. She gets it from her mother.'

'Actually, Aunt, it's not a stupid idea,' said Audrey. 'If they come back, which I am not so sure they will, there will be a big racket when they hit the wires. This will get Mister Wolf going and we'll all wake up.'

'But to what end? It would be better if you silently hid outside to see who it is. Let them come. It was a big mistake not to keep an eye out last night. Whoever was in the garden probably came and left by car. They might do the same again.'

'That's a really good idea,' admitted Bill generously. 'We can take turns at sitting in the boys' car across the street, watching. Your car is too recognisable. We can have hot tea in a thermos, hot water bottles under our coats, maybe some sandwiches... Then if they come, we can tear off in hot pursuit.'

'No pursuit. Silently, stealthily. Let no one see you or you'll be in danger. I don't think you are competent enough to get out of it, once you are in it. Arm yourselves too, just in case.'

'We can't do that,' said Audrey. 'I'm sure that's wrong.'

'Not as wrong as being on the wrong end of the stick. Go to the room at the far end of your corridor. I think there's an old umbrella stand in there. You'll find my father's walking stick. You'll recognise it by the ivory inlay. He always said it was more useful than any pistol, much like my cat turned out to be better than that straggly shaggy thing the boys call a dog. But I suggest this is a watch-only situation. Have you found Karmony yet?'

'Not yet, we've been too busy.'

'Luckily for you, I've been busy too. Karmony and her older sister live in a backyard cabin belonging to the cleaner here. You'll find it easily – I wrote down the address. Ta dah!' She passed them a sheet of hospital stationery with a flourish.

Karmony and Melodee Falconer shared a modest cabin the size of a caravan in the bottom of a deep block that sloped down towards a gully. Tall trees between them and the main house gave privacy, and as long as you weren't fussy about mod cons you would be perfectly happy there. A wisp of smoke curled from the chimney.

Bill hoped that the girls ate cake, because she had bought a whole one from the bakery. It had been neatly entered in the expenses and bribery sheet.

'Yes?' A girl they assumed to be the sister opened the door.

'Hello, I'm Audrey and this is Bill. We met Karmony earlier and wondered if we could speak to her?'

'She's around the back, collecting kindling. You'll see her.' The girl went back to the kitchenette where she had been slicing up some vegetables.

Karmony was snapping twigs under a large tree near the back fence.

'Hello,' she said. 'I recognise you from the coffee shop. Can I help you?' She put the twigs in a basket.

'I'm Audrey and this is Bill.' Audrey motioned with her hand towards Bill.

'And this is cake,' said Bill, holding up the fragrant brown paper parcel. 'I hope you like carrot cake. You must think it strange to have us visit here, but we hoped you could help us, you see. You work at The

Bean, and there is something puzzling us.'

'Worked. Why do you want to know?'

'Look, it's a long shot but we have a friend who is a suspect in this mess and we're doing a little digging on his behalf.' Audrey picked up some wood. 'Might as well help fill your basket.'

'I'm not sure that I can help, but ask away. All that I know is common knowledge.'

Audrey and Bill looked at each other. They both realised that they had no idea what to ask, having rushed in with no plan.

'What were they like to work for? We're looking for a general idea, to get a clearer picture,' said Audrey, making it up as she went along.

'They paid.'

'We can pay you too, a little. Since you have no income, you might be caught short temporarily.'

'Really? I am, a bit. I'd appreciate it, but you're free to have all I know. It's not like it's state secrets or anything. Rick is a bastard who is having his head turned by Anna who is totally self-obsessed. Fabiano is miserable but seeking comfort everywhere. Everyone's greedy for another dollar yet find none to give to me. How am I doing so far?'

'All this is common knowledge?' Bill was shocked.

'To people who spent any time with them, yeah. I guess.'

The grey sky yielded to pressure and rain started

pouring down. They ran for the door of the little cabin, pulling off muddy boots.

'Have a seat,' said Karmony. She pointed to a narrow bench by the kitchen table.

'This is nice, so cosy,' said Audrey.

'If by cosy you mean small, then you're right,' said Melodee. 'But we like it a lot. Who are you?'

Audrey looked out of the window to the rain soaking a green field on the other side of the gully. It was nice to be inside and dry. If you ever needed to fix the roof on a place as small as this, it would not be a big issue.

'Private investigators asking about work,' Karmony answered her sister, somewhat incorrectly. 'How much are you going to pay me?'

Again Bill and Audrey looked at each other, floundering. They had absolutely no idea of what would be a reasonable sum, but judging by the surroundings and the basic meal being prepared they imagined almost anything would be welcome.

'Are you paying for information?' asked Melodee with interest. 'For ten bucks I'll tell you what I think. It was the Frenchman.'

'Why are you so certain of that?' asked Bill with considerable interest.

'It's what everyone's saying. He's been arrested, hasn't he? Well then.'

'There are other suspects. Now, Karmony, in regards

to money, unless you have something else to tell us I think 50 dollars is enough. Why do you find Rick a bastard, as you put it?' asked Audrey.

Karmony started sobbing and rubbed her eyes. Bill handed her a handkerchief, pressed into a neat square.

'Here. What's so bad about Rick?'

'False bastard,' muttered Karmony and wiped her eyes.

'You're upsetting my sister,' said Melodee. 'Give her the money and go. We don't want any trouble.'

'Fine, we'll go,' said Audrey, rummaging for the money. 'Here you are, thank you for your help. I hope that you'll find a job soon. If you can think of anything else, will you call us?' She wrote their number and address on a piece of paper. 'Visit any time.'

Karmony held the hanky out to Bill, who waved it away.

'You keep it, I have plenty.'

'She already has a new job, starts next Wednesday.' Melodee led them to the door.

Outside the rain was now pouring, and they clung to each other trying to shelter underneath Bill's wet poncho as they slid their way on the grassy path up to the road. Water had pooled up around the car and in order to get in the driver's side, Audrey had to stand ankle-deep in water.

'Good thing we splashed out on wellies,' she said.

'My feet are the only dry part of me, though water is starting to run down my legs. Hot bath and dry clothes is what I want.'

'Bags I the first bath,' said Bill.

'Great. Then I can have the longest one. Make sure you're quick and don't use all the hot water.'

Audrey turned the wipers to max speed and tried to wipe the mist from the inside of the windscreen with her sleeve.

'Give me your hanky, I can't see a thing.'

'No hanky, sorry. I gave the only one I had to Karmony. Let's see what else there is.' Bill rummaged around on the floor, and in the capacious glove compartment. 'A sock. Here you go. Looks clean to me.'

The sock worked reasonably well, and they set off towards home. As soon as they pulled away, the rain stopped and was replaced by a pale yellow sun.

'Where was that sun five minutes ago when we needed it?' asked Bill, and draped the sock over the dashboard so it would have a chance to dry.

Audrey used Inez's downstairs bathroom so no one had to wait their turn. The only drawback for Bill was that by the time the hot water reached upstairs, she found that most of it had been used already.

They were getting some life back into the kitchen stove when the boys returned from one of their jobs, carrying a bag full of empty cans.

'We stopped by the tip,' said James. 'Figured you wouldn't have a great deal here.'

'Inez thought it was a bad idea. Thinks we should observe in silence from a car instead.'

'Not bad. I vote we do both. Let them walk in, believing all is well, and then get tripped and run away. Then we follow them,' said Audrey.

'Agreed,' said Bill, who personally couldn't wait to make trip wires, nor do a stake out. As far as the pursuit bit went, she was unsure, but would deal with it if it came to that.

The boys had also brought a reel of strong fishing wire, which they proceeded to rig up at every possible access point into the garden, slightly higher than the height of Mister Wolf so he could pass unimpeded. At every connection they ran a line to a bunch of cans, hidden out of sight. It took most of the afternoon. Holes had to be made in the cans and the system had to be fixed so that it actually went off.

'It's not very noisy,' said Simon after testing a couple of wires. 'We could do with something louder.'

'I wish we had some of those strings of Tibetan bells that Anna has on her door,' said Audrey.

'They hardly make a sound at all, just a faint tinkle,' said Bill. 'I know! There are a couple of cow-bells in the library, sitting on a shelf. I'll go get them.' She returned with two cowbells and a set of pewter mugs. 'No need to drill these, they have handles already.

It's a shame that we only have two bells.'

It was as loud as it was going to get. Whatever surprises night would bring was yet to be seen, but everyone felt much better at the thought of the improved garden.

Dinner was a simple affair of lasagne leftovers consumed in front of the kitchen fire. Bill had a French cassoulet, with most of the ingredients missing. It looked more like a thin soup with white beans, but it was warm and filling.

'And as a bonus I can eat it with one hand, no need to cut anything up.' She waved a spoon.

Mister Wolf fixed a stare on her, his longing for a snack obvious. He trembled slightly and shifted on his feet.

'Leave it. Basket,' commanded James. Mister Wolf moved a few steps away but kept staring. 'Just ignore him, he's already had his dinner. He can have a treat when we're done.'

Simon had been quiet for a time. He looked up. 'The more I think about it, the more I believe that Karmony has a thing going for Rick. She wasn't crying about the job, but the love lost. What do you think, James?'

'Hell hath no fury etcetera. Makes sense to me. Losing the job wouldn't be worth the tears because she had another one already. I said Basket!' Mister Wolf had again edged closer to Bill, a strand of drool slowly gathering at his bristly lips.

'I need a manual to understand these people,' complained Bill, ignoring the dog. 'They say one thing and mean another entirely. It's a foreign language I have no key to.'

'Truth is an optional extra for some,' said Simon. 'You have to come at it from a different angle, Bill. Their game is only an advanced version of you being pleasant to Fiona when you don't want to be. Or like playing cards with the charming Sugar Plum, Ruler of the World, Queen Inez.'

James had parked his car in a strategic position on the corner diagonally opposite Inez's house, where a stout tree spread its dark leafless branches. Since her house spanned the entire corner block, this was a good place to be. You would be able to see anyone approaching in any direction.

'If we sit low and still we should be pretty safe from being discovered,' said James. 'Who's taking the first shift?'

'We'll do it, said Audrey. 'You can relieve us at three o'clock. We can stay awake until then.'

Meanwhile, Bill had been upstairs in the junk room, as directed by Inez. The umbrella stand was not hard to spot. It was filled to capacity with miscellaneous umbrellas, a parasol, two wooden-handled golf clubs and a collection of canes. There was a heavy walking stick too, inlaid with a pattern of black and white. *This must be the one*, she thought. *But how would it help us? Are we supposed to fence with it?* It had a pleasing weight, but she took a golf club as well. Audrey could get a good swing with that.

'That's a handsome walking stick,' said Audrey. 'I can use it if my knee gets any worse but it's hardly a weapon, is it? Just as well, because I don't want one and I'm definitely not going to swing golf clubs at anyone.'

Into a basket they packed a thermos of blueberry tea and one of black coffee, a slice of cake for Audrey and apples and raisins for Bill. Audrey added a packet of crackers and a couple of chocolate bars for energy.

'None for me, thanks,' said Bill and added another apple and some celery from her food delivery.

They dressed in their warmest clothes and made themselves comfortable in the car, wrapping up with extra blankets.

'We should have brought the bird-watching binoculars.'

'Good idea, I'll go and get them.' Bill eased herself out of her cocoon to go inside. 'Have we forgotten anything else?'

'I'm not wearing my watch, are you? Well then, bring yours or we won't know when our shift ends.'

Audrey unscrewed the thermos cap and poured

herself a cup. It was very pleasant being alone in a car in the dark, with the smell of blueberry tea right under one's nose. She could see all the entry points to the garden, unless someone was to come across the back via an adjoining house. That was less likely, surely. She sighed and took another sip.

Her drink was finished by the time Bill returned, bringing the binoculars and her watch.

'You took a long time.'

'Couldn't find the binoculars. Has anything happened?' She tucked herself back in under the blankets.

'Nothing at all. Have a hot drink if you're cold.'

The highlight of the next hour was an owl that flew low over the bonnet and landed in the tree, briefly. The following hour saw the end of the tea, cake and raisins.

'How much longer do we have?' Bill sighed. Stake-outs were not so exciting in the long run. 'We're going to run out of supplies.'

'Hours and hours,' said Audrey. 'Let's play I Spy. You start.' They looked around, but it was too dark to play as you couldn't really see very much.

Time dragged like slowly pouring treacle from an endless tin. Before long, Audrey heard the regular deep breaths of someone falling asleep. She jabbed Bill in the side.

'Ow! What was that for?'

'You're falling asleep.'

'I'm not, I'm just resting my eyes a little.'

'Eat an apple or drink some coffee.'

Bill nibbled shapes in her apple, which took a long time. She made the apple square, then rounded all the corners, sculpting and whittling until only the core remained. Audrey sank deeper into her seat, pulling her scarf up higher.

'Don't get too comfortable,' said Bill. 'If you fall asleep I won't be able to stay awake on my own.'

Audrey blinked hard a few times and yawned. She was about to reach for the coffee when she saw a figure approach in the dark. 'Be still, someone's coming. Hold your breath!'

Bill didn't question what possible good that would do, but they both sat completely still, studiously not turning their heads as a figure walked past the car. The figure, a man walking briskly with his collar turned up against the cold and his hands thrust deep into his pockets, disappeared down the street.

'Phew, that was exciting,' whispered Audrey and exhaled. 'You can move now. Have another apple.'

'I have to ration the snacks, we still have so long to go.' Bill fidgeted a little. 'Let's play the memory game. I'll start. In my suitcase I packed a banana.'

'In my suitcase I packed a banana and an accordion.'

'Banana, accordion, nightingale.'

'Banana, accordion, nightingale, echidna.'

'Banana, accordion, nightingale, echidna, ash bucket.'

'That's two words. But okay. Banana, accordion, nightingale, echidna, ash bucket, tennis ball.'

A slight figure wearing a hooded sweatshirt moved quietly along the footpath, looking directly at them.

'What do we do now?' whispered Bill.

'Pretend to have a conversation with me,' hissed Audrey. They proceeded to talk to each other in an animated way, gesticulating, laughing and slapping each other on the back, completely ignoring the hooded figure coming straight towards the car. Before they could hit the locking button the backdoor was yanked open and the figure flung itself in.

'Hi,' she said cheerfully. 'Where are we going?'

'Penny! What are you doing out so late?'

'You know.' Penny looked sheepish.

'You promised. This is not good enough,' said Audrey sternly. 'A promise is something you keep, otherwise why make it at all? Just so many meaningless words. We'll drive you home.'

'I'm really sorry.'

'Ssh! Car lights approaching,' warned Bill. 'Get down.'

The two women slumped as low as they could, breathing into their scarves with their eyes half shut. Penny slipped to the floor, uncomfortably wedged next to a circular saw and a box of screws that cut into her back. She hastily pulled some debris from the seat over her head. The lights drew up level with their car and stopped. A flashlight shone through their window. Bill hit the locking button.

'What's going on here?' A police officer they hadn't met before stood looking in through the window with a large torch on his shoulder. 'Step out of the car please.'

'How do we know you're a police officer and not a murderer, concealed to look like police? I prefer to stay in the car if it is all the same to you,' said Audrey.

The police officer held out his badge and nodded to the black and white four-wheel drive behind him.

'What's happening here? There's been a report of suspicious activity.'

'We're waiting for a friend,' improvised Audrey. 'Just sitting in the car, waiting. Is that a crime?'

'I need your names and addresses. Driving licence, please.' He took out a notepad. Bill and Audrey looked at each other. Their licences were inside the house, not considered essential for a night of surveillance.

'They're inside the house,' said Bill. 'Over there, that's where we live.' She really didn't want him to go home with them. All that fishing line and tin cans could seem a bit suspicious.

'It's an offence to be in control of a vehicle without carrying the correct documentation,' said the officer.

'That's alright Officer, because we are not in control of the vehicle,' started Bill.

'What she means is it's not even our car,' said Audrey quickly. 'No, scratch that. We are not planning on driving, we are just sitting here waiting for the owners of the car to come and drive it.'

'I might come past later and check that your friends have arrived.'

Another car approached, quite possibly a sedan but neither woman was good at cars. This one looked like any modern darkish car with nothing to distinguish it. It turned into their street, slowed until it was past the police car and drove off into the distance. The police car drove off too, in the opposite direction.

'That was him going past then, I swear,' said Bill. 'We missed it. Where are the nosey neighbours looking when we have intruders in the garden, I'd like to know? We might as well go to bed now. I don't want to have to speak to the police again tonight. The car might not come back for hours, if at all, now that the police have spooked them.'

'Right, Penny, you can come out now, naughty girl,' said Audrey. 'Time to go home.'

'Do I have to?'

'You most definitely do. We'll talk another day.'

Penny gave directions to her house on the outskirts of the village and disappeared through the open gate as Bill and Audrey watched.

'Let's hope the policeman doesn't decide to come

knocking on our door tonight,' said Bill with concern. 'I'm not sure how we could explain the tripwire.'

'We could blame it on naughty nephews.'

'Any nephews we can rustle up are grown men.'

'They're not to know that.'

They gently shook the boys and told them the operation was called off, to which they received grateful sleepy grunts.

Simon made thin pancakes with lemon and sugar as a special treat for breakfast, happy to have been allowed to sleep through the night.

'We have to do something about the traps this morning. If we leave them up during the day, anyone can walk into them,' said Audrey.

'It's going to take too long to take them up and down every day. Why don't we just padlock the gate? Anyone scaling the gate will get what they deserve,' said James.

'Good plan,' said Audrey. 'We have choir practice this evening. Will you sleep here tonight?'

'Sure,' said James. 'We're going to Melbourne tomorrow, so you'll be on your own for a bit. Will you be alright? We can leave you the dog, if you like.'

'Of course.' They were interrupted by clanging from the garden.

'Quick, we've caught something,' cried Bill. They rushed out, dressed in their motley collection of slippers and dressing gowns. Standing in the early morning half-light was Penny.

'You!' Bill opened and closed her mouth, not believing what she was seeing. 'I trusted you.' She turned and went upstairs, deeply hurt.

'You'd better come inside. There's pancakes,' said Audrey, and took her hand more firmly than she intended. 'Come on.'

'Go on, have some. It's my special recipe, they're delicious,' said Simon.

Penny had a mouthful, swallowed silently and put down her fork. 'I'm so sorry.' Tears started building in her eyes.

'I understand,' said Audrey, who didn't. 'Have some more.' She cut off a piece and fed the girl, who swallowed obediently, like a baby bird.

'I didn't mean to. I really was stopping but some girls gave me a dare. I'm so bad.' Now she was crying properly, snot and tears mixing freely.

'Tissue! Here, blow your nose, it's repulsive,' said Simon, arms folded across his chest. 'Pull yourself together. How can you be so bloody weak? These women have been terrified. Inez is in hospital because of you.'

Penny looked up, astonished.

'You'd better believe it. Fell on the ice after she heard you prowling the other night. I've changed my mind. No pancakes for you.' He whisked her plate away and put it on the floor to Mister Wolf's immediate delight.

'How can that be?' asked Penny. 'I only came here now.'

'You mean you haven't done any night-time prowling here before?' asked Audrey.

'I swear.'

'You have not proven yourself particularly trustworthy.'

'I want to be. I want you to trust me. How can I do that?' Fresh wailing erupted.

'Shush,' said Audrey. 'Trust is simple. It goes like this, are you listening? If you want to be trusted, all you have to do is be trustworthy. That's all. Eventually, the world understands that you are. Then, never ever break the trust. It's quite plain. Do you think you can do that?'

'But isn't it being trustworthy, if those girls can trust that I did what they told me to do.'

Audrey sighed. 'First you have to choose between what's right and what's wrong. Once you have, trust in that side only. Even when it appears difficult, the choice never is. Do I make myself clear?'

'Yes. I want to go home now.'

Choir practice that night was at a boutique winery south of the village. The long gravel driveway was full of cars as Bill and Audrey arrived. They parked at the end of the line and started walking up the drive. The fog was heavy but they could see the first few rows of freshly pruned grapevines flanking the drive. When they got closer the winery appeared, a large yellow rendered edifice. The heavy front doors were open and laughter could be heard from within.

'Come in, come in.' Sam, one of the baritones and the owner of the winery, put an arm firmly around each of the two women and steered them into the cavernous space. 'It's a little cold, but the acoustics are excellent.'

The conductor gave them a new piece to work on in preparation for the annual Swiss-Italian festival in spring, with Fiona given a small solo. Though spring seemed a long way off, there were several new songs to be added to the repertoire, in Italian, which made for tricky work.

After singing, there were drinks and nibbles in the cellar door area.

'Hi, I'm Sara, Sam's wife.' A woman in her forties came up to them with a plate of warm nibbles straight from the kitchen. 'I'm not a singer myself, so I had time to be in the kitchen for a bit. The choir sounds great.'

'Sam's right about the acoustics,' answered Bill. 'It's a brilliant space for singing.'

'Here, have a crostini.'

Bill had a glass of pinot noir in her one good hand

and declined, but Audrey took two. A passing choir member took the last one in passing, leaving Sara with an empty plate.

'You're fast learners, it seems.' Sara wore narrow red slacks and a white shirt with a couple of gold chains around her neck. Bill took note of the simple style. It was highly effective. She had penny loafers, a narrow belt and a tumble of brown shortish hair.

'Thank you. We're enjoying the choir immensely,' beamed Bill.

'I didn't mean just the choir. I heard you were doing some digging for Hugo, looking for suspects. I have something for you.'

'Do tell.' Audrey was surprised. She hoped to hear from the masseuse. This was a bonus.

'A close friend of mine was pretty taken by him – Fabiano, I mean. He did have a certain magnetism, wouldn't you say? Anyway, this friend of mine says he planned to leave his wife and go to Brazil with her.'

'Brazil? I thought it was Italy,' Audrey replied.

Sara shook her head slowly. 'No, I'm sure it was Brazil. My friend is in an unhappy marriage and so was he. They were planning a new life together. She gave him her access code to make a bank transfer to finance it. She's fairly well off.'

Audrey had an idea. 'Is she involved with a meditation centre at all?'

'How did you know that? Yes, she does yoga at the

same place that I go to.'

'Just a hunch. Has any money been withdrawn?'

'Around 10,000 dollars,' she said. 'Not exactly spare change. Do you think there's any chance of the money being returned?'

'She'll have to speak to the police. I doubt it. She's not the only one who has given him money. Thanks, that answers a question we've been wondering about.'

'Got to go and check the oven,' Sara said, and moved on. 'I've got a tray of croquettes on the go.' She hurried off in the direction of the back door.

'Do you think she was talking about herself? Did she make the friend up?' whispered Bill.

'I don't know. Maybe, maybe not. It's another piece of the puzzle.'

Audrey and Bill chatted their way through the room, ending up with Ellen, the masseuse. She was standing in the far corner away from the open fireplace, talking about vocal cord care to a couple of the tenors, Jim and Gordon.

'I never drink coffee, tea or alcohol, it is so bad for the voice. Rest, exercise and hydration is the key.' Ellen was a strong-looking woman, rather square in figure with a prominent jaw line. She had solid arms like a wrestler.

'I'm willing to sacrifice a little voice for wine,' said Jim.

'Then you're not taking your singing seriously.

You would find your middle and lower registers have greater colour if you took more care,' said Ellen disapprovingly.

'What's in your own glass?' asked Audrey, taking a sip from her wine, generously provided by the hosts.

'Mineral water.'

'You don't find the endless water dull?'

'Of course not. The complexity of the local waters is astounding. This particular one has a faintly metallic undertone with a tight sparkle of small bubbles. All the springs are significantly different. Like a wine tasting, but you stay sober and get your vocal cords lubricated. I also run a cool mist vaporiser next to my bed, to hydrate my nasal passages. La lalalalala la,' she trilled.

Sam joined them with a tray. 'Are you enjoying the wine? Try some olive tapenade to go with it.'

'Mmm.' Audrey made an attempt to roll her eyes with pleasure, since her mouth was too full to speak.

Bill cast a glance at Ellen to see if she might object to the notion of olives but she seemed not to have any qualms. Bill put down her empty glass and took a cracker spread thickly with tapenade.

'Just the one. Looks divine, Sam. Love the winery too.'

'Ellen, did the appointment we booked get used?' asked Bill impatiently, no longer able to cope with waiting.

'Yes, that was kind of you. I extended the treatment, had no one in after her anyway. She had a relaxing time.'

Bill decided to take a chance. 'It's a pleasure to be able to help, especially mistreated women. We were hoping she would find it healing and soothing, to help her relax a bit.'

'Mistreated women? Is she? I had no idea. She nodded off at the massage table so she was certainly relaxed.'

'Well, that's good to hear, maybe we were wrong.' Audrey nodded goodbye and they walked off. 'As for vocal care,' Audrey muttered to Bill, 'she'd do better herself if she rested her own cords a bit and talked less.'

'So was the nurse wrong? Did she confuse them with someone else?'

'I don't know, but we need a different line to throw. This one was both expensive and disappointing.'

They drove home slowly through the thickening fog. They struggled for a minute with the garage door in the dark.

'The boys aren't home, obviously. Ssh, did you hear that?'

'I can't hear anything.'

'It sounded like a moan. I'm going to get my torch.' Audrey quickly unlocked the house and fetched her torch from the hallway table. They set off carefully into the darkness, avoiding the trip lines. Turning the corner, the yellow torch beam illuminated a figure on the grass near the sundial.

'Penny? Is that you?' said Bill. They bent down on the wet grass. 'Can you hear me?' shouted Bill, shaking Penny's shoulder firmly.

'Huh?' Penny groggily sat up. There was a streak of dried blood on her cheek.

'Can you stand up?' asked Bill. 'We need to take you inside.'

Audrey stoked the kitchen fire and put the kettle on. 'You're frozen to the core,' she said. 'Let's warm you up a bit.'

Bill proceeded to clean Penny's face and head. It didn't look bad, overall.

'I wanted to make it up to you and prove I was trustworthy so I hid in the garden to see if I could catch your bad guy in the act. Then I was hit on the head. That's all. Sorry.'

Bill and Audrey exchanged looks.

'You've proven something important,' said Bill. 'Nothing to apologise for. We now know beyond any doubt that there was someone there, someone with bad intent. What it also must mean is that we're getting closer to finding out who killed Fabiano. You've been so helpful. How's your head? Do you want to go to hospital?'

'No. I feel better now. I can't go to hospital, they'll tell my mum. Can I stay here?'

'Just for a little, then we'll run you home,' replied Audrey. 'You'll still have to tell your mum that you hit your head. She'll need to keep an eye on you. You have to be careful. And don't do that again, it's really dangerous.'

'You can stop fussing now. Are there any pancakes?'

CHAPTER 11

James and Simon couldn't put off their Melbourne trip any further but Mister Wolf stayed on as houseguest. The weather was very pleasant so Bill and Audrey took him out for a stroll down the street.

'Look, there's Anna,' said Audrey. 'She's just coming out of that shop. Let's go and accidentally meet her.'

'Anna, good to see you out and about. Has your friend gone back yet?'

'Yes, there's just me now. I might have another friend up next weekend, we'll see.' Anna smiled at them. She looked pretty relaxed.

'Did you enjoy the treatment?' asked Bill. 'Ellen does a special local's rate if you buy a booklet of ten sessions. Could be useful to know.'

'Oh, I convinced Maria to take the appointment. It was the least I could do, as she'd taken time off from her job to come and stay with me. Money's a bit tight at the moment so it was an opportunity to be nice back. Thanks.'

'You are so welcome,' said Bill, through gritted teeth.

They continued down the street, letting Mister Wolf lead the way. He expressed an interest in going to the butcher's in the hope of a bone. He was rewarded with one to take home and eat later.

'So we're no wiser than before,' said Audrey. 'Anna could be beaten and scarred fore and aft and we have no way of knowing.'

'Could we invite her to join us at the Bath House?'

'I suppose. I think we should give her a rest for a bit, perhaps talk to a few other people. More than anything I want to speak to Rick, but I don't know how.'

Fiona was practising her new solo. It wouldn't have hurt to have a longer one, she felt, but a solo of any length was recognition of her singing. She was the best soprano in the choir, of course, and her Italian pronunciation was quite satisfactory. Repeated holidays to Italy – and one or two Italian boyfriends – could be credited for that.

Even as she sang, she was deep in thought. *I want to be the one who gets Hugo's name cleared. Why should those two busybodies be the ones who get all the credit?* Here was her chance to be properly noticed by Hugo at last.

What she needed was a simple plan to flush out the real killer from the list of possibilities.

Her weekend was spent going over suspects and scenarios. For Fiona, this proved to be very difficult, like playing chess when you don't know how any of the pieces move. Pot after pot of coffee was brewed, and pencils chewed.

Her notepad remained blank except for the margin, which filled up with the word Hugo written in curly script. She sighed. This was not getting her anywhere. She pulled on a warm parka and went for a bracing walk around the lake. When you are need and crave romance, everything romantic can be physically painful. There were lovers embracing on the arched footbridge by the lake, reflecting their unified shape in the dark waters. Others sat on benches, or walked hand-in-hand on the pathway encircling the lake. It felt like a blow to her stomach. Damn these happy people.

She walked on, faster and faster until it was almost a run. When she returned home out of breath and sweaty, she tossed her clothes on the floor and stepped into the shower, letting the water pound her body. A plan was slowly forming, like lifting fog.

She brewed herself a new pot of coffee and curled up on the sofa. Those bloody women didn't seem overly clever with their nosing around. She could do better. By late Sunday afternoon, she had it all nutted out.

She opened a bottle of champagne and poured a glass all the way to the rim.

'Fiona, you are a genius,' she said to her reflection in the window. She toasted herself, bubbles tickling her nose. Exhilarated by her idea she went to bed. 'Tomorrow I start,' she promised.

First on her list was the grocers, where she bought a bag of figs. She waited until she had been handed her change to make her grand announcement.

'I know who did the murder,' she said loudly to the girl behind the checkout, bursting with excitement.

'Who?'

'I can't tell you yet. I just need to do something first, then it will be a simple matter for the police to make an arrest.'

'Really? How clever of you. Are you sure? How do you know? Is it the Frenchman?' The girl looked at her, frowning slightly. 'I hope it isn't him. He's nice.'

'Oh you mean Hugo? Definitely not. I have solid evidence. Yes, I am completely sure. See you later.'

Shame, it wasn't the chattiest operator but she had been loud enough for other customers to hear too. It was certain to work. Just to make sure the process was speedy she went to the newsagent and bought a magazine. The performance was repeated to full effect, the line behind her pricking up their ears. She smiled serenely and went to her favourite bakery where she got a loaf of still-warm pane di casa.

Next was the bank to change a fifty-dollar note into coins. Her patter was practised now, and she elaborated loudly while the teller added up her money. The bottle shop was extra chatty, debating at length the merits of the current government (none) before she could pay for her bottle of premium merlot and interject with her more interesting news. She was going to get some cheese anyway so it was no hardship to pick up a wedge of brie and a small tub of caviar dip at the delicatessen while casually gossiping.

The chemist was next in line. Fiona bought two new shades of nail polish and a tube of lash extender. Gracie, the perky assistant, seemed interested and listened keenly along with the bored customers waiting for prescriptions. The final destination was the post office. A stamped envelope later and a bit of talk and the job was done.

Now all she had to do was wait. Surely it would only be a matter of days before the news spread through the village, like distorted ripples on a pond. If it was a local, of course. If it was an out-of-towner she would give the news a week to take hold. Her money was on a local, though. The best would be if it was one of those pesky ex-nuns who had done it. Either way, she would show them for trying to muscle in on Hugo so bloody quickly. It had been a big mistake asking them for help when he gave her the responsibility to run his business.

She brought her purchases home and relaxed on the sofa, heart beating a little faster. She imagined the happiness Hugo would feel when the real murderer was taken to task. He would take her in his arms and gaze into her eyes. 'Fiona, *je t'aime*,' he would whisper, nuzzling gently into her neck while holding her tightly in an embrace that would never end. 'I have been such a fool not to see...'

She hugged herself in anticipation of countless romantic versions of this scene. A celebratory glass of wine was in order. She lay down on the sofa and kicked off her shoes, gazing out through the trees at the roofline of Le Bouquiniste. Soon.

Tuesday morning she heard the sound of the postman's moped, followed by the clang of her mailbox. There were a couple of usual bills and a leaflet from the hardware store announcing the winter specials: 'Take care of your lawn this winter!' But that was not all there was. At the bottom of the pile was a stiff white envelope addressed by hand in beautiful script. It must have been dropped off locally as there was no stamp. Nor was there any sender and she opened it with some curiosity.

Dear Fiona,

May I have the pleasure of your company for a little fossick in Trentham tomorrow, Tuesday? The weather promises to be good. I shall bring some food, just bring rubber boots and your best smile. Meet me at the Falls car park at 11am. I have a little surprise. À toi, pour toujours. Bisous, Hugo xxx

She grabbed the fence to steady herself. A date with Hugo. Not just coffee at his shop which she usually paid for but a date, a real date, in the privacy of nature. Finally he had woken up to her charms. '*Bisous* to you too, Hugo. Mwah!'She blew a kiss in the direction of the lake and smiled.

Then she realised that Tuesday was in fact today. It must have been dropped off yesterday after the mail delivery. She had very little time. Oh my God. She started panicking. What she would wear? Excitement fluttered in her stomach. There was no time to book a manicure. There was no time for anything.

She dressed with more care than a bushwalk should warrant. The weather was holding up nicely with a cloudless sky but frost had covered the ground overnight. As she didn't want to go on a date with a nose red from cold, she started her dressing with a superfine layer of alpaca thermals to add warmth without bulk. Who wanted to look lumpy and padded? Not her, she would sooner freeze. She shuddered when she recalled the hideous blanket that had covered Bill, top to toe.

She added an off-white thin-zipped cardigan knitted with the softest of possum fibres. Her classic cream moleskin trousers were an excellent fit, and firm enough in fabric to slim her nicely shaped bottom even further. She turned in the mirror and looked over her shoulder. Yes, good. A silk kerchief knotted around her neck was flattering too and gave a flash of colour. A white goose down jacket, left undone, and black rubber riding boots finished the job, making her far too warm indoors. The mirror confirmed her good sense of style. Wonderful. She looked absolutely perfect.

'Hello Hugo, here I come.' She gave herself a little wave.

The falls were only twenty minutes from her house, but being deep in the old forest it seemed like she had travelled to a faraway place. The smells were different to home, like eucalyptus cough sweets and damp earth. She could hear the falls roaring, aided by winter rains, which had encouraged heavy flows of water. The air was saturated with oxygen and she inhaled deeply with satisfaction. Strangely, the car park held not one single car. Had he not arrived yet? It was just past 11.00. There was, however, a red heart-shaped helium balloon tied to a railing with an envelope dangling underneath. It waved gently in the breeze, beckoning her.

'How romantic.' There was a note in the envelope. She opened it, hands trembling.

Ma chérie, take the path leading down to the creek bed.

I have a surprise. Hugo xxx.

She untied the balloon, and holding on to it she walked towards the steep steps leading down to the track along the creek far below. What a wondrously exciting day. She should get out in the forest more often. It must take years off your skin, all this rich air. She inhaled again, drawing the earthy scents deep into her lungs. It made her smile, it felt so good.

The air itself seemed alive as some startled birds fluttered up from a bush. When she reached the viewing platform halfway down she found another balloon. She added it to the one she already had, tying them around her arm so she could have both hands free. The walk was a little difficult and getting more so the further down she went.

There was no sign of Hugo at the bottom. She looked around to see if she could find another balloon when there was a big splash in the creek. As she turned sharply towards the sound, she heard running footsteps behind her. There was no time for anything more. Just a sharp pain, then nothing.

Her attacker dropped the baseball bat and grabbed Fiona under her arms, dragging her out into the creek. Though she was only slight, it was hard going. The down jacket snagged and tore on some spiky brambles, sending grey feathers fluttering. A boot came off as it rubbed against the rocks on the bank. Some brambles had to be cleared to make it easier to lug her down.

Fiona was pulled into the clear mountain waters until it was knee deep, deep enough for the waters to flow unimpeded across her billowing white jacket. Only the balloons tied to her arm were above the surface. Her attacker straightened up and left, picking up the bat on the way back up the hill.

***

'Trentham Falls is the longest single drop waterfall in Victoria, plunging some 32 metres over basalt columns,' said Kim, reading aloud from the visitor booklet to her husband Matthew, who was driving their 4WD over the rutted track. '...Five million years ago, yada yada, molten lava rapidly cooling... '

She looked at him over her reading glasses. 'Do you really want to know the detail? Alright, best remnants of original vegetation in the area, manna gum, messmate, stringybark and narrow-leaved peppermint. Ideal for picnics. Toilets provided for visitors. And here we are. I'm going to use those toilets before we go anywhere.'

Kim and Matthew stepped out from their car, putting on waterproof jackets and woolly hats.

'What luck, I thought there'd be more tourists.' Matthew didn't want to be disturbed in the forest. He liked to watch birds, and that was hard in company. Much as he loved Kim, thirty-nine years of marriage had not taught her to be quiet when needed.

They found the uneven steps difficult to manage.

'Let's just make it to the viewing platform and turn around,' said Kim.

'We'll see how hard it gets after we reach the platform. Might be smoother from there. It's not rated a hard walk.'

'Okay, but fetch my gloves, will you, Matthew? It's freezing,' said Kim, shivering.

'I'm not going back to the car now, put your hands in your pockets.'

'I need my hands to hold on to the railing, and I don't want to slip. It's muddy. You be careful too.' They made it to the platform.

'It's soothing, isn't it?' Kim rubbed her hands together trying to get some friction going. 'All this endless water, just falling, falling. Oh, look at that bird, is it a honeyeater?'

'No, it's a treecreeper. See it running up the trunk? It's collecting insects. They're pretty common around here, I think. Conditions are right.'

'Treecreeper?' asked his wife. 'Are you sure? It looks just like a honeyeater.' They watched the little bird fly down towards the creek. 'Look down there, what's that?'

'Balloons, I think,' said Matthew.

'Balloons? Can't be balloons. Pass me the binoculars.' She focused on the bright red objects. One broke free and rose straight up in the air, an inflated love heart aiming high. 'Oh my God. Matthew,' she said, dropping the binoculars. 'There's someone lying in the water. Hello? Are you alright? Hello there!' She started scrabbling down the steps, cold hands and steep steps forgotten.

'Careful!' Matthew slowly climbed down after her, clinging to the railing. Sections were a bit icy. Maybe the person had fallen.

Down at the creek they found a woman lying face down in the water.

'You must do mouth to mouth, Matthew!'

'She's dead, Kim. Nothing anyone can do.' The woman lying in the creek was white and cold as ice. The sight of her one bare foot made him turn away. So sad.

'We have do something.' Kim gripped his arm.

He glanced up at the embankment, then down to the water. 'She must have tripped or something from up there and fallen, landed on her head... Oh my. Give me your phone, mine's in the car.'

'So is mine. Oh, how horrible.'

Groaning with effort, they made it back up the steep stairs.

***

Le Bouquiniste was closed for the day. Hugo, taking inspiration from Bill and Audrey's paintwork, had decided to deal with some long overdue maintenance.

He decided to skip painting the ceiling, which was fine as it was. Such mess to paint ceilings, but the walls, what could be seen of them, left a lot to be desired. So did the chipped and faded trims around the doors and windows. Satie was playing on the stereo, the fire was crackling, and he had no plans whatsoever for the whole day except finishing this task. It was a good job that the book cases were made from unpainted timber, with no need for more than the odd waxing around the edges.

After finding Fiona and the notes in her pocket, the police wasted no time in returning to their prime suspect. When they arrived, Hugo had nearly finished a second wall and was in an excellent mood.

'What do you mean, Fiona is dead?' Hugo sat down heavily on a chair, wet brush dripping on the rug. 'How?'

'We were hoping you could tell us,' said Rosie. 'We would prefer to interview you at the station, if you don't mind coming in with us.' Though politely put, there was no question that this was an order.

'Of course.' Hugo's mind was reeling. 'Fiona dead? I am stunned.'

They took Hugo into the only interview room at the local station, and showed him the notes which, though wet, were clearly legible.

'But that is not my writing,' said Hugo, relieved, when they were lined up in front of him. 'Nothing like it. I would never write such things anyway. What is this?' He looked at their passive faces but received no clues. 'I am not interested in Fiona other than in her obvious qualities as a soprano in the choir. She was, how you say, a limpet. Clingy. A leetle bit *cuivré*. And why would I kill her? It is obviously a frame-up, no?'

'Where were you this morning?'

'At the shop, painting. I sometimes close on the odd day midweek if it is really quiet. Is normal.'

'Can anyone confirm this? Did anyone come to the door, see you?'

Hugo thought for a minute. He closed because it was quiet. There had been few people down at the lake. A handful of walkers maybe, but nobody had come to his door.

'Sorry, wish I could say they did.'

Hugo did not return. Rumours flew widely across Daylesford. Over all, the sentiments were one of collective relief. It had been unsettling to have a murderer loose. But among the many comments bouncing and drifting around in the doorways like so many stray leaves–'Just goes to show', 'You never can tell, 'Would he have stopped at two?' – quite a lot of people were feeling sorry and confused.

'What a pity, he was alright. You were friends, weren't you?' The nurse checked Inez's blood pressure. 'That's fine. How's the elbow today? Any pain?'

'Can't hear you. Speak up.' Inez was not in the best of moods.

'I said your blood pressure is fine, Ms Pretty.' The nurse had experience of Inez and was happy not to engage.

Bill and Audrey came for a visit, bringing a box of chocolate orange biscuits.

'Ballentine said that you usually like these. How's the arm?'

'I am not talking about my arm anymore, it's all they ever want to talk about around here. Tell me about Hugo.' She slapped the blankets for emphasis with her good hand.

'We don't know more than anyone else. The bookshop is shut and he's gone. I imagine there will be a trial eventually.'

'You can't trust those slick Frenchies. Kissy, kissy one day, knife in the back the next,' she huffed. 'All those dark Latin passions. But at least they're not as dull as some others. I nearly married someone French once. He was unfaithful. They all are, it's in the blood. If you don't have several women, you are not a real man.' She sighed, wistfully. 'Though he was, he really was...'

This was news to Audrey, who only knew of Inez's brief engagement to a Scottish farmer breeding beef cattle on a property north of Bendigo. It had ended badly, and Inez had gone on an extended journey to the continent instead of going through with the

283

intended nuptials.

Le Bouquiniste remained closed until further notice. The conductor of the choir called for an emergency meeting at his house. The tone was most sombre. The situation did not look good, no matter what angle you looked at it. Fiona was dead, and according to the news reports, Hugo was held on a suspicion of a double murder.

'Can I have a show of hands if we all agree on the postponement of practice meetings until further notice?' The conductor's ample whiskers seemed to be wilting. 'Until things have settled down a bit, it doesn't seem proper to continue.'

A sea of hands rose, but Bill's stayed down.

'You don't agree?'

'Well, don't you think it would be a good idea to maybe sing something for Fiona's funeral, whenever that will be? Assuming the family agrees. I think we could meet in a few days' time. Then we'll be prepared just in case.'

There was a murmur of assent. A fresh show of hands proved the choir unanimous this time, and the conductor promised to bring some music to the next meeting, which would be dedicated to preparing themselves for the funeral.

Audrey and Bill rang Rosie Lloyd to ask what was

happening but they got little information apart from the fact that Hugo had been charged with murder and had been to court for a bail hearing. Bail had been refused, so now he was being held on remand pending trial.

They bought a cheerful card featuring a kitten playing with a ball of string strewn with glitter and addressed it to Hugo LeBois, Remand Centre, Brickwell. They wrote a short message inside:

Dear Hugo. We believe in your innocence – we are still untangling the string. All you have to do is trust that the truth will out. Treat this as a little involuntary holiday – maybe catch up with some reading. We will have you out in no time. Sincerely, Audrey and Bill.

They hoped it would reach him, and that they would be able to fulfil their promise. Rosie had said that it was complicated to arrange visits to a remand prisoner, and suggested they just write to him for now. Visits could come later.

***

There was a special morning tea in the hospital staff room. News had got around that Inez was due to go home and one of the nurses had brought in a cake.

'She's worn me out,' said Nurse O'Sullivan. 'She knew me when I was little and in her eyes I have never grown up at all. I have greying hair and three children of my own but she still wants to smack my hand when

I come near.'

'You're lucky,' said a passing doctor, grabbing a piece of cake on the go. 'She actually did smack me when I wanted to listen to her heart. Well, I don't mind a bit of spirit.'

Several staff members stood to attention at the doors when Audrey led her aunt out. They smiled and waved.

'Thank you for taking such good care of her,' said Audrey. This was a very friendly hospital.

Once home, Audrey settled Inez in bed, propped by many cushions. Bill brought a drink and a book, the newspaper being too awkward for the one-armed to handle. Lucy jumped up on the bed and curled up, purring hard.

'Who's a fat cat, then, is it you? Yes it is. You've been overfeeding her again. Is she getting enough exercise?'

'She goes out to the garden when the weather's nice, and she rushes up and down the stairs a lot.' Bill didn't have a clue how to make a cat exercise.

'Hmm. Be a darling and bring me some cake or something to cheer me up. What is there?'

'We'll have to go to the bakery,' replied Bill. There's nothing in the house, we've been dieting, remember.'

'Really? Still? What on earth for? How dull. I will

not participate in this madness. The doctor says I am much too thin. Must make the effort. Off you go, chop, chop.' Inez settled back on the plumped up pillows and picked up her book.

Bill and Audrey walked down to their favourite bakery. The bell above the door gave a joyful little peal as they stepped inside, to be enveloped by the comforting scents of warm baking. The shop was busy and they had to wait to be served. The woman directly in front was the size of a small house, and almost triangular in shape. She was wearing a voluminous dress with a fringe of bobbles at the hem, which nearly reached the ground. Bill couldn't see her feet and imagined she moved on casters. She felt more encouraged than ever to stick with the diet. It couldn't be good for your health, being so large. The woman stepped up to the counter.

'Afternoon Michelle. I'd like three éclairs please, and one of those little sugar mice thingies. A loaf of rye too, please. A length of pistachio twist. Oh, and six macaroons. That's all for today, thanks.' The woman's voice sounded familiar. Bill was puzzled. Where had she heard her before? It was a pleasant voice, well-paced and easy on the ear with a slight sing-song quality, maybe a bit of an accent... It came to her in a flash.

'Margaret!' she blurted out.

'What?' said Audrey, as the woman slowly turned

around like a tugboat changing course.

'Margaret, it's you, isn't it?' The woman's mouth opened and closed but no words came out. Her facial features seemed too small for her face, out of proportion. Small pale blue eyes blinked repeatedly.

'Huh?' said Audrey. 'This is Margaret? Your weight-loss support? You're Margaret? *The* Margaret? She's Margaret?'

'Yes, yes, pull yourself together Audrey,' said Bill. 'Hello, Margaret. We meet in person at last.'

Margaret took out a macaroon from one of the paper bags and ate it.

'Yes,' she replied, and brushed a piece of coconut from her many chins. 'I have a reassuring voice, apparently, and the pay is good. Almost as good as Dial-a-, well you know what I mean, and much easier. You're not meant to actually know who I am. If you want to change support, I understand. Good bye.' She waddled towards the door, bags in hand and macaroon in her mouth.

'No, no, no. Of course I don't. I enjoy your phone calls immensely.'

Margaret stopped. 'You do? Well then. After seeing my generous size, will you still believe I can support you in weight loss?'

'Well, maybe not.'

'Right, we'll see about that. May I ask what you, yes you, are doing here in this bakery?' Margaret's lips compressed into a tight letterbox slot. Her usually soft voice changed timbre and became stentorian.

Bill shrank in shame. 'We're getting treats for Audrey's aunt who's ill. That's all,' she said shyly.

'That's all,' Margaret mimicked. 'A likely story. Don't be so weak. Do you want to get this large? You are a London bun short of a picnic if you think I will fall for the sick aunt story. We're going to buy some carrots for a naturally sweet treat. Follow me.'

Meekly they trotted in her wake to the grocery shop where Margaret, puffing loudly, bought a bunch of fresh organic carrots.

'This,' she growled breathlessly, 'is a real treat. Eat one, go on. You'll feel better.'

She watched them both chew a carrot each. 'Swallow. Good, yes? Now you will go home and if you try the bakery again I will get you blacklisted. I'll be watching you.' She brought two pudgy fingers to her eyes and then pointed towards Audrey and Bill. 'Am I making myself clear?

'Now listen here,' started Audrey, but Margaret interrupted.

'Good. I will call you tonight as usual. Goodbye.' Margaret smiled with satisfaction.

Audrey and Bill stood for a while, debating what to do.

'Well, who are you the most afraid of? Margaret or Inez?' asked Audrey. 'Maybe we can get someone to buy something for us from the bakery.'

'We can't! She'll find out, I know she will.' Bill sounded a little desperate. 'We'll have to go home and bake something. Or give her toast with jam, that's almost cake. We can add some cream on top.'

Inez was unimpressed with their explanation when they returned empty handed. 'I don't want any of your baking, it's awful. Call Ballentine, she'll come over with some goodies for the aged convalescent. I deserve better care than this, you useless ninnies. Put me back in hospital. At least people give you cake.'

Ballentine could not, she explained, come over since she was in the middle of baking but they were welcome to pick some up. They set off immediately, as it was the only way to make Inez stop.

Ballentine lived in a tiny house with low ceilings. At the back she had built an extension that included a small commercial kitchen, totally at odds with the proportion of her little house. She shook her head and tutted when they told her about their problem.

'Here, take these. You're hopeless. Stand up to the woman. She's frail, isn't she? Who can run the fastest? Well then, don't let her bully you so. Now tell me about Hugo. Do you have any news?'

'No,' said Audrey. 'He's being held on remand, I think in Brickwell, but no one is saying. I don't believe he did it. It was Fiona's murder that tipped the scales against him I suppose. It seems so wrong, and there must be other suspects.'

'Like who exactly?'

'Well, Fabiano was a bit too flirty around town. So flirty that at least one woman gave him money as a deposit on an escape to Italy, and another one gave him access to her bank account. There could be others still. He generated strong feelings. The men would have loathed him for the same reasons the women fell for him. Plenty of reasons to kill. His wife, his business partner, creditors, all sorts. There's no reason to focus more strongly on Hugo than the rest, apart from Fiona of course. We have no ideas about that yet. Maybe she knew who the killer was. She was certainly making a stir in the gossip feeding chain about it. Perhaps the murderer found out and set a trap.'

'I like him and I do want him to be innocent, but can we be sure?' asked Ballentine. 'What if he did do it?'

'You have to trust him. He didn't,' said Bill firmly. 'We're on the trail of the real killer and making headway. We have several ideas, and I would like to say that we will know soon. It is not Hugo.'

'Better hurry and prove it. Hugo needs to reopen his shop so I can sell more biscuits. As soon as I have a new reliable stockist they either die or get arrested. There's a lot of people who agree with the police about Hugo.'

'All the more reason to have a little faith,' said

Bill. 'We're on it.'

The evening weight support call came at its usual time.

'Hello Margaret,' said Bill.

'How are you feeling? Happy not to have succumbed to temptation? A bun in the hand today is a bun on the hips tomorrow. Did you fit in the exercise today? You know what they say: don't exercise today, get sick tomorrow. I'm so proud of your hard work. Together we can do it.'

'That's a lot of platitudes for me to chew over.'

'You'll be a success at weighing-in time. You'll lose even more next week.' Margaret kept spouting automatic lines.

Bill was silent for a minute.

'Bill? Are you still there?'

'Margaret, do you want to come for a walk with me tomorrow?'

'Me? I don't walk.'

'I think we should. Ten minutes, tops. It'll be fun. Meet you outside the bakery at nine. You can fuel up afterwards.'

Margaret was sitting in her parked car when Bill arrived. The weather was good, with cool air and a few small clouds, but nothing ominous. Bill chose not to wear the poncho today as it was all too similar in style to the tent Margaret was having to wear.

'Let's go to Jubilee Lake. So glad you came,' said Bill.

Bill hadn't had the time yet to do much exploring of the area but she wanted to see what the other lakes were like. Jubilee was quite different to Lake Daylesford. It didn't have many houses in sight, and the lack of buildings made for more wildlife. Some enormous birds were standing at the water's edge, ignoring them. A startling call broke the serenity.

'Holy cow, was that a klaxon?' Margaret jumped. 'No, look, a peacock.' The bird readied itself for another volley. 'That's horrible. Well, I'm here, so let's do this. To the jetty and back.' The jetty was only a matter of metres to the car.

'Okay,' said Bill. They walked down a gentle incline to the shore and arrived at the little jetty. There was a bench on the shore.

'Let's rest before we go back,' wheezed Margaret. They sat on the bench in silence until she had stopped puffing. 'Who do you think did it?'

'Did what?'

'The murders, of course.'

'I have a theory, but no plan.' Bill shared what she had about Anna, Rick, money, the double-timing Fabiano, greed and lust. 'My money is on Rick.'

'What's your next move?' asked Margaret, looking out over the water impassively.

'No idea,' admitted Bill. 'We've been winging it all along. I'm sure we'll think of something.'

'It's simple,' said Margaret. 'You must break in at this Rick's place and look for evidence.'

'How, precisely, is that simple?' Bill looked at her with scepticism.

'Learn to pick a lock. It's what burglars do. If they can learn, surely you can too. Or are you telling me a burglar is smarter than you? Should take your mind off cake for a while, anyway. Let's go back. Can't wait to hear how you get on with it all. I'll call you as usual.'

'We should walk a little further before we turn back.'

'Work up an appetite, perhaps?' Margaret said. 'Why not, a little further.' They kept walking along the water's edge.

'Break and enter is a crime. I'm not sure I can do it.'

'Don't be such a wuss. Of course you can. How else will you find out? Or are you prepared to let this gorgeous man languish in the dungeons?'

They debated this moral dilemma in such depth they didn't even realise they had walked around the whole lake. It wasn't a very big lake, but they were pleased with themselves all the same.

'I have an idea,' said Bill. 'When you ring me I will support *you*. How about it? You'll still get paid. It'll be fun. What do you say? Plus a walk tomorrow. Same time.'

Margaret stopped and caught her breath. 'I'll think about it.'

'Margaret thought of a brilliant plan,' said Bill when she got home. 'We must break in at Rick's place. Sooner rather than later. We need a little preparation time, but tomorrow should do.'

'Oh no, we mustn't.' Audrey shook her head vehemently. 'I'm not breaking in anywhere. Margaret can do it, if she's so keen.'

'We certainly must. He can't be allowed go around killing people hey-willy-nilly. Who knows how many more people are in danger? Anna, for starters. I know it's him. I can feel it. You think so too, admit it.'

'Well, yes I do, but a feeling is not enough evidence. You need to give me more reason than that before I agree to breaking in, at my age.'

'What's wrong with your age?' asked Bill. 'It's the same as mine more or less and you won't catch me carrying on about it. We're in danger ourselves, or have you already forgotten the garden intruder? If he knows that we're on to him, he'll be plotting to get rid of us as well. You can bank on it. Well, who else has such good motive and opportunity? Fabiano spent all Rick's money but claimed not to have any of his own. He lied, tucking away his own money and used Rick dreadfully. Surely that would make him furious. Not only did he have financial motive, there's also Anna. Don't tell me there wasn't something going on there before Fabiano died. He knew all the movements, was trusted, had a key to the place, and is easily the most unpleasant slimy toad in the whole line-up.'

'Are you rushing to conclusions because you don't like him and don't want it to be Hugo? It could just as easily be the miserable sisters, or at least the jilted one.'

'Think about it for a minute. It makes sense. Margaret's right, we need to have a look around his house to see if we can find any clues. Karmony is only a skinny slip of a girl. She wouldn't have the power to knock down a grown man. Why would she anyway, if the boys are right and she had a thing for Rick? Wouldn't she be more interested in knocking Rick off? I'm right, just wait.'

'What possible clues would he have lying around, just like that? A detailed plan of how he was going to do it?'

'I don't know. That's what looking for clues is all about. You don't know what they are until you see them. There could be poison, papers, anything. Oh come on, you can't say you're not curious.'

'I can't think why there would be poison,' commented Audrey drily.

'You're too picky. Maybe he sedated Fabiano before doing all that trussing and choking. I don't know, do I? Hugo is in a lot of trouble. We can help him, you know we can. We got him into this in the first place, remember.'

'We'll be the ones in trouble if you're wrong. How do we know he won't be there?'

'He's staying with Anna, isn't he, doing the dastardly comforting. What could possibly go wrong?'

'Assuming I agree, how are you planning to get in there? Just out of interest.'

'Easy. We learn how to pick locks first. We can practise on Inez's back door today.'

'Alright. If, and I mean if, we can learn to open a door without damaging it, I'll say yes.'

They went in search of possible equipment and found a screwdriver, a paint scraper, a plastic card and an Allen key. Later, Simon and James arrived with bags of shopping to find the ex-nuns crouching at the back door, labouring over the lock.

'Locked out, girls? We have a key.'

'We're learning to lock pick,' explained Audrey. 'It's not easy unless we damage the lock mechanism or scratch the paintwork. Nearly got it. Ah, no I haven't. If I pry away the wood surround I might be able to get it but I need to do it invisibly.'

'You have some unusual hobbies.' James looked at the tool selection, which by now had grown to include several kitchen implements. 'Just wait until I unload the groceries and I'll dash home.'

He returned in a short while with a bag. 'Here we are: snake rake, torsion wrench, half diamond. Couldn't find my pick gun. Bump key, hammer. You can forget about your whisks and whatnots.'

'Hammer?' said Audrey. 'We don't want to break

anything.'

'Just to hit the bump key with. Let me show you. This lock shouldn't be hard.' He fiddled around for ages, carefully manoeuvring the picks.

'Shall I make you a cup of tea?' Bill asked. 'I thought you said it wouldn't be hard.'

'I said it wouldn't be hard, I never said it would be quick. That's for the movies. If you waited for a lock to open in real time in the movies the credits would start rolling before the story had time to come to its gripping conclusion. Not long now. There.'

'Let me try.' Bill relocked the door with the key. 'Like so, then this... Now what? Oh yes... No. Drat, it doesn't want to open. How on earth did you learn to do that?'

'Useful skill when you're a general handyman. If you want to learn, you should start with a simple small lock and a couple of paper clips. Go and get a padlock and I'll teach you this afternoon.'

Audrey was a quick learner. Soon the little padlock opened willingly. She was enjoying herself hugely. Bill, with one hand only, was not able to do much except watch. The back door lock was a more difficult task but under James's tutelage they were eventually able to do it. Bill took step-by-step notes.

'Thanks ever so much, James.'

'Not a problem.'

CHAPTER 12

'We need to go and buy a couple of baklavas,' said Bill.

'I thought you didn't eat cake anymore?'

'The black things you put on your head, silly.'

'The word you seek is balaclava, and you can hold your horses. I may have agreed to breaking in to someone's house, but I will not look like some common robber whilst doing it.'

'How about a common house-breaker? Okay.' Bill sighed. 'But at least let's wear some dark stuff so we can hide in the dark. I need a black hat or something – my hair is positively luminous nowadays. We can use the driving gloves from the car. Don't want to leave prints.'

The closest they came to a balaclava upstairs was a felted navy cloche hat smelling faintly of mothballs. It didn't fit either of them so they popped out to visit the charity shop a few minutes' walk from Stewart House. Audrey picked up a black acrylic beanie with Black

Sabbath embroidered on it in purple.

'Yes, darling, that's just the ticket. Look at this.' Bill had found a black fascinator with a silk rose and crumpled tulle ruffle.

'Do you want me to do this or not? Find something useful or I'm going home.'

'What about this one then?' The headgear in question was not a hat at all, but a shiny black wig cut in a page style. Bill put it on.

'Perfect,' said Audrey. 'Full black coverage. I'm getting this, too.' She had pulled on a black tracksuit. 'It will give me freedom of movement as I run away from the filth.'

'With your knee I don't think there'll be any running. If we're caught, which we won't be, just bop whoever on the nose while I run. Or I can give them a hard knock with my plaster cast.'

They selected some sneakers for sneaking, a pair of dark roomy trousers with plenty of pockets for Bill and a black jumper. They completed the outfit with a small black vinyl satchel for the equipment and any evidence they would find.

'This is exciting, isn't it?' said Audrey. 'Shall we get some sleep first and break in later, or shall we stay up and practise?'

'I'm afraid I wouldn't wake up in time. Let's stay up and go at midnight.'

'What are you two being so cheerful about?' asked Inez when Audrey went to check on her before bedtime.

'Don't know what you mean. Cheerful? We're just happy to have you home again,' said Audrey, mostly truthfully. 'Good night, see you in the morning.'

Bill filled a thermos of coffee and went up to Audrey's room where they crept into the warm bed to wait out the hours. Audrey practised opening the padlock while Bill read another Christie.

'It's really fiddly. You would be better at this. Shame about the arm.'

'Yes, shame,' agreed Bill and reached inside her cast with a knitting needle. 'It's really itchy.' She turned another page. 'Hush now, I'm getting to an exciting bit.'

By 11.00pm they were starting to feel sleepy so they had a mug of black coffee each and got dressed in the new gear.

'Honestly, Bill, if Mother Superior saw us now...' Audrey broke out in a fit of giggles. 'Your wig is truly hideous. I love it.'

Quietly they went down the stairs and out the front door, hoping Inez wouldn't choose the next hour or two to ring her bell. The night was particularly well suited to their purpose as it was blissfully dry, despite a solid cloud covering. This meant that there was no moon either, and a good chance of avoiding being seen. As their car was both noisy and distinctive, they went by foot along the deserted streets. First they walked past Anna's place to see if Rick's car was parked there. It was, reassuringly.

'Let's make sure he stays put until morning.' Bill placed a hefty nail – thoughtfully brought from the shed – wedged upright behind his tyre. 'This is Margaret's idea, really. She has so many good ones. He'll reverse into this, see. Then he'll decide that whatever he wanted to go home for can wait till morning. We'll remove the nail on the way back. It won't do any harm unless he tries to drive anywhere right now.'

'You're bad, you are.'

'No. I'm really, really good.'

Rick's house was completely dark. It had a little side passage with a tall gate, which opened with only the faintest of squeaks. The back door had an old style lock that looked similar to Inez's.

'Hold the torch and read the instructions.' Audrey was getting the tools organised. 'Ready.' They followed the steps carefully, but no result. They used method number two. Still no result.

'We'll just have go and ask James for help,' said Bill. 'He'll understand.'

'Will he? In the middle of the night? Glad that you're so confident.'

To walk all the way to the boys' house was further than they would have liked, but it was too late to change their minds about the car now. At lease there were no steep hills in that direction, and Bill's exercise would be well and truly covered for the next couple of days. They sped up to a brisk pace and were panting a bit by the time they arrived. The cottage was as dark as all the other ones they had passed.

'It's a good job it's one storey. I'd hate to try to wake *us* up in the night. You'd have to be a good shot at throwing gravel,' whispered Audrey and tapped on what they both hoped was the bedroom window.

James was dreaming. There was a raven, pecking at something. Peck, peck, peck. He turned over in his sleep. The noise continued. He opened his eyes.

'Simon? Simon, wake up. I think there's someone knocking on the window.'

Mister Wolf, who liked to sleep with a blanket pulled over his head, gave a couple of muffled yips.

'Go back to sleep. It'll be the fridge doing the defrost cycle. Or a tree branch.'

'But there aren't any trees outside the window.'

Tap, tap, tap. They could both hear it clearly now. Simon got up and raised the blind. He gasped, jumping back when confronted by the shocking sight of Bill in a black wig and Audrey looking like an ageing rocker in a Black Sabbath beanie, both smiling and waving enthusiastically. It took him more than a second to even realise what he was looking at. It was a hideous apparition.

'What on earth are you doing, dressed like that?' he hissed. 'Come round the front and I'll let you in.'

As if they had arrived at a dress-up party not only on the wrong day but definitely at the wrong time, Bill and Audrey walked in the front door with great enthusiasm, kissing both boys on the cheek and explaining their quandary.

'I see,' said James. 'You want me as an accomplice because of your inabilities to pick a simple lock.'

'Yes, that's it exactly,' said Bill cheerfully. 'I told Audrey you'd understand.'

'Alright. Maybe your plan is okay, but if we find something we're not removing it. I'll bring a camera and we can photograph it instead. You can't remove evidence or it won't be usable.'

'I'm coming too.' Simon put on a pair of brogues and tied the laces tight. 'There's no way I'm letting you do this on your own.'

The women were getting a little weary on their feet by now and were thankful of the boys' decision to drive. First they drove past Anna's to double-check Rick's car. It was still there with all four tyres fully inflated. They parked a street away from Rick's house and walked the last bit.

James crouched down by the back door and did a

couple of smooth manoeuvres. The lock clicked open without any issues at all.

'You went wrong here, see. It's just a matter of practice.'

They went inside in a gathered troupe, moving slowly in a small beam of torchlight.

'You two start with the bedroom, we'll take this one,' said Audrey. She and Bill were in a room that probably served as Rick's office. They were opening drawers full of exasperating amounts of paperwork when they heard a shriek. They rushed over to the bedroom.

'Are you alright?' whispered Bill.

'It's hideous! These sheets!' moaned Simon. 'With that lamp! No one can have this bad style and not be guilty.' He gave the women a sideways glance. 'Obviously with the exception of your own style tonight. I'm sorry, I'm just a little tense. Keep looking.'

The bedroom hid nothing incriminating (apart from bad style) that they could see, nor did the office, though with so much paper it was a hard room to search. They figured that evidence was less likely to be in paper format, so they concentrated on finding things that would stand out as odd, or things that were hidden behind other things.

The boys were just going through the kitchen when they heard a sound from the front door. A key was turning smoothly in the lock.

They dashed to Bill and Audrey, who were going through the bathroom.

'Quickly, run, someone's here,' hissed James.

'We can't. Audrey's knee has locked up. Shush. Turn off the torch.'

The four of them stood completely still in the tiny bathroom, packed like sardines, hardly daring to breathe. They heard footsteps, then the front door opening and closing. They stayed in the bathroom, listening hard.

'All I can hear is my own heartbeat,' whispered Audrey.

'I can hear your heart from here,' said James. 'I think he's gone. Let's go before he comes back. Can you walk, Audrey?'

'Yes, gently. I'll just have to pop the knee back, hang on. Glad you brought the car.'

They decided to leave via the front door, which would lock as they closed it behind them. Next to a coat rack was a chest of drawers with a canvas bag on top.

'Just a quick look and then we'll go.' Bill was reluctant to give up. She had been so sure they would come up trumps. 'Bingo. I was right. Look at this.'

She held open the canvas bag. It held a coil of orange nylon string that looked exactly the same as what they had seen when they found Fabiano. There was also a roll of packing tape and a tear-off dispenser.

'All we need is a couple of coffee beans and the evidence is complete. Photo please, James,' said Bill.

'Can you tilt it at a greater angle?'

Bill obligingly angled the open bag and on cue, a scattering of coffee beans rolled out.

'Spooky or what? Let's go,' she said.

Once safely driving away they let out whoops and hollers of triumph like a bunch of teenagers. 'We did it! Are we good or what!'

They stopped a little up the road from Anna's and Bill quietly walked back and removed the wedged nail. There was no sign of movement or light from the house.

Safely home again, Audrey put on the knee brace given to her the last time her knee had popped. 'I have to rest it for a while. Any further shenanigans you want to involve me in will have to wait.'

'Don't tell me that it wasn't worthwhile. We are further than ever, and still safe. That was exciting, wasn't it?' Bill's eyes glittered. 'Inez will be thrilled. Priority one now is to warn Anna. What can we tell the police? We can hardly say that we broke in.'

'I have an idea. Tomorrow, we'll go and knock on his door with some excuse.'

'Like what? It would have to be really good.'

'Easy,' said Audrey calmly. 'We'll pretend that we're collecting things for charity, and we'll be surprised to see him there as we clearly have no idea where he lives. How's that? Then, we can go to the police and say that we saw the bag when we were in the hallway, which is completely true anyway.'

'You know, I think that could work. Good thinking. Sleep tight.'

Inez woke to a silent house the next morning. She put her hearing aid in but still couldn't detect any movement in the house. Unusual. Bill and Audrey were from habit up very early. Could they have gone out for something? She closed her eyes again and tried to get back to sleep. It wasn't until an hour later that clanging and banging from the kitchen alerted her to the fact that breakfast might be on the horizon.

'You're late this morning,' she said as Audrey appeared with a tray.

'Sorry, we overslept.' They had decided not to tell anyone just yet, not even Inez. 'Do you need any errands run this morning? We're heading out in a little while.'

'You could get the paper. I want to see if they've published my letter.'

Bill was already dressed and much too impatient to even think about breakfast, but Audrey made her have some porridge.

'It will do you good. You won't think clearly on an empty stomach.' She spread apricot jam on some toast for herself and started to eat. 'We'll need to look as if we've done some collecting already. When we've finished eating, we'll get a couple of large carrier bags and pack some stuff from the house.'

Into the capacious bags went Inez's best grater, an unopened bottle of cat shampoo, a collapsible umbrella that everyone hated because of its uselessness as shelter, and a ceramic mug with the text '25 years reunion – Bremen High School 1983' on it along with a picture of happy little Bremenites, slightly faded with the years gone by.

'Is that enough?' Bill looked at the bags with scepticism.

'It'll be fine. He's not to know how long we've been collecting for.'

'You,' said Rick, opening the door. 'Will you not leave me alone?' He started closing the door but Bill already had a foot in the way.

'Please don't be upset,' she said. 'We didn't know this was your house. We're just helping to collect jumble for an upcoming bazaar for the needy. We'll leave. Accept our most sincere apology. So sorry.'

'I see. Maybe I should be the one apologising, for hastiness. Since you're here I might as well give you something. How about this bag?' He took the bag from the chest of drawers and looked inside. 'Just some twine or something, but the bag is pretty reasonable. I don't know where it came from actually, but you can have it. Bye.' He closed the door.

The women stared, lost for words, at the closed door.

'What on earth just happened?' asked Audrey, holding up the offending bag. 'That's it, we are going back to the police. I don't understand a thing.'

'But why would he…' started Bill. 'I don't either.'

At the front desk of the police station stood the sergeant they had encountered on their last visit. They handed him the bag and explained the bits of the story they felt that he needed to know.

'So, if I understand you correctly, you went to the private residence of someone you consider to be the prime suspect in an official murder investigation you have nothing to do with. This is a man who is grieving the loss of his friend and business partner. There, you claim to have been given a bag of critical evidence by someone you feel, with no evidence whatsoever, to be a murderer. You are aware, aren't you, that it's a serious crime to impede a police investigation?'

'But the police are always asking the public for help. We're the public, aren't we? And this is help.' Bill smiled hesitantly, her cheeks a bit red from the scolding.

'This isn't help, this is an offence. It is also a crime to masquerade as charity collectors. Give me the bag of things you've collected. You will hear from us in due course.'

'But we haven't collected these things. They are our own, to make us look more official. We're just carrying them around,' protested Bill, cheeks even redder.

'Give me the bag.' He held out his hand and Audrey reluctantly let go of the bags.

'You will not do anything more, you understand? If I see or hear of either of you again in relation to this case I will arrest you. Go away before I change my mind and do it now.'

'That didn't go so well,' Bill admitted as they trundled home. 'I thought they would get happy and excited. All that happened is that we lost things that weren't ours to lose and got told off into the bargain.'

'Buck up. I don't think Inez has ever even been to Bremen. She won't notice it's gone. And cat shampoo! That's never going to get used. What's more important and urgent is to warn Anna.'

Catching Anna on her own so they could warn her about this most delicate and dangerous matter was difficult. Rick appeared to be back at her place and they didn't want to stand outside and wait for Rick to leave. It was just too obvious.

'What if we split up and go to a corner of the street each?' suggested Bill. 'We can just walk around a bit and look inconspicuous. And when he leaves he'll have to come in either direction and we'll know to go to her.'

'Sounds like a sterling idea. I'll go left.'

They shivered on their respective corners for over an hour. To get warm they marched back and forth, stomped their feet (or in Audrey's case, foot, as her knee pained her rather a lot), rubbed their hands (except Bill, who only had one arm to rub) and generally had a miserable time. An hour is exceedingly long when you're standing somewhere cold and you can't leave your post. Bill was beginning to intensely dislike surveillance on foot when she spotted Rick's car turning left. She hunched into her coat and walked away, as if she was just on her way somewhere important. She glanced at the car as it passed her. Oh no.

'Audrey, ahoy!' She half ran towards the other corner. 'They were in the car together,' she puffed.

'Well, isn't that dandy? Here we are, trying to save her from a murderer and she goes off in the car with him just like that. Pouf! Enough of this for now. I need hot chocolate.'

They walked to the main street and sat down in a cafe, thrilled beyond belief to be inside. Audrey moaned aloud when she swallowed the first few mouthfuls of hot liquid.

'So good. My teeth will soon stop chattering.' She

slammed her mug down, sloshing chocolate on her saucer. 'There she is, run, Bill! My knee...'

Bill ran out the door as Anna turned the corner.

'Oh Anna, are we glad to see you. We have to talk.' She propelled Anna back to the cafe and her still-warm chocolate. 'We thought you had gone somewhere with Rick.'

'I had, yes. He just dropped me at the post office corner and I was walking home after my errand. Is something the matter?'

'Yes, we're very much afraid that there is,' Bill replied. 'You must understand that we're not completely sure but still we must warn you. There's a strong possibility that Rick killed both Fabiano and Fiona.'

'Rick? What? Oh my God. But I... But he...' She unbuttoned her woollen coat and fanned her face. 'Hot in here, isn't it?'

'There have been so many shocks for you,' said Audrey. 'Would you like something to drink? Chocolate?'

'Nothing for me, thank you. Oh, some water maybe. Why do you think it's him? I don't believe you.'

'A lot of reasons. We need you to take care, and pull back on the amount of time you spend alone together.' *Like all of it*, thought Bill.

'You two are so sweet, you really are. I love your

concern but you're wrong. He loves and protects me. It was that Frenchman who did it. He's still safely locked up, isn't he?' Her hands trembled slightly as she smoothed a strand of hair away from her face.

'He is certainly suspected,' said Bill. 'But until this is solved you are not safe. Two people have already died, remember. At least promise us you'll think about it. Take note of anything suspicious he does or says.'

'I will. I feel I can trust you two. Do you mind if I ask you something?'

'By all means. Anything we can do to help.'

'If it turns out that you're wrong, as I am sure you must be, how long do you think I should wait until I marry again? Rick asked me last night. I said yes.'

'You absolutely must wait until it's settled, promise? Other than that, you should wait until you feel truly ready. Some people wait a year, some more.' Bill sighed and shook her head. 'Cool your heels a bit.'

'A year? I don't want to wait a whole year. I've already waited my whole life for someone like Rick.'

'Then at least wait a while. You'll need some time, even if it doesn't feel that way. You're young.'

Margaret tutted at this when Bill told her.

'Mmm. I've had another thought. You told me the nail was still behind the tyre, and so the car could not have been driven. Unless, and this is really unlikely, he saw it, moved it and replaced it. What do you think that means? Did he walk in the middle of the cold night when he had his own car available, just sitting there? He didn't try to drive his car or he would have a flat tyre. I've changed my mind. Unless he used a different car, someone else came. Not him. Who else is on your list, especially someone with access to a key to Rick's place? Now prove it. But please, be careful. Go and find those boys of yours and hope they can be of help. Don't be alone at all. I will go on as many walks as you like, just promise you'll stay safe.'

James was out shopping when they rang him on his mobile.

'I'm almost at the grocery shop. You can meet me there or wait and I'll come to your place in a while. I have a couple of errands. What's so urgent?'

'We can't say on the phone,' said Bill. 'Meet you there in five minutes.'

Audrey and Bill swept into the shop with an air of bubbling excitement.

'We're just so happy to see you. We've got it this time,' said Audrey. 'Remember the nail that didn't puncture Rick's tyre? Do you understand the significance of this? It means that he didn't drive, so it wasn't him who came and dropped the bag off.'

'He could have walked,' suggested James.

'No, I'm sure he wouldn't. He didn't even try to drive.'

'I see what you mean,' said James. 'Oh my God, that leaves us with Anna. It must be her. Who else could it be?'

'Well, I can't see anyone, with the possible exception of Karmony,' said Audrey. 'She could have had a set of keys. But I'm not sure...'

'Anna could easily have taken his key when he slept,' said James, 'or even had a key of her own. She would have used her own car, bringing the prepared canvas bag ready to plant evidence. Then the next day, she could anonymously inform the police.'

'I don't understand why she would do that. Isn't she having an affair with him?' asked Audrey.

'Can't you see?' said James. 'As long as anyone but her is sentenced for this, she'll go free. As Hugo's case isn't watertight, she needs to spice up the next suspect. Enter Rick, a readymade villain for her to use. I think that if we are right in any of this, you might find that she, not he, was the one prone to violence.'

'What about poor Fiona?' asked Bill.

'Fiona might have found out the truth by herself. You two were perhaps not the only ones with an interest in clearing Hugo. She was always smitten with our charming Frenchy.'

They turned into the next aisle and came face to face with Anna, staring straight at them.

'You?' she spluttered. 'You're all wrong.' She took a few steps backwards. 'It wasn't like that at all.'

'Anna, calm down,' commanded Audrey.

But Anna had no intention of calming down. She turned and grabbed a glass bottle of mineral water from the shelf, smashing the base off in one swift movement. Adele was doing her shift and was peacefully stacking canned goods when she heard the breaking glass. She rushed over to see what had happened and stopped sharp, face to face with a wild woman armed with a broken bottle.

'Don't come near me. Any of you.'

Adele reversed as the woman brandished the bottle in front of her, water pooling over the floor, then grabbed a meat tenderising mallet from the rack with her other hand.

'I'm warning you. Everybody step back. Nobody calls the police.' She edged closer to the exit, waving her weapons, black hair wilder than ever.

'Anna, put those things down.' Audrey took a step towards her, empty hands outstretched in a gesture of peace. 'No one wants to harm you.'

Adele looked as if she really, really wanted to. She caught the eye of Louise behind the till who was surreptitiously digging in her pocket for her mobile phone. She slowly eased it out and started to film.

Anna lunged forwards with the bottle, nicking Audrey's arm. Audrey flinched as the bottle connected. A trickle of blood started running down her arm, dripping on the floor. She clamped her other hand over the gash firmly but remained where she was.

'With my bad knee I can't move as fast as you, Anna. I'm going to take another step towards you now. Put the bottle down.'

As Anna raised the bottle to take another swing, a missile hit her hand and the bottle fell.

'You will not hurt my friend, you total and absolute cow,' Bill cried as she readied her arm with another potato. 'Audrey, stand back.' A second potato followed the first, missing its intended target. Anna roared.

'You bitch!' She hurled the tenderising mallet. A huge stack of plastic Coca Cola bottles trembled and toppled as the tenderiser struck. The heavy bottles bounced and rolled as they landed. The ones that fell from the top of the stack bounced the highest, some exploding midair, showering everything and everyone with Coke.

'Hello, what's happening here?' Simon came in through the door just as the final bottle landed. 'What have I missed?'

Anna turned to look at him crazily, now cornered and unarmed, having lost both mallet and bottle. She wavered back and forth. Simon quickly grabbed a newspaper from the pile by the door and rolled it up. As she decided to take a run at the open door behind Simon he stabbed the rolled newspaper firmly into her stomach. She fell to the ground, clutching her middle with a groan.

'Quickly, grab her!' They rushed to hold what they could grab, a flailing arm, a thrashing leg.

'Ow! She bit me.' Adele pushed Anna's face away from her arm, a blue imprint of her fangs indented in her bare arm.

Louise, the checkout girl, ran to the shelves of household equipment and came back with a coil of general purpose utility rope. Simon did an expert knotting job as the rest held her down.

'And this is a clove hitch, see? This bit goes here, and then you can tighten and undo it easily as you need to.'

'Simon has always been a star with knots,' said James proudly.

'You'll pay for this, you bastards. I'll kill you all.' Anna continued shrieking.

'Stop carrying on, save it for when the police get here,' said Audrey.

'Such language,' said Simon. He brushed his hands on his pants. 'I think you might have to close for a minute and clean up. There's a lot of wet glass on the floor. Not to mention sticky. Bill, could you bear to do some one-handed first aid? She's bleeding. Must have cut herself. Has anyone called the police yet?'

'Not us, they've forbidden us to interfere,' said Bill, busily wrapping up Audrey's arm using supplies from the pharmaceuticals display. The cut didn't look deep, but was bleeding a bit regardless. 'I'll get to

Anna in a minute.'

'I'll ring,' said Adele and fetched her mobile. 'Hello? Yes I'll hold. Can someone make her quiet please, I can't hear myself speak.'

'You're a bit of a banshee, aren't you?' James came from the cleaning aisle with a plastic mop bucket and upturned it on Anna's head. This didn't stop the abuse but it came out more muffled.

'Yes, I'm still here. I'd like someone to come and collect a prisoner please. Yes, I know. Well, it's complicated. I'll explain when they get here. The corner shop in Daylesford. Yes. Anna from The Bean. My name is Adele Tylden. Thank you, I expect to see someone here soon. Goodbye.'

'They're a bit outside Newstead, so will be about 35 minutes. We'll wait for them here, and I don't think we should clean up yet. They might want to see the scene.'

'Well, if you don't need us here for cleaning, we'll see you later.' Bill and Audrey turned to leave.

'You can't go, you're witnesses. There's even footage of it here.' Louise waved her phone at them.

'We promised not to interfere,' said Bill plaintively. They'll only be angry and look sternly at us, and I just want a cup of tea and some clothes that are not soaked in soft drink. We're probably in shock, which can be dangerous at our time of life.'

Adele looked at them sceptically. 'But...'

'We couldn't help it that she happened to be here,' added Audrey. 'Let us pay you for the water and potatoes and rope and bandages and stuff.'

'No one goes anywhere,' said Louise firmly. 'It will be even worse. I'll go and put the kettle on. Choose some nice biscuits from the shelf, Adele, we'll have a cuppa here while we wait and we'll all feel better for it.' Louise went to the entry doors and bolted them closed, just in the nick of time as a handful of customers approached. She flipped the sign over to 'Closed'.

Adele returned shortly from the staffroom with a tray of steaming mugs. The shop was always pretty chilly and they all enjoyed the simple comfort of holding onto a hot mug. They sat down on the floor well away from the incessant abuse coming from the bucket. Adele selected a packet of Dutch Speculaas and passed the packet around.

'Yum, Spéculoos,' said Audrey.

'I thought they were pronounced Specky Lass,' said Louise and took a gulp of her tea.

'In German it's Spekulatius,' said Adele, who had done three years of German at school. 'Delicious in any language, aren't they? We're going to need a second packet.'

'My eyelashes are sticking together, I can only open this eye,' said James and squinted. 'Coke is sticky stuff.'

'Never touch it myself,' Bill giggled. 'But now I'm

stuck to the floor with it. Oh, just look at us.' She laughed. 'We did it! We actually did it. No jail for Monsieur Hugo.'

'You have an impressive arm, Bill,' said Louise. 'You should enter the Ladies Boot Throw contest at the New Year's Games in Glenlyon.'

Maybe. I wouldn't stand a chance if that one entered, with her hammer arm.' She nodded towards Anna. 'Somehow I think she'll be unable to attend.'

'Bill played cricket in the convent for years,' said Audrey.

There was a rapping on the glass doors. Fortunately it was Rosie Lloyd who had responded to the call. Still, even with her capacity for understanding and prior knowledge it took them a little while to sort out what had happened. There seemed to be a whole lot of groceries involved.

Rosie replaced the rope with handcuffs. Anna, freed from her bucket, glared at the ex-nuns.

'I should have killed you when I had the chance,' she shouted as Rosie led her out to the waiting car.

It wasn't long before Audrey could drive to Brickwell to collect Hugo. He was inordinately pleased at his sudden release and gave her a big hug.

'I believe I have you two to thank for this. We have missed the Beechworth excursion but perhaps you will let me cook you dinner soon as a tiny beginning of countless acts of gratitude?'

'There's no need to thank us at all, really, Hugo. It's nice, of course, but not necessary.' She smiled. She wanted to add that it had been a lot of fun but since two people had died tragically it was not the correct response. She would just accept some of these countless acts.

As the freshly polished two-tone car majestically rolled into the car park by the lake, the conductor raised his baton. He led his choir in a rousing rendition of *La Marseillaise*, it being the only French song they knew.

When Audrey and Bill returned home late that evening ever so slightly tipsy on champagne and gratitude it was to find a large parcel wrapped in brown paper on the hallway landing, tied up with garden twine. There was also a small flat one, addressed to Audrey.

'What's this now? I'm a little weary of surprises and general thank yous now,' said Bill.

'Oh, go on, the danger's over. It's probably some of Hugo's countless ways,' said Audrey. She opened the flat parcel to find a small framed pencil sketch of Lake Daylesford in winter, mist hovering, seemingly moving over the paper.

'It's beautiful.' She turned the paper over. 'To Audrey, with my apologies. Alastair.'

'That's nice. And will you? Forgive him, I mean.'

'Forgive, yes. Forget, no.'

Audrey and Bill unpicked the knotted string with fingers made clumsy by the late night and all it had contained. They tore at the paper with some caution just in case the content would explode. Fortunately for all, it didn't, and opened to reveal an old wooden cupboard, about a metre high. It closed with a door at the front, which had an assortment of locks mounted to it. In the base was a drawer with a set of lock picks and another note:

The cupboard is for the dextrous Audrey. There is a present inside for Bill – go get it. Love, Simon& James.

'Open the cupboard, Audrey. I want my present. You've had one already!'

Audrey looked at her. 'In time, comrade. All in good time, and now it is the time for bed.'

***

It was nearly spring. You could smell the difference in the air. The sun had started to warm the ground, prompting fresh growth and if you looked closely, the tiniest hint of tight buds were starting to appear on the previously bare branches. Audrey and Bill were having breakfast in the window seat of a Raglan Street cafe. They had decided to celebrate the opening of the last lock and had taken Margaret and Penny out for a treat. Inez had been invited too, but had declined, saying it was an outing for the young ones.

Bill's gift, finally found, had come on their first outing. It was a pair of handsome leather lace-up shoes, and the women admired them as they sat waiting for their orders to arrive. The fit was as perfect as the Dior dress she was wearing, and Bill found they made her walk with a real bounce in her step. Why the dress fitted so well was something she couldn't account for. Maybe it was the frequent walks with Margaret, maybe it was the general stress. She hadn't done anything else special.

'Those boys are truly the sweetest, aren't they?' She turned her feet this way and that, to properly observe them from every angle. 'They must have been expensive. Should I feel guilty at accepting?'

'A gift freely given,' said Margaret. 'Of course you shouldn't feel bad. They are meant for you to enjoy. I could do with some new walking boots. Feel like looking at the shops after we've finished?'

A man stopped outside the window and waved.

'Good heavens, it's Rick,' said Audrey. They waved back.

The bell above the door tinkled as he entered.

'We are really, truly sorry for pointing the finger at you,' said Bill demurely.

'That's okay, I can see how it looked. Just thought I'd let you know that I'm getting out of the lease and will be returning to Melbourne. I leave tomorrow.'

He sighed. 'I did love her, you know. I visited her last week. Foolish, I know, but I had to talk to her.'

'Things can sometimes go so wrong, despite our best hopes and wishes,' said Bill. 'And once they start going wrong, they can speed up rapidly until everything is a blur and you're no longer able to get off the train. We are curious. Why did she do it?'

'She suspected something was going on. He'd been acting strangely. She went to the shop just after Hugo had left. Fabiano was in the storeroom in a worked-up state when she arrived, sweeping up a broken cup. They had an argument and he told her he was leaving. They fought often, but this time it was different. She threw a bag of beans at him and it split open all over the floor. He slipped, knocking his head on the edge of the shelves.'

'So it was an accident?' asked Margaret.

'It might have started as an accident, but ended in murder all the same. She had the presence of mind to put on some food prep gloves before tying up his hands and feet. Then she took handfuls of beans and shoved them in his open mouth, finishing with a few layers of plastic food wrap. I think she only meant to have a fight with him to try to find out what was happening, but when he fell she just did what came naturally. It simply happened. It was her good luck that he slipped in the storeroom. She wouldn't have been able to drag him there herself. This way, she could decide herself when he should be discovered. As it turns out she picked you two for the job. I would say she chose pretty badly, don't you?'

'She led us to him with all that ruse about giving coffee to the choir,' said Audrey. 'She's a convincing actress.'

'Not all that good actually. He was the actor out of the pair. She had tried and failed to get cast in the TV series he worked on.'

'We didn't doubt her. What about Fiona, what was going on there?' asked Bill.

'Anna heard a rumour going round the village that Fiona knew who the killer was and she had to silence her in case it was true. She killed two birds with the same stone, you could say, by choosing her method to firmly implicate Hugo. It was also pure luck for Anna that he had no alibi. She killed Fabiano on a spur of the moment, but she had enough wits about her to try to implicate people. Hugo had left his prints all over when they argued, so that was already in place, but she didn't know that. She added the coffee beans to the mouth to make it look like someone was angry about his coffee, having overheard the end of the argument between them. If the witness hadn't come forward about Hugo, she would have done some pointing herself, you can be sure. She planted that evidence in my house, remember.'

'We remember,' said Bill, blushing.

'Then she just slipped back into bed with me. She is so beautiful, it's hard to believe she could be bad. I thought she loved me back but she was ready and willing to let me take the blame.'

'Beauty,' snorted Audrey with disdain after he had left. 'Since when did beauty provide immunity from badness?' She sat up a little straighter and turned her profile to the street.

Outside, a tourist took a quick snap with his camera.

'Ah, beautiful,' he breathed with admiration.

And it was. The picture had captured two women in the window like an artfully designed display. One of them with a sharp profile, sitting ramrod straight. She was dressed in some unusual kind of tailored suit topped with an outlandish hat. She seemed to be angry about something, which only served to put more fire into her already interesting features. Her friend clapped her hands girlishly as a waitress laden with plates approached.

Gnarled vine branches snaked around the edges of the window, forming a frame. He observed the tableau for a minute, sighed, and walked on down the sunny street.

www.ingramcontent.com/pod-product-compliance
Lightning Source LLC
Chambersburg PA
CBHW021401110726
47901CB00008B/2015